Enjoy this

Paul Walford
2005

ncben252@yahoo.com

"Cotton Exchange"
in Wilmington
May 28, 2005
w/ Thomas

A Man and a Mule

By

Ben Watford

authorHOUSE

1663 LIBERTY DRIVE, SUITE 200
BLOOMINGTON, INDIANA 47403
(800) 839-8640
www.authorhouse.com

First published by AuthorHouse 10/21/04

ISBN: 1-4184-8543-8 (sc)

Library of Congress Control Number: 2004095314

Printed in the United States of America
Bloomington, Indiana

This book is printed on acid-free paper.

Table of Contents

A Man and a Mule

The trail was dusty and sun baked, it meandered across a broad overgrown meadow. In the distance, about five hundred yards, at the far edge of the meadow was a stand of stately pine trees their tops reaching skyward seeming to blend with the wispy clouds filling the horizon. On the right side of the trail was ditch filled with water from a recent rainfall. On both sides of the trail small bushes grew and made a feeble attempt to cover the route and, at a few points, they almost succeeded. The ditch on the right and the bushes served as a boundary between the meadow and the trail. The entire meadow was covered with small scrub brush, grass and other plants mingled with wild flowers. Communities of yellow golden rods grew in random patches across the meadow, as if placed there by some demented farmer with an eye for the grotesque. The scrub brush and small trees grew tall along the ditch between the meadow and the trail like an elongated oasis in some foreign desert. When the land was cultivated, some time in the past, these plants were cut down, now nature was reclaiming a part of the terrain.

At many points along the trail the foliage was so thick that the meadow beyond could only be seen at intervals. The leaves of the plants nearest the trail were dust covered, an indication that the trail was frequently used. Occasionally, there was a rustle of leaves as some small animal scurried to the safety of the underbrush. A small herd of deer grazed in a grassy patch near the edge of the woods. The deer seldom wandered far from the woods. The smell of a rider and mount coming down the trail caused them to raise their heads and sniff the wind. Catching the strange scent the deer moved closer to the edge of the woods. They continued grazing while keeping the strange pair in view. Suddenly one large buck raised his head and rushed into the woods. The rest of the herd followed him.

The land, on the side of the trail, was farmed in the past, now it was left uncultivated, as it would no longer produce crops. Like so much land in the South, when it became unproductive the farmers moved to more productive land. There was always more land.

The sun's last red emissions gave the landscape an eerie glare and signaled the onset of night. It was late evening, and a tranquil quietness descended over the land. The only sounds heard were birdcalls as they staked out their territory and attracted mates. Endlessly stretching out along the meadow, the trail appeared to end where the pine trees of the forest intervened, far in the distance.

Along the trail came a solitary rider. His mount was a mule, brown and dusty, with oversized ears. He rode at a leisurely pace. The rider and his mount appeared to have infinite time to get to where they were going. He rode as if he had no destination in mind. He rode as a man just out for a ride on his favorite mount. He rode with the ease of a man who understood animals. The rider carried no crop and wore no spurs and allowed the mount to move at its own pace. From a distance one would surmise that the animal was leading the man.

Eventually, the man dismounted and allowed the mule to drink from the ditch. He looked at the sun and then surveyed the landscape. He used his right hand to shade the bright sunlight from his eyes. When the mule had finished drinking he attempted to mount it and the mule quickly moved sideways to avoid being mounted. The man pulled the reins of the mule close and whispered in its ear. He then mounted the mule without further problems and continued on his way.

The solitary rider's skin was jet black. He stood six feet, six inches tall. His lips were thick and his nose was broad. His arms were muscular and his legs were long. His forehead was covered with beads of perspiration. The rider had a beard of kinky hair. He wore a pair of bibbed overalls and no shirt. His shoes were brogans with metal clips at the top and laced with haywire. He wore no socks. His left hand contained only two fingers and the thumb. The little finger and the finger next to it were amputated at the beginning of his hand.

Riding since the first light of day, he had stopped only to water the mule and to allow it to graze. The dust from the road had encrusted his forehead. He wiped the sweat and dust from his brow with the back of his hand. His hand covered with dust from the trail merged with the dust on his forehead and left its mark. He talked quietly to the mule and then continued his journey.

His six foot, six inch frame clung to the back of the mule. He leaned forward, patted the mule and spoke softly to it. It was a one-way conversation. The only acknowledgment from the mule was a slight flicker of it's ears as they continued their journey.

Had fate proved more compassionate, he would have been an African warrior or the chief of some African tribe. Today, December 4, 1866, he was just another free black man in search of work and a meal. His only possession was the mule on which he rode bareback.

Riding for several more hours both the man and the mule were tired. He dismounted near a stream and allowed the mule to drink. After the mule finished drinking, he drank from the stream. The rider then encouraged the mule to graze.

While the mule grazed, he rested near the stream with his bare feet in the water. Before leaving the stream, he washed and took a final drink of water. He waited for the mule to finish grazing. After the mule had finished grazing, he again spoke softly in it's ear, he mounted the mule and continued his journey, letting the mule to set the pace.

The Early Years

He was born Jumo Gumasaka in the village of Gome in West Africa. His father was a rich man by the tribe's standards. He owned a herd of twenty goats. From the time that he was old enough to walk, he had tended goats for his father. He enjoyed goat tending. It allowed him to pretend that he was a warrior, protecting the livelihood of the entire tribe. He usually daydreamed of being an elder with many goats and many wives. He dreamed that some day he would be the chief and protector of his people.

During the summer months he would take the goats, early in the morning, from their enclosure. He would lead them to a valley fifteen minutes walk from his village to graze. His father and mother were pleased with him, proud of their little man. He was the oldest of their six children. The other children envied him and yearned to be the one who cared for the goats. Jumo was proud of his position in the family. Being the oldest carried with it privileges that the other siblings did not enjoy.

One summer morning Jumo went to the enclosure, opened the gate, and fetched the goats. He called his dog and led the goats toward the nearby valley and feeding ground. It would be late in the afternoon before he returned to the compound. He carried his staff, his lunch, and a container of water.

His dog always followed him to the grazing area and helped him herd and tend the goats. He started out on an effulgent summer day. The sky was clear, none of the rain clouds that plagued this time of the year were visible. A slight breeze moved the leaves on the scrub brush that dotted the plains. Jumo heard the call of the morning birds and the sound of the doves in the distance. He was familiar with all the sounds he heard. They were part of the landscape, part of his environment. He barely noticed the familiar sounds. Any sounds out of the ordinary would have attracted his attention. There were no strange sounds to be heard. The day was like all the other days he had taken the goats to graze in the valley. Jumo detected no difference in the sounds coming from his surroundings that were unfamiliar to him. He ignored the sounds and went about the business of tending his family's goats.

He used his staff and his dog to herd the goats and to keep them together. If any goat strayed from the herd he would send his dog after it. His father had found that Jumo was adept at tending to the safety of the herd. He trusted Jumo's competence at goat tending. Jumo's father was not concerned about the goats since Jumo was with them, yet, he cautioned Jumo about their safety before he left each morning.

Jumo knew that he was the most important sibling of the family. He knew and accepted his duties as part of the process of becoming a man and a warrior. He had said "goodbye" to his mother and father and started on his way. His father had given him the same instructions day after day since the first time he took the goats alone to the valley.

"Stay alert and if wild animals approach, make as much noise as possible. Don't allow the dog to attack, keep him close to you. Herd the goats and bring them back home."

On the day that the slave catchers caught him, he was tending the goats not far from his village. Armed only with a staff he was easy prey. He was young and healthy just what the slave catchers wanted. The journey they planned for him was not for the weak, old or feeble. Only the strong would survive the journey that the slave catchers had in store for him. The slave catchers captured Jumo as he sat eating lunch and watching the herd of goats far from his village. He was more concerned with the fate of the goats than his own safety.

Jumo knew that his father would be angry with him for leaving the goats unattended. Releasing the dog he uttered a single word, which meant, "Home." His dog ran for the village. He knew that when the dog reached the village, his father and the other men would come for him. The slave catchers knew this also and they hastily bound him and carried him rapidly from the area.

At first he thought the raiders were after his goats and he tried to protect them. It was only after his capture that he realized he was the prize they sought. He had no idea what they intended to do with him. His main concern was the fate of his herd of goats. When his father and the men from the village reached the grazing area, the goats were safe; there was no sign of Jumo. They tracked and hunted for him for many days without success. Weeks after the abduction, his father continued the search alone. He never found any trace of his lost son. He never lost hope that his son would be found and years later he was still searching in all nearby villages for Jumo. He searched in vain. The rest of his life would be spent in a futile search for his first-born.

Jumo, with his hands bound behind him was marched to a holding pen where other black men and women awaited their fate. Later the entire group of fifty-six blacks was marched west toward the ocean. There was little food or water, most were weak and weary by the time they reached their destination. They were placed in holding pens to await their fate. Two days later they were led to the waiting ships. Their long journey was about to begin. The life that they had lived, their friends, family and villages no longer existed.

Jumo was placed on the ship and shackled far below deck. He still believed that his family and tribe would rescue him. Jumo was convinced that the members of his tribe would find him and punish his abductors. He waited in vain to be rescued.

They were nearing the shores of the islands in the South Atlantic before he gave up hope of a rescue. He had difficulty accepting what had happened to him. All that he wanted was to return to his home. He missed his mother and father, his siblings, his herd of goats and his village. He heard new sounds, sounds that were not familiar to him. He saw new people, people who spoke a language he could not understand. For the first time in his short life, he experienced the queasiness associated with seasickness. Gradually, he began to feel that all was lost. Finally, he began to realize that his life in the future would be radically different from that of the past.

His parents, his home, his friends were all gone. The village that was so familiar to him and all its occupants were but a dream. The old familiar sounds and smells were no longer there. Still Jumo, did not give up hope. He made a vow to the Gods of the trees, the mountains and the forest that he would someday return. Those Gods had protected his family for untold generations. His covenant with the Gods was that he would one day return to his homeland. He would see that his abductors were punished.

The ship that carried Jumo was bound for the new world. He was only one of one hundred fifty blacks aboard the slave ship. He would eventually be sold as a slave someplace in the Americas. All the rights and dignity of human beings were denied him. He would become property to be bought and sold. His former tribe, parents and friends couldn't help him. He had no friends, and no one who cared about him or his fate. Those like him on the ship were too concerned with survival or death to show concern for one lost black boy. Jumo would become a slave.

Jumo watched in horror as three women threw themselves into the sea during one morning wash down. He saw the sea turn red from their blood as sharks attacked them. He wondered if the life that he was about to begin was so horrible that death was the only alternative. He thought of following the women into the sea and death, but thoughts of his village, his parents, his brothers and sisters and his goats kept him alive. He fully intended to survive this ordeal and return to his village.

His seafaring journey ended on the Island of Jamaica It was Jumo's twelfth harvest. Here he would work in the cane fields. Jumo became a part of the commerce triangle, slaves, whiskey, and various staples produced by the American colonies.

In the early 1800's the shipment of new slaves directly to the continental United States was outlawed. The Shipment of slaves was banned by all states except South Carolina and Georgia. Slave traders brought slaves into the United States illegally from the Caribbean islands. The influx of slaves into the United States continued.

Coming by way of Jamaica, Jumo was placed on the slave block in Charleston, South Carolina. He had seen fourteen winters. He had no understanding of the events taking place around him. Jumo had no control of his fate or destiny.

Jumo still considered himself free and the master of his fate. To Jumo, the chains that bound him hand and foot did not make him the property of someone else. He had no idea, no concept, of man as property.

Everything around him was strange and different from his homeland. Men of a strange pale color came and examined him, looked into his mouth and pressed his muscles. He was sold. He had no rights, no father and mother, no sisters or brothers, no headmaster and no tribe to protect him. All that he had known was lost to him. He could no longer tend the goats of his family. He could not become the warrior of his dreams. Jumo's future was uncertain; he lived only for the present.

Jumo became the property of the Jacob Latimore Plantation. The boy, who wanted to be a warrior, became a slave. His destiny and his future lay in the hands of others. Others would control his life and his future; he had no further control of his destiny.

Life on the Plantation

The Latimore plantation was located in Beaufort, South Carolina. The massive plantation contained sixty slaves, producing cotton, corn and peanuts. It was typical of the plantations of South Carolina. The big house, the slave shacks and tended fields, all controlled by the master and the overseer.

After arriving at the plantation he was examined by the overseers and then told to report to Jim for work assignment. Jim was a large black man. He was in charge of field assignments. He wore overalls a shirt and no shoes. He was the largest black man Jumo had ever seen. He treated Jumo with a sort of fatherly kindness. He showed him his living quarters and introduced him to the cook as the new boy. Using sign language he explained what was expected of him. He taught him to use the hoe. Jim watched carefully as Jumo went about his expected duties.

Jumo was given the name Frederick by his master Jacob Latimore. To all the plantation slaves, he became known as Fred. He shared a slave shack, located behind the big house, with three other boys. His shack was just one of many that lined the dirt path behind the big house. His new home was superior to what he had left in Jamaica. Jumo realized this; he also realized that he was still not free.

Tom, Randy and Joe were his bunkmates. Randy, born a slave, he knew no other way of life. He was a jet-black lad with big teeth and large ears. Life on the plantation was all that he had ever known.

Thomas came to the Latimore plantation by way of Jamaica. He was a mulatto and preferred the farms in the United States to the sugar cane fields of the islands. For Thomas, coming to America meant an easier life than he had ever known. In the sugar plantations of the islands, black men were old by the age of forty. Most of the sugar plantations workers were dead by the age of fifty. The work in the cane fields, harsh treatment and disease took its toll on the workers. Lacking families, health care, poor food and inferior living conditions, most slaves in the cane fields of Jamaica died at an early age.

Joseph, or Joe as the rest of the slaves called him, was the oldest of the three boys. By his own reckoning he had seen eighteen harvests. He was the one that maintained order in the cabin. Joseph made sure that each boy did his share in keeping the place tidy.

Joseph was born in Africa and lived there until he was three years old. He and his mother, captured by the slave catchers were sent to Jamaica. Too young for the cane fields, he was sold and placed on the slave block in South Carolina. The Latimore plantation purchased him at the age of six.

Joseph's mother, stripped of her son, was sold to a different landowner, someplace in North Carolina. He had not seen his mother since that fateful day on the slave block. He had no recollection of his father. The Latimore plantation was the only home that he had ever known. His mother was sold when he was six years old. The only mother that he knew was the plantation cook. He did not remember his early life in his African village. The only life that he had ever known was the life of a slave. Freedom was an idea that had no meaning for him.

Randy was the youngest member of Fred's bunkmates, he had seen nine summers and his mother was sold when he was four years old. Randy was shy, he never smiled and did whatever Joseph or Jim asked him to do. He had no known relatives on the plantation. He had never known or met his father. Knowing no other way of life he accepted his fate and his insignificant role on the Latimore plantation.

Fred became close friends with Thomas. They understood each other's dialect. Even though the vernacular was slightly different they could understand each other. This was the first person that Fred met that spoke a language similar to his. Thomas, being older, taught him the duties required of field hands. He spent many nights trying to teach Fred the strange new language of the white man. In return Fred recounted stories of life in Africa before his capture.

He described his village, its inhabitants and its wealth. He told Thomas of the village headmaster or chief, how he resolved disputes and generally controlled the affairs of the village. He described the herding of goats and how he was the one member of his family allowed to take the goats to pasture. He explained to Thomas the role of the women in the village. He elucidated in detail how the women tended the crops that were grown and the nurturing of the children. The idea of extended families was most difficult for Thomas to understand. He could not conceive of how one could have many mothers. Thomas was filled with many questions about life in Africa. Fred did his best to make him understand what his former life was like and how much he missed his tribe, his family and his village.

Both boys were captured by slave catchers and had lost their families and their tribes. They longed for the day when they could return to their homeland and join their tribes. They worked side by side on the plantation and both dreamed the dreams of freedom in their African homeland.

Their meals, such as they were, were cooked and served in the common slave kitchen by a three hundred-pound black woman. All the slaves knew this black woman as Aunt Sal. Aunt Sal was born a slave and the years of her life in slavery had not been kind to her. She had seen her seven children sold one by one. She loved them although they were not the black children that she wanted but those of the white men. To Aunt Sal this made little difference, they were still her children.

It pained her to see them sold one by one, realizing that she would never see them again. Aunt Sal had given up on life and looked forward to the hereafter. To Aunt Sal the idea of freedom was not a part of her physical existence. All that she had ever known was life on the plantation as a slave.

The life of a slave was all that Aunt Sal ever expected from her earthly existence. She accepted slavery as a way of life. She was devoutly religious. Aunt Sal had adjusted to her position in life, harsh though it was. She believed there was a better life coming in the hereafter and Aunt Sal lived for that time. Being devoutly religious, she spent many long hours trying to get the other slaves to accept the white man's God.

Life was harsh on the plantation. The four young slaves centered their conversation on escaping to the North. The most feared white man that Fred, Thomas, Randy, Joseph and the other blacks on the plantation encountered was not the master Jacob Latimore. They rarely met him or even saw him. It was the white overseer, David Dunlop.

The overseer took delight in punishing the slaves for the smallest infraction. The first lashing that Fred received at the hands of the Dunlop was for breaking a hoe while chopping cotton. After his third lashing at the hands of Dunlop, Fred decided to run away, to escape to the north and become a free man.

He longed for the freedom that he had known as a very young child in Africa. After the fourth lashing for talking back to the overseer, Fred went to his cabin and planned his escape. He knew that he would need food for the trip to freedom in the North. He had overheard conversations of older slaves describing life in the north. There, black men were not slaves and could live free, have families and work for wages.

Fred knew that water could be obtained from rain or streams, so his major concern was food. For several weeks Fred saved part of his bread and hid it under his bunk. He told no one of his plans. Fred had heard the older men talking about the drinking gourd in the sky. He had heard them say that following it; one would end in the North a free man. Fred spent many nights looking in the northern sky locating the drinking gourd and the nearby stars. After a time he was so familiar with the night sky that he could locate the drinking gourd with a single glance.

Fred had no idea of the distance he would have to travel or the hardships that he might meet. He only knew that some place in the distance was a land where men could walk free and earn money from their labors. He had learned this from the conversations of the older black men on the plantation. Fred wondered why none of them had tried to leave and follow the drinking gourd to freedom. To Fred it seemed a logical solution to the problems that blacks faced. To Fred it was a better solution than working until death on the plantation with no family and no friends.

In his childish dreams he saw himself going back to his village in Africa. To go home to Africa, Fred would have to cross the big river. In his dreams, even that journey was possible. He planned carefully and for the right moment to make his escape. He had saved enough bread to last him for several weeks. The bread he had hid under his pine straw mattress. He was sure that his supply would last long enough for him to reach the promise land. He planned to supplement his diet with the capture of small game such as rabbits or squirrel. He also hid a small length of rope to use as a snare to capture small game on his journey.

One night, after the other boys were asleep he left the cabin, crept out into the moonlight. He wanted to be far away from the plantation before the first light of day. Walking outside the cabin, he located the drinking gourd and headed north.

The sky was clear, the stars competed for visibility with the moon, and the drinking gourd hung low in the northern hemisphere. He had little trouble heading in the right direction. He listened for sounds of being followed and heard none. He knew that everyone was asleep. A dog started to follow him. He picked up a stick and ran the dog back to the plantation. On this journey he wanted no company.

Fifty yards from the plantation, Fred started to run and ran as fast as he could. He made sure that the drinking gourd in the sky was in front of him. The drinking gourd was his ticket to freedom. Soon he would be his own man.

Fred knew that he had to avoid contact with white men, plantations and other slaves. With the thought of freedom in his mind, he ran the first five miles without stopping. He finally rested under a large oak for a few minutes and then continued his journey toward the drinking gourd.

Ten miles and four hours from the plantation he first heard the dogs. The baying of the hounds told him that his escape was no longer a secret. Each minute the sound appeared closer and closer. He started to run and ran as fast as he could. He knew that he could not outrun the hounds, but he had to try.

"How could they have known so quickly?"

Fred had left the plantation by his reckoning just a few hours. He had placed pillows in his bed to make the other boys think that he was asleep. No one should have known about his absence until at least the next morning. Even if his bunkmates discovered his absence, surely they would not tell anyone. He started to run faster. He had no idea of where he was going. Fred only knew that he did not want to go back to the plantation.

The sound of the dogs came closer and closer. With the dogs hot in pursuit he knew that his newfound freedom was doomed. With the dogs closing in, Fred climbed a tree and just waited. The first voice, other than those of the hounds, was that of the overseer Dunlop.

"Climb down from that tree nigger or be shot down."

Fred climbed down the tree while the overseer and three other white men, that he did not recognize, restrained the three hounds. Once on the ground they set the dogs on him and watched as they tore at his flesh. Finally, they called the dogs away and put the leg irons and handcuffs on him. They mounted their horses and he was half walked and half dragged back to the plantation. It was still dark when they arrived at the plantation. The overseer tied him to a tree and waited until daybreak before summoning the slave population.

The sun was rising in the east on this mild summer day and there was a fine mist in the air. It was beginning to rain and the raindrops began to fall on his face. Fred, tied to the tree, did not notice the rain. His thoughts were on what his punishment would be at the hands of the overseer. Fred fully expected another lashing and was determined not to cry out. He would endure the pain in silence. All the blacks watched as the overseers meted out the punishment for the runaway. Fred was untied from the tree and lead to a chopping block by Dunlop. The overseer stretched Fred's left hand on a block of wood and cut off one of his fingers on his left hand.

Dunlop said to assembled slaves, "Every time a nigger runs away I am going to cut off one of his fingers. When I am done with the fingers, off comes the arm."

Fred was handed over to Aunt Sal, the cook, who tended his wounds and nursed him back to health. She showed little patience for what he had done.

She called him a dumb nigger and said to him, "Yo taking off done made it bad for all us."

He asked her, "How dey know I gone so soon."

She just laughed.

"Nigger, you got a lot to learn."

"lak what."

"Lak who to trust, who not to trust."

"When you runs away you don't tell no one and you makes sure don't no one know which away you goin."

"I done all that Aunt Sal. Still someone told and I don't know who it was."

Finally, she said, "Go and ast yo friend Tom."

He didn't have to ask Tom. He overheard Dunlop saying to Tom, "You a good nigger Tom, come up to the big house later today after finishing work. I will give you some old clothes."

It was difficult for him to believe that Tom had gone to the overseer about him. Yet, he had to believe when Tom discovered that he was gone, he had told Dunlop. That would explain how they managed to catch him so quickly.

He stayed with Aunt Sal for two weeks and finally, she put him out and told him, "You ready to go back to work."

His first act upon returning to his shack was to face Tom. Tom was older than Fred. That did not matter to him and he intended to confront Tom about informing the overseers of his escape attempt. Neither boy knew their true age as size was more a measure of the years lived than any other indicator. Thomas was about six inches taller than Fred. To Fred it did not matter. He was going to pay Thomas for snitching on him. He met Thomas outside the slave quarters.

"Tom why you tell on me."

"Nigger you git us all in trouble running way like dat."

With his good right hand he hit Tom smack in the mouth removing his two front teeth. The other two boys pulled them apart. Tom went straight to the Overseer and told him what had happened. Dunlop waited a full day before exacting punishment. He wanted Fred to think of his punishment and to agonize over it. He finally called Fred again to the chopping block. With the entire slave population watching he removed another finger. Fred was again in the care of Aunt Sal. Aunt Sal showed little sympathy for him or his action. Yet, Aunt Sal did what she could to ease his pain.

"You, the dumbest nigger I ever seed, don't you ever learn nuttin. Ain't no use in fighting what is, just try to stay outta trouble."

For ten years Fred worked as a slave on the Latimore plantation. He played the role of a good slave but he never accepted it. Fred took Aunt Sal's advice about how to act and to behave. Fred's lashing came less frequently as he became more of a model slave. He avoided trouble, did the work required of him and stayed out the way of the overseer. He kept within him his feeling about the institution of slavery of which he was a part. Fred never shared his thoughts with any of the other slaves. Aunt Sal had taught him well. He avoided trouble by learning the role that slaves had to play to survive.

The War Years

When the War Between the States started he was still a slave on the Latimore plantation. Little news of the progress of the war reached the slaves. Most slaves had no idea what the war was about or what their stake was in the conflict.

Only the absence of white men on the plantation and in the surrounding area suggested that a war was in progress. Fred wondered why there was such an absence of white men realized that most of the eligible white men had gone to fight in the war. Like most slaves, he had little idea of the reasons for the war but he was pleased that it had come. He began to speculate from the conversation that he over heard that if the north won the war he would be a free man. That was the gossip that spread through the slave quarters. When he asked his fellow slaves about it, some were sure that was the case, others were doubtful. The only person that he could go to for factual advice about the war was Aunt Sal. He knew that Aunt Sal was truly a slave but she was loyal to the blacks on the plantation. Fred knew that Aunt Sal would be honest with him and that Aunt Sal would not tell anyone if he questioned her about the war.

Aunt Sal said to him when he asked her about it, "Don't you fret over it they ain't gonna never set us free. We is slaves and we is gonna be slaves, war or no war."

"But Aunt Sal why is white men fighting each other"?

"Cause white men hate each other as much as they hate niggers".

"Why do they hate each other"?

"It's none of my business or yours, what will be will be and the war, it don't concern us".

"But why"?

"I done told you it's none of yo business".

"But why are they fighting?"

"Jist wait and see what happens, you ask too many questions bout something that is none yo business, now git outta here, I'se got work to do."

As Fred left Aunt Sal he was more confused than before. He wanted to believe her. Yet he still hoped that the gossip surrounding the war was true. He wanted to believe that one day he would be a free man.

There were rumors that the union soldiers were within the borders of South Carolina. The whispers of the slaves carried news that the war was not going well for the South. The slave gossip was that the new president was going to free all the slaves and give them all forty acres and a mule.

Fred was beginning to believe that soon he would be free and with forty acres and a mule. That was more than he could dream of. He would finally be free and with the gift from the president he could make a nice living just farming. He could even marry and have a wife and a family.

Fred dreamed of being a free man. He wanted to be a person without a master and a man free to make his own decisions. He wanted to have a family and live without fear. As the war came nearer and nearer to the plantation, Fred was convinced that soon he would be free. He heard rumors that the war was about to end and he rejoiced.

On the first day of January 1863 President Lincoln proclaimed, in his capacity as commander-in-chief of the army, "all persons held as slaves within any state or designated part of the state, whereof shall then be in rebellion against the United States shall thenceforward, and forever be free." This proclamation applied only to those states that were in rebellion against the union. South Carolina was one of those states.

By 1864 there were no adult white men left on the plantation, they had left to join in the futile attempt to stop the Northern troops. The mistress of the plantation called all the slaves together and explained the situation to them.

The mistress said to them, "You are free to go and those of you who want to stay and work on the plantation are free to do so".

"Those that stay will receive wages for their labors".

Older slaves went back to their shacks to prepare for the days work. They had no money or means of livelihood and no place to go. The forty acres and a mule that was the dream of the slaves after emancipation would never materialize. Most of the slaves in the south had no education, money or land. They had no place to go so most stayed where they were. Only the young left the plantations and most headed north or joined the war effort against the South.

Fred's first act upon hearing the news was to leave the plantation and head for the nearest union line. For days on end he dodged the confederate troops and finally found his way to the union camp. He was joined by hundreds of other blacks following the union troops.

He wanted to become a soldier fighting those that had enslaved him. He finally got a job with the Union troops. Contrary to his wishes he was not given a gun to kill white Southerners. He was made a cook and spent the next three months cooking for the union soldiers. This was not what Fred had expected and he had no desire to serve the white soldiers in any capacity. He wanted to carry a gun and fight in the war against those that had enslaved him.

At the end of three months he left the all white union army in the dark of night. He located and joined the First Regiment of South-Carolina Volunteers, an all-Negro regiment. All the officers, including the commanding officer Col. T. W. Higginson, were white men. This Fred did not mind because he was now in the army and could carry a gun. He would be allowed to fight in the war.

Fred shipped out with the regiment from Beaufort, South Carolina. The expedition took them deep into the interior of Georgia and Florida. They were repeatedly under fire. At Township, Florida, a detachment of the expedition fought a cavalry company that met them unexpectedly. The attack took place at midnight as they were marching through Florida. The attackers were beaten off with a loss of one Black man killed and seven wounded. Fred was sure that he would never live to see the end of the conflict. As the standard bearer for the First Regiment, Fred was always in the forefront of the battle.

He fought with First Regiment of South Carolina Volunteers until the end of the war. Four hundred men made up the original group that had left Beaufort, South Carolina. Only two hundred twenty-five men of the Regiment survived the hostilities. Fred was one of the survivors. Against all of the odds involved in the conflict of warfare Fred came through without being shot. The Civil War came to an end on the day that General Lee met General Grant at the Appomattox Court House and surrendered the Army of the Confederacy. It was a day of rejoicing throughout the north, most blacks in the south failed to understand the consequences. They placed no faith in the white men of either side. To most of the southern blacks it was just another aspect of life on the American continent. They suspected that nothing would change the harsh conditions of slavery, especially since white men were still in control. Little did the blacks of the southern states realize that life in the future would be radically different from the past. The old south was gone forever and would never return. The young could adapt to the changes but many of the older blacks longed for the old days.

Sometime during the month of May in 1866 Fred was discharged from military service. Fred's mustering out pay consisted of ten dollars and his uniform. The Union Army took his musket. Like all the other blacks from his regiment, he had fought bravely for a cause that he barely understood. At the end of the war he headed for his former plantation.

It took him two months traveling by foot to reach his former plantation. He did not know why it was necessary to go back to the old plantation, only that all the people that he had known were there. He arrived at his former plantation and found nothing but ruins. Where the big house stood, only the chimneys remained. Even the slave shacks were burned to the ground.

Sherman's army, as it passed through South Carolina, left little standing in its path of destruction. Fred had no idea what had happened to the former slaves of the plantation or where they had gone. He went to the black burial ground where he found an old head stone made of wood. Carved on the head stone, were the words " Aunt Sal, rest in peace."

Fred had never liked Aunt Sal. He could never like any Black who accepted their place in life as Aunt Sal had. Yet, there was sadness in his heart at her passing. He remembered that she had nursed him back to health. In the end it was her advice that had taught him how to survive during his days of slavery. With his last ten dollars he purchased a mule and headed west.

A Mule Called Nellie

Fred and his mule headed northwest. He passed through North Carolina. The days passed like the falling of the leaves during the onset of winter and he kept no track of time. Fred saw the beautiful landscape that the changing of the seasons brought. He was a free man and to Fred that was all that was important. With no special destination in mind, no place to go, he continued west.

The one thing in the universe that Fred understood was the mule. All of his life Fred had worked around mules. In the South that Fred had known mules were as prevalent as dogs. His mule, called "Nellie" was not just his means of transportation but his friend and traveling companion. He talked to Nellie as if she were another person and Nellie responded with all the stubbornness that mules possess. Fred had seen horses on the plantation work until they collapsed and died. That had never happened with the mules on the plantation. When Nellie got tired she just quit walking. The mule just sat or grazed and Fred knew better than to force her to continue.

He understood mules from his days on the plantation. Fred knew that treating mules with kindness got more results that anything else. Fred regarded Nellie more as his friend than as an animal, his means of transportation or a beast of burden. He always made sure that she had the time to graze and that water was available. Nellie was the one that he talked to because there was no one else around.

He passed through the battlefield of what had been the siege of Perryville, Kentucky. Near the trail he spotted a shiny object. The light was coming from the bushes about twenty yards off the trail. Deciding to investigate he gave the necessary commands to Nellie. Fred moved close to the source of light. His first thought was that the light was coming from a mirror. Upon closer inspection he discovered that it was an insignia on a hat. Closer inspection revealed the remains of what had been a Union soldier. The Union soldier had been dead for many months. Only his bones remained. Even his uniform had been almost destroyed by the scavengers.

By his guess the man had been an officer. His shoulder bars were still attached to his uniform. His remains were scattered over a wide area. The scavengers had moved his remains over almost an acre.

21

He located most of the uniform and he confiscated the hat. Near a group of bones he found a colt forty-five peacemaker revolver. He found one hundred twelve of rounds of ammunition and a holster. The gun had started to rust and the holster was badly chewed and mold ridden. Though the pistol had been exposed to the weather for many months it was in working condition. He picked up his finds including the wallet of the union soldier. He buried the remains in a shallow grave. Fred took the wallet and all the papers that he could not read. He decided that he would make a map of the area. He would return the papers to the union military department when conditions and time permitted.

He found a small sack containing five twenty-dollar gold pieces and one ten-dollar gold piece. Fred decided to keep this in return for burying the remains of the soldier and returning the papers. He took a piece of string and tied the sack containing the gold coins around his waist under his overalls. It was more money than he had ever seen at once in his whole life

The items that were of most interest to him were the colt revolver, its ammunition and holster. Traveling on until nightfall he and mostly Nellie decided to call it a day. The first stars were beginning to appear like beautiful diamonds in the sky. It was a warm night and the evening breeze was just beginning to cause a slight movement of leaves of the trees. Most of the small animals had finished feeding during daylight and only the owls were heard as they started the nightly hunt.

That night he made camp near the Fish trap Lake and caught a rabbit in a snare for his evening meal. He dared not shoot the gun that he had found for fear of being discovered with it and he was not really sure that it still operated. Fred knew that black men were not allowed handguns in most of the Southern States. He did not want to be caught with the gun and ammunition.

He cooked and ate the rabbit over an open fire. Fred used the fat from the rabbit to clean and shine the colt revolver. He cleaned the gun with all the care that he had given his musket while serving with the South Carolina Volunteers. He knew that weapons work best when clean of grime and grit. In a few hours he had the handgun looking almost new. With the remaining fat from the rabbit Fred cleaned and polished what was left of the holster. Fred fell asleep with the colt under his head. His last thought before falling asleep was how he was going to use the gun in the weeks and months to come.

The next morning he got up before dawn and took care of his mule. He rubbed her down and made sure that she had plenty of water. With no one else around to talk to, he had a long conversation with Nellie, the mule. He told Nellie that she was beautiful and that she was his best friend. He explained to her that they were going on a long journey. He told her that at the end of the trip they would rest and that all would be well. It was a one sided conversation but it made no difference to him or the mule. It was only then that he mounted the mule and set off heading northwest.

Fred was filled with the anticipation of trying out the gun. When he felt that he was far enough away from civilization he was determined to try it. Fred learned to shoot while serving in the army. He had only shot the long musket and he was not sure that the colt would shoot the same way.

He knew that the gun would be useless once the rounds of ammunition were gone. Fred was determined to make it last since the gun would be of little value without ammunition. Spotting a rabbit in the dense woods, Fred dismounted and crept to the spot where he had first seen the rabbit. He crept within about twenty feet of the spot. When rabbit ran out of its hiding place he shot at it. Much to his surprise he missed the rabbit by almost five feet.

He knew that much practice was needed if he were to use the colt revolver effectively. He decided that he would not waste more ammunition. He would practice with the weapon until he learned how to control it. Fred cut the flap from the holster and greased it with rabbit fat. He then spent countless hours practicing how to draw and aim with the colt.

He traveled mostly at night and always took the back trails staying in the dense woods whenever it was possible. Fred avoided towns and contact with civilization. It took longer traveling this way but he considered it safer.

After about eight months he had traveled through the states of Kentucky, Missouri and had reached the border of Kansas. He had learned to draw and shoot with the gun. With hour upon hour of practice he became a sharpshooter with his colt and it became an extension of his arm. The more he practiced with it the more his confidence in the gun grew. Finally, he found that he could hit a rabbit on the run at twenty feet.

He realized that his weapon, with its short barrel, was ineffective at greater than this range. Fred continued to practice with the colt. Eventually, he was convinced that he could draw and shoot as accurately as any man using the short gun. Fred became an expert marksman and could draw the short gun with lightning speed.

On the Kansas border he had his first opportunity to test his skill with the gun. While riding his mule near the Arkansas River, Nellie jumped and almost threw him. Fred looked in front of Nellie and saw a large snake directly in his path. He immediately drew the pistol. Simple reflex actions motivated Fred's movements. He did not think about what he was doing. He reacted to a situation and the colt appeared in his hand almost as if by magic. He did not consciously consider his actions or that he was aiming the weapon.

All the months of training that he had endured put his natural ability into action. He fired the pistol. Even Fred could not have analyzed his reaction. Fred hit the snake directly in the head. The snake, moving in the agony of death, represented no further threat to Fred or his mule.

He had become a master of the fast draw and was extremely accurate with the pistol. Fred cut the head off the snake and cooked the remains over a slow fire. He ate the snake while Nellie grazed nearby.

The colt revolver was now a part of the man. It was an extension of the man. Shooting the colt was as natural to him as breathing or sleeping. Fred had mastered the use of the short gun. Never again would he fear any man or any animal he would encounter. He was not just a person with a colt revolver he was the colt revolver.

While traveling, he kept the gun and its holster in a bag tied around the neck of the mule. Whenever he passed a town or small village he made sure that it was not visible. When traveling in the back woods he kept the colt in its holster.

He had forty-six rounds of ammunition left. He had no idea what he was going to do when it was gone. That problem lay in the future but he knew that somehow he would obtain more. He still had the money in the sack around his waist. He would go to a settlement and buy more ammunition when his was all gone.

Life With the Indians

As Fred was traveling through Kansas, four Indian warriors riding toward him suddenly surprised him. The warriors were about one hundred yards away when he first saw them. He stopped Nellie and just waited for them to reach him.

His colt was strapped to his waist, he realized that he could draw and drop the four warriors before they could use their weapons. Their bows and arrows were no match for his colt. Yet, Fred had no desire to kill them.

He knew that the Indians had suffered under the white man's rule just as he had. Fred was willing to take the chance that he could deal with them. When they were about thirty yards away he raised his left hand in a form of salute.

The Indian warriors signaled back with raised hands and approached cautiously on their ponies. They were perplexed by his black skin and hair. Upon seeing their first black man, they first thought he was a God of the Underworld. They spoke in sign language for a few minutes. Fred had some difficulty explaining what he was, where he was from, and where he was going.

They used sign language to show that they wanted food. He signaled that he had none. Finding that Fred had no food the warriors turned their attention to the strange pony that he was riding. The warriors pointed to their ponies and then to Nellie.

Fred said, "Mule."

They had no idea of what a mule was and just laughed at the strange pony with the oversized ears. Using sign language they finally made him understand that they wanted him to accompany them to their campsite. He agreed to go with them and the five of them took off for the Indian village.

On the way to the campsite they learned of his accuracy with his side arm. A deer bounded out of the woods in front of the group, without a second thought Fred's revolver was in his hand. A single shot to the head of the deer dropped it in its tracks. The Indian warriors could not believe what they had seen. They made him repeatedly demonstrate his ability with his side arm. They finally realized that they were dealing with a man that could have killed all

26

of them. The Indian warriors had a new respect for this black man so different from themselves. They slung the deer across one pony and headed for their campsite.

The group arrived at the Indian village, in a valley bordering the Pawnee River. The children hid behind their mothers or ran into the teepees. The women and children had never seen a jet-black human before. The Indian village was small and consisted of about thirty teepees. The small Indian village set in a clearing adjacent to the river. Nearby there was a small patch of cultivated land. Fred suspected that they were trying to grow corn or some other edible plant. In an enclosed area, there were about ten more ponies. There was a large fire pit in the center of the village. Stones surrounded the fire pit with two stakes on either side for hanging pots or other cooking apparatus.

The men removed the deer and the women went to work on it, they had not had so much meat for sometime. With only their bows to hunt with there were relatively few deer kills. From the fish drying in the sun and the hanging nets Fred surmised that they lived mostly on the fish caught in the river. He was brought before an elderly Indian warrior. Fred assumed he was the leader of this little band of about fifty Indians. He sat in a circle with the rest of the braves as the pipe passed from one to the other. As the pipe was passed no one spoke. The four warriors that brought him to the village were part of the circle of Indian men. There were no Indian children or women present at the meeting. After everyone smoked the pipe the conversation started.

After pipe ceremony, the four warriors described the incident with the deer. The Indian warriors told the gathering how they had met Fred on the trail. They described in detail Fred's uncanny ability with the colt. The leader spoke to one old Indian who spoke and understood just enough English to convey some of the elderly Indian warriors words to Fred. The old Indian warrior spoke to Fred.

"Me Shining Light, your name?"

"My name is Frederick."

"You stay with us, many braves gone to meet Great Spirit, many women need men, you pick."

The leader spoke again to the English speaking Indian and again he addressed Fred.

"Your name, Running Deer."

After the circle of warriors had broken up and most of the men went to their teepees, the children came to look at the new warrior, Running Deer. The children approached cautiously but were no longer afraid of this strange man. They rubbed his arms his and face while Running Deer sat very still. The children, like many of their elders, had never seen a black man. He was strange to them. Even his hair was different. He also spoke a language that they could not comprehend. The story of his exploits with the short gun had spread like wildfire around the village and the children were curious about this new warrior. They talked to him and even though he could not understand them he smiled and that was all that was needed. The children of the village accepted the new member of their tribe.

Fred had made no comment about staying or leaving. The choice was not left to him. The leader had spoken. He put Nellie, his mule, in the corral with the ponies. Nellie did not like the village or her surroundings. The smells, the sounds and the ponies were strange to her. Fred talked to her for a few minutes to calm her down. He fed and watered her and started walking away. Nellie followed him to the entrance of the corral unwilling to be left alone with the strange ponies. Fred spent a few minutes talking softly to her and then left her in the corral.

Few of the Indians had ever seen an animal like his mule. They were surprised that it understood commands and would obey orders like their dogs. They were also surprised to see a man talk to an animal the way Running Deer talked the Nellie. They were reluctant to mount and ride it though Running Deer, in sign language, offered to allow them to do so.

"Try to ride her, its OK, she is a good pony".

The warriors just shook their head and there were no takers. No one wanted to ride Running Deer's ugly pony.

Nellie also received a new name from the Indians. They called her "Ugly Pony With Long Ears." Running Deer was escorted by a brave to a Teepee and motioned to enter. A young woman gave him a pail of water and a rawhide robe that barely fit. He was left alone for three hours and finally the young woman came back for him.

The deer that he had killed had been cooked and a feast was in progress. The meal consisted of deer meat, roots, herbs, a corn meal like mush, and assorted fruits and nuts. He ate his fill and they informed him, using sign language, that in the morning they would hunt deer again.

The next morning Running Deer and five braves set out on their hunting trip. The braves armed with bows and arrows and Running Deer with his side arm. He now understood why the braves had problems hunting deer.

With their crude bows and arrows they had to get very close and then hope for a lucky shot. Even if they hit a deer they would have to track their kill for many miles. Often the scavengers would find the kill before they did.

He had difficulty explaining to the hunters the limitations of his handgun. Running Deer had the same problem with his short gun that they had with their bows. He could not shoot deer that were more than twenty or thirty feet away. Running Deer finally convinced them that there were ranges to his weapon and that beyond that range it was ineffective.

They tied their mounts and began to creep upon three deer eating in a little clearing on the edge of the woods. Moving down wind from the deer so they could get within range of Running Deer's deadly colt revolver. At thirty feet from the trio of deer, Running Deer drew his colt. In a blinding show of speed and accuracy he dropped two of the deer.

Running Deer, convinced that he had hit the third one, saw it run into the woods. The braves were in hot pursuit of the wounded deer. Two hundred yards away they found the dead deer. They put the three animals on their ponies and headed back for the camp.

It was late in the afternoon when they returned to the camp. All activity ceased as the returning warriors approached. The women stopped their work and the old men welcomed them back to the village. When they entered the camp the children met them. It was different from his previous entry into the camp. The children no longer hid from him. They came to him and held his hands, vying for his attention. They patted Nellie and moved quickly out of the way when she tried to nip them.

The entire tribe greeted the returning braves and Running Deer as conquering heroes. The meat that they were returning with would serve them well in the cold winter days to come. The survival of the entire tribe depended on its' ability to store food in the seasons when there was plenty. In the winter month's food would be scarce. The women of the tribe spent much of their time digging tubers and preserving fish for the winter months. Much of this deer meat would be dried and stored for use later. A part of each deer killed and each fish caught was dried and placed in a common storehouse for the entire tribe to use. Nuts, corn, and roots of various plants were also gathered during the spring and summer months. No matter how much food they stored for the winter months, there was never enough.

During winter, the entire tribe depended upon the storehouse of food prepared by the women. In long and severe winters one or more of the ponies were slaughtered to provide much needed food. The winter months were hardest on the women and children. Many younger children and the very old members of the tribe did not survive the cold winter months despite the efforts of the entire village.

The braves again described to the leader the events surrounding the hunting expedition. They had to recount the event often, first for the chief, and other braves and then for the women and several times for the children. They raised their hands and made the sound of the gun and then fell over as if they were the deer. The children never tired of hearing the story and soon they were mimicking the event.

The women stripped the meat from the deer and hung portions in the sunlight to dry. They knew that the winter month's food would be scarce and they intended to be prepared. They dried the meat and put it in storage as they did the roots, nuts and corn. Running Deer took part in the feast following the day's kill. Running Deer was happy and felt that he was among friends.

He counted his ammunition and found that he had twenty-four rounds left. He had no idea what he was going to do when it was gone. That problem would come sometime in the near future. He still had the money in the sack around his waist. He could go to a settlement and buy more ammunition when his was all gone.

The Marriage

The lazy summer days passed into autumn and then winter finally came. Running Deer remained with the Indian Tribe. He frequently hunted with them and together they killed enough game to last through most of the long winter. He was concerned because his ammunition was running low and he had no place to obtain more. He used his remaining ammunition with caution. He shot only when he was sure that he would hit his target.

One evening Running Deer sensed a change in the mood of the entire tribe. There was a festive breeze blowing through the camp. It was as if every member of the tribe knew of some impending event but Running Deer. Even the children were busy preparing for the coming event. Every Indian woman was cooking and preparing for some special festival. Only Running Deer had no idea of what was about to take place.

The men put on their finest outfits. They painted their faces and the face of Running Deer. That evening the men came to the campfire. The women and children retired to their teepees and the men sat around the campfire talking quietly to each other. The old leader of the tribe called for silence and the talking ceased.

The leader called Running Deer and took his right hand in his left hand. In his right hand he had a sharp knife. Running Deer had no idea of where the knife came from. He did not know what was about to happen. He could speak their language. Yet, he was not sufficiently fluent to follow them in normal conversation.

Running Deer was always saying to them, "Speak slowly."

The leader took the knife and in one quick motion cut a small wound in Running Deer's right hand. He released Running Deer's hand and cut each adult male's hand in the same way. Each man pressed his hand to the bleeding hand of Running Deer. Running Deer became a blood brother of the tribe.

His next act was at the insistence of the Tribal Leader. The Chief told him that he must select a mate. There was no question of what he should do. The leader had spoken. It was not a suggestion but a command. He explained to Running Deer that there were not enough males in the village and that, as a member of the tribe; it was his duty to select a mate of his choosing.

Since entering the camp, all of eligible females had competed in doing small favors for him. They brought him water, wood for his fire and followed him around. They would put on their best outfits and parade around the campsite until Running Deer noticed them. Each eligible maiden was determined to make Running Deer her mate. They knew that with his skill and hunting ability they and their children would never be without food.

The women noticed how patient Running Deer was with the children of the tribe. The children climbed all over him at each opportunity. They followed him around. He had unlimited patience in dealing with them. He spent time teaching them to make bows and arrows. He carved dolls out of wood for the small girls. The children of the tribe called him "Black papa." No brave in the tribe was more liked by the children than Running Deer.

The selection was not an easy one for him. There were ten maidens to choose from. From those eligible females of the tribe Running Deer had to select one. He was to make his choice by going to her and wrapping her in his robe. He chose one who had lost her mate in an encounter with the blue coats. Her name was "Tree Flower." Tree Flower was a beautiful Indian maiden of twenty seasons. She had long flowing black hair and moved with the grace of an antelope. Running Deer selected her because of all the maidens she appeared most serious in her actions toward him. Tree Flower was pleased that he had accepted her. She had no children and was sure that such a renowned warrior would not select her.

Running Deer had noted that she did not smile frequently like the rest of the maidens. When Tree Flower smiled the sky lit up for Running Deer. He had often seen her bringing water from the river or collecting wood for her fire. She had never followed him around or tried to get his attention. She was one of few available Indian maidens that did not vie for his attention. Occasionally, he would catch her looking at him. When he looked her way she would turn her head and continue with her chores. He was convinced that he was making the right choice.

Shining Light walked over to him and said, "She good cook and hard worker will give you many strong sons."

It pleased Tree Flower to become the woman and mate of an important hunter. That evening the tribe gathered for the marriage ceremony. Each member dressed in his or her finest outfits. Painted with red iron oxide dye and wearing her marriage clothes, Tree Flower emerged from her teepee. To Running Deer, she was the most beautiful woman he had ever seen. They were both very happy. She walked over to the Chief. He took her hand and placed it in Running Deer's hand. Running Deer wrapped her in his cloak and then the leader of the tribe joined them in marriage.

The feast and dance that followed lasted far into the night and Running Deer was very happy to see it end. Finally, the two were free to go to their teepee as husband and wife. The next day Tree Flower moved their teepee near the center of the camp. She had married the most important warrior of the tribe and it was her right.

Tree Flower was the envy of all of women of the tribe. Running Deer was devoted to Tree Flower and treated her differently from the way the other Indian braves treated their mates. He would not allow her to bring the heavy skins of water from the river but did it himself. He gathered the wood for her cooking fire and always held her hand when they were walking together. For Tree Flower, Running Deer was willing to do woman's work, work unbecoming of a warrior. He had much to learn about the Indian way of life. Running Deer was deeply in love with Tree Flower and treated her as an equal.

One day she said to him as he was returning from the river with water.

"I am strong woman. I can do that."

She saw the look of sadness come to his face and she kissed him.

She said, "I like it when you do it."

He laughed and said, "Do what?"

She gave him a tap on his buttocks and ran into the teepee and he followed her. The other women in the tribe began to demand the same treatment from their mates. Some women received the new treatment demanded. Some did not. Winter turned into spring and

Tree Flower was with child. Running Deer was happy and content with his life. He enjoyed his relationship with the tribe. After all of his wanderings, he had at last found happiness. The little village brought back fond memories of his village in Africa. The way each member of the tribe cared for others of the tribe reminded him of the way his village was. He was especially impressed with the way the children were treated. Children belonged to the entire tribe and each member of the tribe took turns caring for them. It was as Running Deer remembered from his brief boyhood experience in Africa.

Tree Flower taught him her language with the patience of a mother toward a newborn child. He helped her gather succulent roots, nuts, berries and fruit an activity that most of the braves considered beneath them. Tree Flower was pleased with the attention and caring that he showered upon her and did all that was possible to please him. When the leaves on the oak tree were the size of a squirrel's foot, Tree Flower's time had come. It was during April that Tree Flower gave birth to a baby boy.

Running Deer was not allowed at the birthing as the women of the tribe handled it. He walked around the camp in a daze and the other braves joked about his concern. They considered the birth of a child, a natural occurrence, like the coming of winter or the first snowfall. It was not their way to worry about events that were the domain of the Great Spirit. There was little thought given by them that anything could go wrong. Only Running Deer was nervous and excited by the birth of his child.

The elders of the village simply said, "It will go well or not well, it is the will of Mother Earth."

Running Deer found their attitude disquieting but he said nothing. One brave, Black Bear, came over to him. He was with the four braves that spotted Running Deer on his mule nearly two years ago. Black Bear took him by the hand. He led him to the corral where they rubbed down the ponies and the mule. Black Bear wanted to engage Running Deer in some activity that would take his mind off the events that were occurring. He was successful in his attempt. While taking care of Nellie, and the other ponies, Running Deer became engrossed in the activity. For a few moments he almost forgot that a new life was beginning a few feet away.

He talked to Nellie as he would another person. Black Bear watched astonished at the man who talked to animals as if they were people. Finally, an elderly Indian woman came for him. She did not speak but took his hand and pointed to the birthing Teepee. At first he started to run, but with all the braves watching him, he had to act the part of a man and a brave. He calmly walked to the teepee and lifted the flap and went in.

There were three women in the teepee and one was holding a blanket containing the newborn child. He ignored her and went over to the corner where Tree Flower lay with her eyes closed and took her hand. She opened her eyes and smiled at him and with all the women watching he took her in his arms and held her tightly. He kissed her and then turned his attention to the woman holding the newborn baby. His new son was strong and healthy. Running Deer was sure that all the happiness in the world belonged to him. He held the baby boy for so long that one woman finally came over and took it from him. She gave it to its mother for a feeding.

A few weeks after the birth of his son the women cleared a patch of land and planted corn. The women put a fish heads just below the seeds in each row of corn. Cultivating the ground with digging sticks, they went about their work and Running Deer watched them. He asked his wife about the fish heads. She explained, as if talking to a child, that they would make the corn grow strong and produce much fruit.

The fish in the Pawnee River were plentiful. During this time of the year there was plenty of food. Much of it was dried and stored in the common teepee for use later. The tribe would always need food during the winter months. There never seemed enough food for winter no matter how much they preserved and stored. Running Deer still had to hunt during the winter to provide the extra needed food.

Running Deer had never in his life seen a group of people so dedicated to each other, sharing and caring for the needs of all. The children were the most carefree lot of the entire tribe. Even the seasoned braves deferred to them. Teaching them the way of life prescribed by the tribe was the duty of all adult members.

Disciplining the children was also the role of all the adult members of the tribe. It was difficult to decide which child belonged to which parent. All adult members of the tribe were teachers and parents. Summer passed into fall and his son was just beginning to take his first steps.

The women of the tribe were harvesting the crop of corn. Running Deer was helping them with the task. The women did not mind that he was doing women's work and accepted him as one of them. A few of the younger women giggled when he showed up and started helping them. The stern looks from the older women and Tree Flower soon put a stop to that in short order. That night the women were inside their teepee and the men sat around a campfire. The leader of the tribe spoke to Running Deer.

"Why do you do woman's work, you are one of our bravest warriors?"

"I love my wife and enjoy helping her with her work."

The old leader smiled and nothing more was said about the matter but more of the young braves starting doing woman's work. The old ways die-hard but change was taking place and Running Deer was responsible for the small changes.

He was loved by all the tribe and more than one young Indian maiden longed for his favors. Yet, he remained faithful to Tree Flower. Their love grew stronger with the passing of the days and the seasons. In the fall of the following year he found her making another baby basket. When he asked her why, she smiled. Then she told him that the spirits were kind to them. This time it would be an Indian maiden. He chased her around the teepee. When he caught her they hugged for a long time, their love was enduring and eternal. They were happy with their love, their family and their tribe.

Death in the Indian Camp

The tribe had put away enough fish, corn and meat to last through the severe Kansas Winter. Running Deer counted his ammunition and found that he had three rounds left. The year had been good to him and the tribe. He had wasted very few rounds of ammunition. It was almost as if the Great Spirit had controlled his aim. Whenever, he aimed and shot, he hit his target. He was the most respected brave in the entire tribe.

With plenty of stored food the tribe waited for the snow that was soon to come. The tribe rejoiced in its good fortune and waited for spring. They knew that no matter how harsh the winter, spring would come. With the spring came the renewal of life. Spring brought the promise, as always, that times would be better.

Running Deer discussed his diminished supply of ammunition with the tribal chief. The chief called Shining Light and explained the problem to him.

Shining Light said to the chief, "I get more."

The next day Shining Light took five of the decorated clay pots made by the women, mounted his pony and rode off. He returned five days later with thirty rounds of ammunition. Shining Light did not speak to anyone but the chief; he then walked over to Running Deer and gave him the ammunition. He did not say where the ammunition came from. His only words to Running Deer were almost an apology.

"Later I get more."

Running Deer thanked Shining Light profusely he then thanked the chief. The chief said to him, "You good hunter, you kill much game, soon we kill more."

He wanted to ask how he was able to acquire the ammunition but decided if Shining Light wanted him to know he would have told him. He had enough ammunition for many months and that was all that mattered. Running Deer would let the matter rest.

Spring finally came and the food that they had stored lasted through the long cold winter. Tree Flower gave birth to a baby girl. This time Running Deer acted more like a brave and Tree Flower complained about this.

She said to him, "You are becoming more like an Indian warrior. You are not the person of kindness that I took to be my life mate."

"I am trying to be more like the people of the tribe."

"I don't want you like the people of the tribe, I want you like you were. You must not change, be who you are."

He took her in his arms and calmed her fears and promised that he would never change. That he would always be there for her when she needed him. He held his new daughter in his arms. He thanked his wife. She understood that he had come from a different world.

Tree Flower knew that his ideas of life and living were different from the tribe. No matter how much he wished he could not become an Indian warrior. He would always be different. She loved him and part of this love was because of this difference.

Their very existence depended upon the Pawnee River and its bountiful harvest. They drank its water, harvested its fish and lived by its rules. They had all of their needs taken care of by their warriors and the Pawnee River.

The young Indian Maidens in the group were always flirting with Running Deer. They took every opportunity to do favors for him, bringing him fruit, nuts and berries. This did not go unnoticed by Tree Flower.

One day Running Deer was lying under a tree and a young Indian maiden came up with a branch. She sat beside him and started fanning him with the branch. Tree Flower had more of this than she could endure. She grabbed the young woman by the hair and would have torn it out by the roots had Running Deer not intervened. It was the first fight Running Deer had witnessed, a tragic disagreement among tribal members. He felt responsible for causing the fight. Running Deer was determined that it would not happen again. Back in the teepee that night Tree Flower would not talk to him. Finally the next morning he kissed her and asked her what was wrong.

"I don't want the other women around you."

"She meant no harm."

"You are my man and if you need fruits, water or fanning I will provide it."

Running Deer was convinced that he would never understand women. He agreed with her. After the talk Running Deer accepted

39

no more gifts from the women of the tribe. He avoided being caught alone with any of the Indian women and peace reigned in his teepee.

His wife made him a deerskin pair of britches and a vest. They were not as comfortable as his overalls but he put them on and wore them to please her. He allowed her to paint his face and upper body for the fall festival. The night of the festival his wife put the children to sleep and joined him in the festivities.

At first he had some difficulty with the dance steps that the braves did but he caught on quickly. They danced late into the night and then retired to their teepee. He held her close, told her of his love for her and calmed her fears about other Indian maidens. Running Deer counted his blessings and was sure that few men experienced the happiness that they enjoyed.

It was a bright clear autumn day when he set out with three of the braves to hunt deer early in the morning. The dew was still on the leaves of the plants when they left the village. The sunlight reflecting off the water on the leaves gave the trees the appearance of crystals. The day promised to be one of those early spring days when everything would go perfectly. The birds in the trees welcomed the day with their song.

Tree Flower had prepared a small sack of food and water for him to take with him. He held her for a long time and then kissed his sleeping children and joined his hunting companions. He mounted his mule as they selected their ponies and the four hunters started on their journey. Leaving early in the morning he promised Tree Flower that they would return before the end of the day.

They traveled some distance from the camp since the deer stayed in the deep woods. Five miles from the camp they spotted their first deer. Coming upon it from upwind the deer caught their scent and ran deeper into the forest. They could not get close enough for any attempt at a kill. They made a wide circle ending up about ten miles from the camp. The hunters came upon a large stag and two doe grazing in the woods.

They circled again making sure that they were downwind from the group of deer. Tying their mounts to trees, about a quarter mile from the deer, they started to creep back toward them. Quietly and creeping from tree to tree and bush to bush they closed in on their quarry. Thirty feet away Running Deer raised his weapon and took careful aim and dropped the big buck in its tracks. The female deer ran into the dense cover and he did not attempt to shoot it. The other braves asked running Deer why he did not shoot the other deer. He tried to explain that they were female.

This made little sense to the other three and they said, "One can eat female deer also".

"Female deer bare young and someday will produce more deer for us to kill. If we kill all the females there will come a time when deer will not be plentiful as they are now. This big buck will provide all the meat that we need for the present."

The three braves started to tackle the problem of getting the large buck back to the camp. It was too large to sling over the ponies. The pony could carry the buck but one of them would have to walk the ten miles back to the camp. The braves cut two long poles using their tomahawks. They made a cradle of vines and place the poles on either side of the pony.

They carefully loaded the deer, mounted and started the journey back to the camp. Half way to the camp Running Deer saw how tired the pony was becoming and halted the group. He attached the poles to a complaining "Nellie" his mule and friend and that started the journey home. After about two miles, Nellie sat on her hind legs and refused to go any further with her load. A brave picked up a stick to beat Nellie into continuing. Running Deer would not allow him to use it. He went over to Nellie and whispered softly in her large ears. Nellie got up and he walked beside her for the rest of the trip.

As they approached the camp Running Deer sensed that something was drastically wrong. There was an unnatural quietness in the air. The children were not coming up the path to greet them. There were no barking dogs. There was the smell of smoke and burnt flesh in the air. Running Deer left Nellie to continue the journey alone and raced for the campsite. What Running Deer found of the campsite overwhelmed him.

Where the campsite had been nothing stood and there were dead bodies everywhere. There were no signs of a fight and there were no strangers among the dead. The signs suggested that the tribe had no time to resist the onslaught of the attackers. Running Deer looked for strange bodies among the dead and found none. Nothing moved in the campsite, even the dogs were dead. The teepees were still smoldering. In panic he called for his wife and children and received no reply. He rushed for their burnt teepee and there he found them, dead like the other members of the tribe. Tree Flower had been shot twice, once in the head and once in the chest. Both children had been shot as she held them trying desperately to protect them.

He held the lifeless body of his wife close to him as tears streamed down his face. Running Deer could not imagine who could have committed such a crime. Running Deer knew that if it were another Indian tribe that committed this act they would have spared the women and children. They would have taken the women and children with them after killing the braves. It would be unusual for the blue coats to attack an unarmed village.

He heard movement from the bushes behind his teepee and his hand went for his gun. Seconds before he was ready to pull the trigger, a whimpering Indian boy of nine seasons, emerged into view. The other three braves had joined him and they were busy yelling at the distraught boy who could only utter:

"Mama, Mama, Mama."

The camp was in total disarray. There was destruction everywhere. Running Deer held his wife in his arms and cried. His world, his life was destroyed. He could not imagine whom or why such a crime would be committed. He picked up his children and brushed the dried blood from their clothes as if this act would bring life back to them. Like his wife, Tree Flower, the children had been dead for many hours.

Running Deer said aloud, "Why did we go hunting today, why did this have to happen?"

No one could answer his question.

A brave who had been talking to the lone survivor came over to him and said, "pale face."

Running Deer could only utter a single word, "Why."

The boy had been play hunting in the woods, when the attack occurred. They desperately tried to get him to tell who was responsible for the destruction of the camp. The boy was of little help. So distraught was the boy, it took sometime to get him to explain to them what had taken place.

It took almost an hour for the boy to calm down enough to tell them how the destruction of the village was accomplished.

He said to them, "When the sun was high in the sky. A band of about twenty-five white men came. They had sticks that kill. They killed all the people. When they finished killing everyone, they set fire to the teepees."

He had come out of the woods when he first heard the thunder of the sticks that the white men carried. He hid behind a tree and watched as the men destroyed the camp. He alone had survived the carnage. He survived because he was outside the camp when the men arrived. Even the small babies and children were shot. They took nothing and destroyed everything. Even the ponies in the corral were shot. Of the small band of fifty-five Indians there were five left. The three braves, Running Deer, and a small Indian boy were all that was left of the tribe.

It took the four of them five days to bury all the dead. The ponies they did not bury but left them for the scavengers. This would help prevent the scavengers from disturbing the graves. The remaining braves wanted to burn the dead. Running Deer explained to them that such a large fire and smoke would attract the attention of the attackers. They would return and kill the remaining members of the tribe.

They buried the dead in shallow graves and piled stones on the top of them. On Tree Flower's grave and those of his children he placed crude crosses. He had seen this done on the plantation and upon the graves of the soldiers killed during the war. He was not sure of the significance of crosses but it seemed the right thing to do. When the braves asked him about them, he explained that he was calling upon the Great Spirit. The Great Spirit would take them safely to the hunting grounds. He spent sometime at the grave of his wife and children. Finally, one brave came over to him and signaled that it was time for them to leave. There was no point is staying in the camp, where they would go they had no idea.

After the burial, they took as much of the dried meat and other food as they could find. Much of the food was burned and useless, they picked through the ruins of the storage Teepee and took what they could. They filled their water skins from the river and the five of them started on their journey. The small boy, still in a state of shock was place on a pony with one brave. They wanted to get as far away from the white man's civilization as possible. They headed southwest deeper into Indian country.

Quanah, Last Champion of the Comanche

They did not speak of the destruction of their village. Yet, each man wanted to avenge the death of the members of the tribe. In seven weeks the small group had crossed the Oklahoma territory into Texas. They wanted to contact and join the Indian groups fighting the white man. The braves realized that their small group stood little chance against the white man's guns. They intended to join the Indians fighting the white man, and with them, kill as many white men as possible. They were determined to avenge the destruction of their village and their tribe. Who ever was responsible for this macabre sequence of events would eventually pay dearly for what they had done.

Near the North Palo Dura, Running Deer and his companions met a band of Indians lead by the Comanche half-breed, Quanah. Quanah's, mother Cynthia Ann Parker, and was captured by the Comanche in a raid on Parker's Fort. She was nine years old when the raid occurred. She had grown up with the Indians and knew no other life. She became the wife of Quanah's father, Peta, the young chief of the Noconas. Early in her marriage she gave birth to Quanah. Quanah looked like a full blooded Comanche except that his eyes were blue-gray. She gave birth to Quanah's brother Pecos and his sister Prairie Flower. Cynthia Ann was proud of, and content with, her husband. She refused to allow ransom to be paid for her when it was offered. She told those who would ransom her that she had children to care for. She did not want to leave because she loved her husband.

Like all Comanche children, Quanah grew up on horseback. He learned to ride as soon as he learned to walk. When Quanah was six, he had his own pony and was practicing with the bow and arrow. Rough play and daylong rides were the lot of Comanche boys who would someday become warriors. He grew up envying the Comanche warriors who paraded around the camp before going on raids. As a young Indian boy, Quanah's one desire was to grow up and become a true Comanche warrior.

When Quanah grew to be a man he took his father's place as chief of the Noconas. He was a fearless and able Indian warrior. Quanah led his people in their fight against the white man. Quanah and his band were spreading fear through most of Texas. His quick raids and narrow escapes from the United States Cavalry were rekindling war fever among the plains Indians who were still free. Those Indians on reservations sought any news of his exploits, hoping that he might reverse their fortunes.

Running Deer had no idea who the group was nor did his companions. They watched the group for about five hours from a hill one half mile away before deciding to join them. They were determined to find a group of Indians still fighting the white man. They thought that this was such a group they so decided to make their move.

After much discussion, it was decided that one brave and the young boy would ride down to the Indian Camp. They were to ask if they could join them. By taking the young boy, they could more easily explain what had happened to them. They wanted show that they were intending to wage war on the white man. They wanted to prove that they were not there to steal horses from them or to harm them. Running Deer and the other three braves stayed where they were to await the outcome of the meeting. Two hours after leaving, only the brave returned. He informed the other three that the chief wanted to talk to all of them. Running Deer asked if their band had been receptive to their plans of joining them.

He was told what the chief had said, "We can always use more braves."

They decided to go into the Indian Camp.

When Chief Quanah saw Running Deer, he was not pleased and accused him of being a spy for the white man. The other braves of Running Deer's group recounted his uncanny ability with the six-shooter. Quanah was not impressed with their disclosure. He would have proof of Running Deer's skill with his weapon.

It took hours of telling and recounting the fate of their tribe before Quanah made his decision. He set the conditions that would allow the four men to join the group or be killed. It was a test of courage and ability and Running Deer was the warrior selected to perform the task.

He asked Running Deer for his gun and took it in his hand and examined it carefully. Quanah finally announced his decision. He had his braves bring a log near the campfire and placed seven stones on the log. He then told Running Deer that he would have one chance of joining his group and fighting the white man. He first had to pass a test.

If he failed the test, Running Deer and his companions would die. Only the life of the young boy would be spared. Using his six-shooter, Running Deer would have to shoot the seven rocks off the log without reloading.

When one brave held up his hand and showed six fingers and pointed to the seven stones, all Quanah's warriors began to laugh. They knew that the task was an impossible one. One of the Indian braves with Running Deer started to protest, stating that the task assigned was not fair. One of Quanah's braves put his spear in his chest. He would kill him on the spot if he protested further. This silenced Running Deer's small group.

They knew that death was the outcome of the trial. There was nothing that they could do about it. They would have to await the outcome. They would accept the outcome and die as bravely as possible. Quanah had given Running Deer an impossible task. Death awaited Running Deer and his companions when and if he failed.

Running Deer was moved about twenty yards from the log and Quanah returned his gun to him. There was nothing but silence as he moved into position with his gun in its holster and prepared to draw. He realized that Quanah was serious about their deaths and he had one chance to save the four of them.

His hand speed was a blur of light as the gun appeared in his hand. In rapid secession the first five stones flew from the log then with a second hesitation he fired his final round. He hit the sixth stone on the side. The stone slid into the one next to it and both fell from the log. A shout went up from the two hundred warriors assembled in the camp. The warriors were amazed at what had taken place. Quanah had given Running Deer an impossible task and he had accomplished it. Quanah raised his hand for silence. It was a few minutes before silence was restored and then Quanah spoke to the assembled warriors.

He said, "My word is as sacred as the great mountain where the sun sets. The Great Spirit honors both a man and his word, any man that does not keep his word is not worthy or honorable in the eyes of the Great Spirit."

"As my father and my father's father before him, the word of a Comanche leader cannot be false. If the leader's word is false, misfortune falls upon our people. Therefore, these four will become members of our tribe. They will become our blood brothers and help us drive the white man from our lands."

"Running Deer is not the name of a true warrior, tonight we will celebrate the new warrior and give Running Deer a new name."

Running Deer had to prove repeatedly, his ability with his six-shooter. They had him demonstrate his shooting ability while riding a pony. They were impressed with his accuracy. When mounted on a moving pony he was as accurate as standing. He was more accurate with the gun when moving as opposed to standing still. Though many braves had guns, none could shoot as rapidly and as accurately as Running Deer. One of Running Deer's companions put a pipe in his mouth. At twenty yards, Running Deer shot the pipe out of his mouth. This little group had found a home with the fighting Indians of the plains that would allow them to avenge the death of their tribe.

That night the braves danced. Late into the night they began planning the raid of a settlement some fifty miles away. Their scouts had just returned and explained the layout and the war council was busy making plans for the battle that would take place the next day. Quanah, true to his word, gave Running Deer a new name. To his new tribe he would be known as "Eagle Eye." The young boy was turned over to the women to be trained in the fashion of warriors.

Eagle Eye's mule Nellie was placed in the corral with the ponies. Eagle Eye had to spend more time than normal convincing Nellie that everything would be all right. He made sure that she had plenty of food and water, and then walked away from her. The other Indian warriors were curious about the mule. They accepted Eagle Eye's word that she was as good as any horse but not quite as fast. For the upcoming raid, Quanah had provided Eagle Eye with one of his ponies. This act by the chief showed the rest of the braves that Eagle Eye was a special warrior and had gained his respect.

The next morning, two hundred warriors left the campsite located in Palo Duro chasm. They headed west for the settlement of Pampa about thirty miles away. They rode their ponies hard and left behind a cloud of dust. Scouts sent out in all directions kept them informed of any blue coats in the area of their passage. They came within ten miles of the settlement and camped for the night. Scouts were sent to get information about the settlement. The number of horses in the settlement was of special interest. Quanah's men did not need ponies, yet, to the warriors of Quanah's tribe, stealing horses was almost as important as taking scalps. They realized that if the winter was particularly severe and no buffalo were available, the extra ponies could be used for food.

The success of this mission was almost a forgone conclusion. There were careful plans laid about the escape route. Spare ponies were selected to insure a swift return. These spare ponies were left at the temporary campsite ten miles from the point of attack. The plan called for them to cover their tracks by crossing rocky terrain and traveling through streambeds.

The Texas frontier was too extended to defend all points against surprise attack. The raiding party knew and understood the terrain that they would cover. There would be scouts in front and behind them. Quanah was a capable warrior and leader. He did all that was possible to protect his men and their ponies.

Eagle Eye had killed men during the civil war, but had taken little pleasure in doing it. Now it was different. He envisioned the white men camped outside his tribe's camp and how they planned to burn and destroy the village and kill its' occupants. The white men had killed his wife, his children and his tribe without mercy. Now his turn would come to destroy one of their villages and to avenge the death of his wife, his children and his tribe. Eagle Eye looked forward to the coming raid and the destruction of the white man's village. His reasons for wanting to destroy the village were personal. Nothing would stand in his way and no white man that he encountered would survive.

The chief held a planning session and it was decided that they would strike at first light. Not a building was to be left standing. No one in the settlement was to be spared. The ponies and any other available supplies were to be taken back the camp by the warriors.

The warriors put on their war paint and readied their weapons and at first light they hit the village. Only the barking of the dogs greeted them as they entered. The attack on the village was a total surprise to the occupants.

Eagle Eye headed directly for the general store. He dispatched the shopkeeper and the two other occupants. He took all the rounds of ammunition that he could find. He did not intend to ever run out of ammunition for his weapon as long as there were white men to kill. He took what ammunition was available and set fire to the structure.

Quanah's warriors set fire to all the building in Pampa. They shot the inhabitants as they emerged from the buildings. The surprise attack left the village defenseless. Every building in the village was destroyed, burned to the ground.

Eagle Eye was at Quanah's side. He dropped the first six men in their path before they could shoot their weapons. He reloaded and continued to fire until there was nothing left to shoot. His thoughts were not centered upon what he was doing. His thoughts were of his wife and children. With each white man he shot, he recalled the vision of Tree Flower, and his children, Little Sparrow and Small Running Deer.

The destruction of the village was complete. Only one warrior was lost. In two hours there was no one alive in the village. The warrior rounded up the horses took the few remaining supplies from the burned out general store. They took their dead warrior with them. He would be given a hero's burial when they reached their camp. True to the Comanche proverb, "A brave man dies young" the slain warrior had seen only fifteen winters. They mounted their ponies and headed out before the blue coats could arrive.

The warriors left while the village still burned.

Scouts returned during the raiding parties rest stop. They informed Quanah that a troop of about three hundred fifty blue coats were about three miles away and were closing in fast. Quanah was preparing his band to move out. Seven aged warriors stepped forward.

They said to Quanah, "We will stay."

Quanah said to them, "It is the will of the Great Spirit. We will remember you around the campfire. We will meet you in the happy hunting ground. Give regards to our ancestors."

Eagle Eye did not understand what was happening. He only knew that the old men were to be left behind. He objected to this.

He said to Quanah, "I will stay behind with them."

"No it is not your time."

Eagle Eye said, "They will all be killed."

Quanah said, "Let it be Eagle Eye, later you will understand why those brave warriors chose to stay behind."

Eagle Eye did not understand but he bowed to the wisdom of Quanah. He turned and took one last look at the seven aged warriors who had decided to stay behind while the rest of them rode on. Eagle Eye then joined Quanah and the rest of the braves and they moved rapidly from the area.

The seven said their good-byes to their chief. They mounted their horses and rode off to meet the oncoming blue coats. Running Deer, called Eagle Eye by the Comanche, marveled at the act of bravery of the old men. In all his life, he had never witnessed such an act of bravery. Seven aged warriors, alone, facing three hundred armed blue coats. He wanted to join them but was prevented from doing so by Quanah. He had much to learn about Comanche customs and way of life.

The soldiers pursuing the Comanche raiding party came within view of the aged warriors. Quanah's aged warriors watched, then they dismounted and removed their moccasins, a sure sign they did not intend to leave the spot alive. These aged warriors were ready to meet the Great Spirit. The old men fought bravely killing six soldiers and wounding five before they died riddled with bullets. While they made their brave stand, the Comanche raiding party escaped.

Later at the campsite, as the men were feasting and recounting the events surrounding the raid, Quanah called his commanders into his tent. He signaled for Eagle Eye to enter the tent with them. It was here that he got his first lessons in the ways of the Comanche.

Quanah wanted to explain why he would not allow Eagle Eye to stay with the old men. He asked his medicine man Isa-tai to do it.

Isa-tai said, "You are young and strong. They were old."

"Why did they choose to stay?"

"Their fighting days are numbered, and only those who are able to fight are considered warriors."

They are fortunate for they picked their time and place to die. Few men can pick their time and place to meet the Great Spirit. It is better to die in battle than to become an old man unable to care for one self."

Quanah said, "Your time to die will come. Try to die a hero in battle as our companions did today. Tonight we will honor them."

Eagle Eye had learned one valuable lesson about the Comanche and their way of life. Comanche men hunted to live but lived to win honors and booty in war. He knew that someday his time would come to meet the Great Spirit. He hoped the he would die as bravely as the old men. Stories went around the camp of Eagle Eye's exploits and his role in the raid. It embarrassed him when the other warriors vied to see who would sit next to him at the campfire. Yet, he was pleased that he and his companions had been accepted. He could now avenge the death of his wife and children and his tribe.

He finally got up from the campsite and went to the corral to talk to Nellie. Nellie was pleased to see him. Nellie showed her pleasure by trying to kick him. He calmed her, rubbed her, fed her and then left her in the corral with the rest of the ponies.

The next raid was designed to remove some blue coats that were searching for the Comanche Camp. The scouts had located the soldiers about twenty miles from the campsite at Staked Plains. Quanah called his war council together and made plans for the attack. The plan involved taking the two hundred fifty warriors and meeting the pony soldiers in the open plains. They would come in from the east and west to engage the blue coats in battle.

A temporary site for the conflict was selected in the open plains. An escape route was decided upon and the warriors were divided into two groups. Fresh horses were placed at a site five miles from the scene of the battle. This would insure the warriors that they would have fresh mounts for the return trip.

Eagle Eye was not pleased with the plan. He explained to Quanah that many braves would die if they attacked the blue coats on horseback in the open plain. He suggested that they lie in wait along the rock-strewn passage of the canyon where the troops would pass. There they would wait until the pony soldiers were in sight before shooting them from their horses. Most of the warriors objected to this plan.

They said, "Comanche warriors do no hide when they fight. Comanche warriors face their enemy in open battle. They accepted death if it comes."

Eagle Eye said, "Death will come to many if we meet the pony soldiers as planned."

"Many braves will lose their lives uselessly unless my plan for the battle is followed. The pony soldiers have many long guns and they shoot as well as I do."

"We have seen no white man who shoots as you shoot."

"The pony soldiers have long rifles, they are more accurate over a long distance than I am. Their guns are accurate as high as the eagle flies and as far away as a spent arrow."

A heated argument followed as many younger braves were for meeting the pony soldiers head on and fighting them to the death. They held to their view that a Comanche warrior does not hide from the enemy. The wisdom of Quanah prevailed. The plan that was suggested by Eagle Eye was the chosen one. It was not because of Eagle Eye or Quanah but the medicine man, Isa-tai.

Isa-tai said, "I wish to recount a dream that I had last night."

All listened attentively as the medicine man told of his dream.

He said, "I dreamed that a wounded fox was starving. The fox needed food. For many moons he had very little to eat and only water to drink. The fox could not catch game because he only had three good legs. One day the fox spotted a rabbit and he wanted to eat the rabbit. He knew that with his three legs he could not outrun the rabbit. He hid behind a rock and when the rabbit passed he pounced upon it and had his first good meal in many moons. From then on the fox was never hungry. He learned to hide and wait for his meal to come to him."

Everyone in the room looked at Eagle Eye's left hand and saw the three remaining fingers. There was no doubt in the minds of the council what was to be done. They might question the wisdom of Eagle Eye or another warrior or even their leader Quanah, but none would question the wisdom of the medicine man. The words of the medicine man, Isa-tai, was above even that of the leader, Quanah.

The Indian scouts followed the trail of the pony soldiers, counted their number, their horses and their guns. Their scouts and trackers reported to Quanah and Eagle Eye that the soldiers would pass through Rocky Canyon the next day at noon. Quanah's band of about two hundred fifty warriors, much to the dismay of many young warriors, left the campsite on foot. The Indian warriors took their weapons and supplies on five packhorses and headed for Rocky Canyon. Each man was given instruction by Eagle Eye and told not to fire or be seen until they heard his six-shooter. No warrior was to leave his position until all the pony soldiers were dead. They were to continue to shoot from their hiding place.

For the first time, the warriors realized there would be no hand-to-hand combat. Many warriors were not pleased. Eagle Eye explained that the pony soldiers shoot very well, almost as well as he did and that any man who exposed himself would die.

Isa-tai spoke up and said, "It was my dream that made this possible. I want to accompany the warriors to learn the truth of how the Great Spirit speaks to a person in his dreams."

Quanah stated, "This is the work of warriors. A medicine man is too valuable to the tribe to be lost if the attack does not succeed. The pony soldiers fight well and die well."

"The Great Spirit has told me in my dream that not one warrior or member of our tribe will be lost in this attack. I will accompany you without fear".

Quanah said to Isa-tai, "You will be allowed to accompany us in this attack on the pony soldiers. Since it is the will of the Great Spirit."

There were warriors who disagreed with the battle plans; yet, there were none that voiced the opinion that the medicine man should not accompany them. He would assure their success in the battle. This time Isa-tai would accompany the warriors on a raid and it was to be a very dangerous raid. Even the Comanche avoid the pony soldiers whenever possible. In the past conflicts with the pony soldiers they had lost many braves. Isa-tai's desire to go on the raid convinced the warriors that it would be a success. If they carried out the plan as outlined by the medicine man and Eagle Eye, they could not fail.

The next day when the sun started its journey across the sky, when the owl was asleep in his tree and the ground squirrels were in their borrows, Quanah, Eagle Eye and the rest of the warriors went to meet the blue coats. When the sun was at its zenith, Quanah and his raiders were hidden among the rocks on the side of the canyon. Quanah told them that even loud breathing was not allowed. They must remain as silent as the eagle that soars in the sky if the plan was to succeed. All objects, which would reflect sunlight, were to be left behind in the temporary camp. Nothing was left to chance.

Two warriors had killed the scout for the troops one hour before the arrival of the Indians in the canyon. Eagle Eye was at the end of the line of warriors hidden in the canyon. He waited until the standard bearer was even with him. The rest of the troops were strung out in a column of two passing through the canyon. He dropped the standard barrier with a single shot. From every rock in the canyon bullets and arrows fell on the column of soldiers. The soldiers and horses dropped like the leaves from an oak tree during the onset of winter.

There was no place for them to hide or run. The Indians commanded both sides of the canyon. In twenty minutes there were no pony soldiers still standing. Two braves had been wounded. They went down into the canyon floor and finished off the wounded soldiers. They took scalps, horses, guns and as much ammunition as they could find. They loaded the horses and headed back to their campsite. The raid had been a success and the Comanche had learned a new way to fight. Isa-tai was assured that he could talk to the Great Spirit. Eagle Eye had learned that an idea is not enough. One must have the man who speaks to the Great Spirit on his side. Without Isa-tai, the Comanche would never have accepted his battle plan.

The Comanche changed their campsite to McClellan Creek, which was at the edge of the Staked Plains. They knew that more blue coats would come looking for them. Their old campsite was no longer a safe haven. They arrived at their new campsite late the next day. The ponies were put in a makeshift corral and the warriors prepared to celebrate their victory over the blue coats.

They danced and celebrated late into the night. Eagle Eye was made second in command with fifty braves under his control. He was given new clothes made of buffalo hide. Except for his skin color, Eagle Eye was pure Comanche.

Adobe Walls

A ll was not well with the plains Indians in the year 1873. The buffalo were all but gone in Kansas. With the buffalo depleted in Kansas, the hide hunters moved on to the Texas panhandle. There was an agreement made by the white man that the few buffalo remaining would be spared by the hunters. It was an agreement they never intended to keep. They would destroy the remaining buffalo and by doing so, destroy the Plains Indians. With the buffalo gone, the Plains Indians would be left to the mercy of the white man.

When white hunters moved into the Texas panhandle the government made no effort to stop them. The white hunters were encouraged to move in the area by the government. The government realized that with the end of the buffalo, the life and times of the plains Indians would end. The end of the buffalo on the plains would force the hostile plains Indians into dependence on reservation rations. With the Indians dependent upon government rations, the government could starve them into submission.

The presence of the white buffalo hunters in Texas fueled the flames of hatred in the Plains Indians. They knew what had happened to all the buffalo further north and they wanted to prevent it from happening in the buffalo's last refuge. It was this action that forced Quanah and his band to take drastic measures for their survival.

The Comanche, Kiowa, Arapaho and Cheyenne bands rallied around their Indian leaders and formed an intertribal federation. They would fight for their rights and the lives of the remaining buffalo. Two of the leaders were Quanah and his second in command, Eagle Eye.

The white hide hunters set up a base near the deserted trading post of Adobe Walls on the South Canadian River. The intertribal federation met and they decided they would attack and destroy Adobe Walls. Quanah would lead the combined forces in the attack. Isa-tai, the great Comanche medicine man stated at the tribal meeting that the Great Spirit had approached him. The Great Spirit had taken him to heaven. There the Great Spirit had talked with him and had given him magical powers.

The most important was the formula for a magic paint that would make the horses and men impervious to the bullets of the white men. He prophesied that the attack would drive the white men away and return the buffalo to the plains. He urged the Comanche to hold a ghost dance to prepare for the attack. Eagle Eye and Quanah approved the suggestions of the medicine man. In the spring of 1874 the Comanche celebrated their ghost dance. It took place at the junction of Elk Creek and the North Fork of the Red River.

After the celebration, Quanah, Eagle Eye and the other chiefs met in a war council. The council agreed there would be an all out attack against all whites. Adobe Walls would be the first in a series of attacks by the Federation. Quanah and Eagle Eye would lead the combined forces. On June 26, with eight hundred warriors, the two men attacked Adobe Walls under the cover of darkness. Eagle Eye came with two hundred warriors from the west. The remaining force under Quanah attacked from the east.

There were twelve buildings about fifty yards apart in Adobe Wall and one hundred twenty men and women occupied them. The combined forces of the Comanche destroyed the small settlement and burned it to the ground.

No one survived the onslaught. Eagle Eye had his mount shot out from under him and had to crawl to cover behind the carcass of a dead horse. Moments later he was briefly stunned when a bullet, spent after its flight over long range, ricocheted and hit him in the chest. He caught up with a horse without its rider and continued the fight. Eagle Eye proved again that he was a true Comanche warrior. The stories of his exploits were told around the Indian Camp sites until late in the night. Eagle Eye was rapidly becoming a legend among the plains Indians.

After Adobe Walls, the Indians scattered and vented their fury in attacks from the state of Texas to Colorado. White men were killed in such numbers that Washington sent an ultimatum to the Indian tribes.

They were informed that all Indians who did not enroll on the reservation by August 3, 1874 would be hunted down and killed by

U. S. Forces. Soon after that, ten columns of cavalry and infantry were sent to attack the Comanche strongholds.

Their first effort met with little success. Eagle Eye had so changed the fighting patterns of the Indian warriors that the pony soldiers could never find a real target. The Comanche ambushed the pony soldiers and vanished into the hills.

The End of the Buffalo

Unable to stop the Comanche raids of Quanah and Eagle Eye, the military embarked upon their master plan. The plan was designed to bring the Indians to their knees. To the plains Indians, the buffalo represented a continuous source of food, fuel and the necessities of life. The wild horses on the plains allowed the mobile way of life that the plains Indians had become accustom to.

The army and the United State's government set out to destroy the plains Indians. Buffalo were slaughtered to take away the Indian's livelihood. When the slaughter of the buffalo was complete, less than five hundred of the sixty million were left on the western plains. The horse population was also systematically destroyed. The end was in sight for Quanah, Eagle Eye and all their warriors.

Many Comanche tribes succumbed to the white man's pressure and entered the reservation. Quanah, Eagle Eye and their warriors were not among them. They continued to raid and kill whenever possible. They attacked the blue coats and settlers in quick raids and then vanished into the surrounding hills.

The United States government was determined to finish the Comanche raids and make Texas safe for settlers. In 1870 the command of the Fourth Cavalry was assigned to put a halt to the raids. Under the command of Slidell Mackenzie, the 4th Cavalry set out to mount an invasion of the Comanche homeland.

Mackenzie's command attacked the Comanche warriors of Quanah and Eagle Eye. The wily chiefs remembered the fight in the canyon. They refused to fight a pitched battle. Eagle Eye led his warriors in lightning raids on the 4th Calvary's rear guard and then vanished into their hiding place.

In October, Quanah and Eagle Eye led a wild charge through Mackenzie's camp, ringing bells and flapping buffalo skins to panic the cavalry horses. The Indians warriors rounded up the stampeding horses. The raid netted Quanah and Eagle Eye seventy prime mounts. During the winter some older mounts of the Comanche had to be used as food and they badly needed new mounts and the new mounts would serve to fuel their raids for only a few months.

With the onset of winter, more Comanche bands surrendered to the reservation. Without the buffalo the Comanche bands were starving to death. Eagle Eye and Quanah, with about four hundred of their people, held out.

Quanah and Eagle Eye were out hunting what buffalo they could find in the spring of 1875, when a white doctor, Dr. Joseph Long, learned of their whereabouts from reservation informants. He was commissioned by the United States government to deliver a message to Quanah and his renegade band of Indians.

He located the Comanche holdout and delivered a message from the United States Government. If the Comanche would come to the reservation, they would be treated well. The United States Army would take no further action against them. If they continued to hold out and fight, the federal troops would exterminate them.

Quanah called his council together. He decided to accept the white man's offer. Many younger warriors were starting to take off their moccasins. They were stopped by the words of Isa-tai.

"The Great Spirit has spoken and his words of wisdom say that this is the only course of action left to us. With the buffalo gone, there is no other way our people can survive. We will follow the leadership of Quanah."

Quanah said to Eagle Eye. "You are a true Comanche though your skin is different. My eyes are also different from most Comanche's, but we are all brothers. Where we go, you go. Where we pitch our tents, you pitch your tent. When we smoke the pipe by the campfire, you smoke the pipe also. We owe you much. You must go with us to the land that the white man has set aside for us."

Eagle Eye was silent for a few minutes and then he spoke.

"My brother Quanah and fellow warriors, we fought the enemy together. We ate together and rode together. There comes a time when all brothers must part. If I were an old man, I would take off my moccasins and prepare to meet the Great Spirit. My time has not yet come. The pale face will not allow me to go with you to the new land. I am a black man. We must say our good-byes. The time of parting is near."

Quanah said to him, "I will insist that they accept you as one of us. If you cannot go, then none of us will go, we will continue the fight."

"My life and my existence are not as important as the survival of our people. You and your people have been my only family for many moons and my continued existence isn't as important as that of our tribe."

Quanah said, "I will accept your decision though I do not agree with it. You are my brother and I am willing to die for you or with you."

Eagle Eye answered, "My love for you and our people is strong, yet each man is responsible for his own destiny. I have made my decision."

"So be it."

They celebrated late into the night and at first light Eagle Eye arose and went to the corral to get Nellie. Waiting for him at the entrance was Quanah.

"You would not leave without saying goodbye to your old Comrade in arms."

They talked of old times and hugged for a long time and finally Eagle Eye mounted Nellie and rode off without looking back. Again, Eagle Eye and Nellie were on the trail without family or friends. He had accomplished much of what he set out to do. He had avenged the death of his wife, Tree Flower, and his two children. Many white men paid for their deaths.

The New Mule

Nellie was beginning to show her age. Eagle Eye had to find another mule. He preferred mules to horses because he understood them better. Mules were all that he had ever owned. He knew that mules were more surefooted than horses and could traverse the rough terrain of the plains with less difficulty. He still had the gold pieces found along with the Colt Peacemaker. He decided to purchase another mule. He cautiously approached farming villages. He was looking for one where other blacks lived. He felt that if the people had seen other blacks and were accustomed to them, there would be less chance of trouble.

After spending weeks traveling through Oklahoma and the southern tip of Kansas, he spotted a farming village in southern Colorado that contained a few black families. He had no idea of what his reception would be upon entering the village. He knew that he could not ride in wearing the colt revolver. Yet, he wanted it where it would be within easy reach just in case he ran into unexpected trouble. In the distance he saw a family in a buckboard, apparently on their way to town.

In his travels he had lost tract of time, he had no idea what day of the week it was. He assumed it was Saturday because that was the day that people went to town to purchase supplies for the week. Most farmers that he knew and was familiar with could not afford to take time from their labor to go to town during the middle of the week. Much to his surprise, the buckboard contained a black family. The mule pulling the buckboard was strong, young and healthy.

He said to himself, "I would sure like to get my hands on that mule."

Eagle Eye approached them. He did not want to frighten them, but he desperately needed to talk to them. He put his gun in a bag around Nellie's neck and rode off to meet the first blacks that he had seen in many years.

He said to Nellie, "Ain't no use in scaring them by being a black man with a gun. They might think that I intend to do them harm. Then they might just panic and make a run for the village. Then what would I do?"

The family consisted of the man, his wife and three small boys. He rode up to the buckboard and signaled that he wanted to talk to them. The man was reluctant to stop but his wife saw that Eagle Eye was unarmed. She reasoned that an unarmed man was not out to cause them harm.

She said to her husband, "Stop the wagon I think he wants to talk to us."

Eagle Eye said to the man, "How you doing today?"

"I seen better days but ain't no use complaining."

"How de do, ma'am?"

"Fine, How de do?"

"Good boys you got there."

"You wont think so if you owned them."

"To the man he said, I am looking for a mule, my Nellie has seen the best of her days."

"You got money?"

Eagle Eye removed the pouch from around his waist and showed the man two gold coins. The black man's eyes lit up with the sight of the gold coins. In all of his life he had never seen so much money.

"Yes, I can pay in gold."

"Then there ain't a problem I own three of the finest mules in these parts. Come home with us and take a look at them."

"That's right good of you. Where yore place."

"Bout five miles from here."

"Where a black man git so much money, you rob a bank?"

"I was in the war and saved all of my pay for five years."

"You shore a rich man. I've got jist the animal that you looking fer. You plan to do some mining."

"No, just need a mule for riding."

"What we jawing fer? Come on and follow me to my shack."

The black man turned the buckboard around and headed back the way he had come.

His wife was not pleased with the turn of events and said to her husband, "What you doing? We got to git the supplies for the week."

"We kin always come back later. I got too many mules and that man's got too much money. You jist be quiet."

Eagle Eye fell behind the buckboard and they proceeded to go to the farm of the black man.

The three little boys on the wagon giggled at Nellie. The oldest one who was about seven years old said, "That old mule will never make it to the farm"

His mother gave him a swat and said, "You be quiet when grown-ups are round about."

The five-mile journey was punctuated with laughter of the children and conversation of the adults. Eagle Eye learned that the black man had been a slave in North Carolina and after emancipation he had spent five years locating his wife. She had been sold two years before he was set free. After finding her, he moved west and farmed a homestead of thirty acres of land.

He managed to eke out a living while waiting for his boys to grow up and help him. His wife worked in the fields beside him, desperately trying to make a success of the little farm. To date they had managed to stay ahead of the bill collectors and the money from the sale of a mule would improve their position.

They arrived at the homestead and Eagle Eye was invited to join them for a repast. The woman was hard at work in the kitchen trying to coax the wood stove into heating the meal she was preparing. The men sat on the porch with a jug of corn whiskey and talked about the weather and condition of blacks in the area.

"I wouldn't let the whites know that you are a rich black man. They wouldn't take kindly to the idea."

"I am not rich and my most prized possessions are my colt revolver and my mule, Nellie. I have been with Nellie since I was a free man and I really hate parting with her. She wasn't young when I got her. She is getting too old now and I have to replace her with a younger mule. I plan to just let her go free on the open plain and let her live out the rest of her days."

"She won't live long on the open plains with all the wolves around."

"Well I am willing to let her take her chances."

"Why not let her live here with us. I will give her to my youngest boy and he will take care of her. She still has two or three years left in her. He would be the happiest youngling in these parts to have her as his own."

"That ain't a bad idea. Let me think on it for a spell."

"I still don't know your name, or where you hail from. My name is George Washington Jones. My wife is Mary. I got my name from the plantation that my folks worked on in North Carolina. I was born on that plantation and lived there until I was freed by Mr. Lincoln."

"I was a slave on the Litamore plantation until the war."

"That down near Beaufort?"

"Jist a few miles North of Beaufort."

"I was down that way once, with a load of cotton being sent out some place by boat."

"I have lived with the Indians for the past few years, I was married to an Indian woman until she and my children were killed by white raiders. I have had many names during my lifetime. My name was Jumo Gamasaka when I was a young boy in Africa. When I was sold on the slave block in America my name was changed to Frederick. Most people on the plantation just called me Fred. When I first went to live with the Indians my name was changed to Running Deer. Later when I went to live with the Comanche my name was changed again and I was called Eagle Eye. As you can see I have been called many names but the name that I like is Running Deer. It reminds me of my wife, Tree Flower, and my children."

"'Tis a sad yarn that ye spin. I'se sorry that you had sich a hard time. You still alive though and you can thank God fer that. Most blacks on this earth gonna see trouble."

"It don't matter, them days is gone forever."

"You think of settling down and working a piece of land someday. With yore money you could git a right good piece."

"Given it some thought, maybe one of these days."

"This area ain't bad for niggers, the whites leave you alone, long as you don't git too high. How good you with that sidearm that you carry?"

"Come out near yore barnyard and I'll show you."

Eagle Eye strapped his gun and holster on and the two of them went out to the barn and George threw rocks and cans in the air. Eagle Eye shot them without a single miss.

"Man, you good with that thing. I ain't seed no man shoot like dat where you learn to shoot like dat?"

"I taught myself."

"You shore good with that gun, I can't shoot my scatter gun that straight."

One boy came up to the two men and said, "Ma wants you to come and git something to eat and she said come right now."

"We better go eat. That woman don't take kindly to keeping food waiting after her done fixed it."

Eagle Eye sat to a meal that he had not seen in many years. He ate his fill of biscuits, collard greens, salt pork and yams. After the meal and after thanking the woman for such a splendid repast, the two men went to the barnyard to look at the mules. The first one that he looked at was a large gray. Eagle Eye walked to the gray and tried to open her mouth. The mule moved her head aside to prevent him from opening it.

"Troublesome bastard ain't she?"

"Ain't all mules that away?"

He finally got the gray to open her mouth and noticed that some teeth were missing and the others were well worn.

"This mule is older than Nellie. I need a young mule. This the best you got."

"You shore know mules, can't blame a man fore trying. Look at this one, ain't quite two years old, She the best I got. I shore hate to part with her. I named her Mary cause she stubborn like my woman. She got a mind of har own."

The mule was all that George said she was, young with a full set of teeth. Eagle Eye liked the ugly creature. They started to talk about the price.

"How much you want for your mule? I am going to leave Nellie here for your boy."

"I'm a poor man and I need to get as much as I can for my best mule, don't know when I be able to ford another one. Would you think twelve dollars being too much for the asking?"

Eagle Eye said, "I got no change so I am going to give you twenty dollars in gold for the mule. I wish you had some type saddle to throw in the bargain."

67

"Got jist what yer looking fer."

He went to the barn and came back with a saddle. It was a little worse for wear but usable. Eagle Eye handed him the Gold pieces and he bit down on them with his molars to test the quality.

"Ain't many times in my life that I had the opportunity to test gold and it shore a good feeling."

"I want to give your wife something for that fine meal and ask her to prepare a small sack of food for me. That will save me a trip into town. I need a few items, like coffee, sugar and some fatback. Think she can do it for me?"

"Give it to me and I will see that she gits it and that she makes you a good traveling meal."

"I will give it to her myself, I want her to know that I appreciate the meal that she prepared for me."

He walked to the house leading the mule while George carried the saddle.

"Mary git out here."

When Mary came to the door Eagle Eye handed her a ten dollar gold piece and she was overcome with joy. She did not test the quality as her husband had done.

She said, "I can't accept this for jist fixing you some vittles. It's too much money."

George stepped in and said, "Keep it woman and go fix him some vittles to take on the road. Give him some coffee, sugar and some fatback too."

"I sure appreciate this Mr. Eagle Eye, and George you ain't gonna see one penny of it. I mean to use it to fix up this old shack and to buy the boys some clothes."

Eagle Eye knew that she meant every word. Try as he might George would never get his hands on that gold piece. Mary returned a few minutes with a burlap sack filled with coffee, salt pork, beans and flour. She had added a tin of brown sugar.

He spent a long time talking to Nellie, trying to explain why he was leaving her in this strange place. He started to walk away and she started following him. The oldest of the three boys came up and patted her gently and led her away. He left knowing that she would be secure. They said their good-byes and he mounted his new mule and headed west.

Eagle Eye knew that he had paid almost twice what the mule was worth. Yet, he was helping another black man survive in this hostile land. That gave him a sense of pride. He considered the fact that they had been good to him and George offered to let him to live with them as a sign of friendship. He had more money than he knew what to do with anyway and helping another black man seemed the right thing to do. In his subconscious mind he envied that black man, after all he had a wife and children. His thoughts went back to Tree Flower and his own children. He realized that it was in the past and nothing he could do to bring them back. That part of his life was gone forever.

Eagle Eye decided that he would name his new mule Flower after his wife. As he thought of his family his eyes felt hot with tears. Why had life dealt him such a hand of cards, It was more than he could understand. To him life would never be the same with out his wife and children.

Trouble in the Town

That night, with his new mount, he camped beside a quiet stream. He let his mule drink from the stream and then tied her to a tree on a long rope to allow her to graze. He ate from the supplies that he had obtained from the Jones family and went to sleep under the stars.

It was a quiet night; only the howling of the wolves in the distance broke the silence. The howling wolves did not bother him, but his new mount was nervous. Flower was concerned about the wolves. Eagle Eye knew that they were too far away to be considered a problem. He went over to her and assured her that everything would be all right. He then made a fire and went to sleep. He kept his gun within easy reach.

In the morning, he mounted Flower without incident and started his journey. He traveled ten miles before spotting a settlement. Taking the high ground he observed the small town before deciding to venture into it. He saw only a general store and about five other buildings, including a saloon. Eagle Eye decided to observe the settlement for about an hour before entering, he wanted to make sure it was not crowded with people. If he spotted many residents, he would by pass it and find another that was less crowded. He saw only one man during his observation period. The lone man walked across the street and entered the saloon. Eagle Eye finally decided it was safe to enter the settlement and purchase his ammunition.

Eagle Eye was positive that such a small settlement would have no law official and the residents would have no knowledge of him or his role with his adopted Indian tribe.

Cautiously, he approached the small settlement. He rode Flower directly down its one dusty street without incident. He stopped her in front of the general store and tied her loosely to the hitching post and entered the store. At the door he scanned the interior of the store. There were five white men in the store. Four of the men were sitting at a table in the back of the store and one, that he assumed was the shopkeeper, was behind a counter working on the store register.

As he entered the store all conversation stopped. No one in the store spoke and all eyes were on him. The shopkeeper interrupted his accounting duties and the four men at the table stopped their poker game and stared at him. He ignored them and went directly to the counter and said to the shopkeeper.

"Mister Sir, I want to buy some shells for my revolver."

"Nigger, you got money."

"Yes Sir, this here is a two dollar gold piece."

"Nigger, where you get so much money."

"I was in the army and this was my mustering out pay."

The shopkeeper bit into the gold piece and said," How much ammo do you want?"

"Two dollars worth."

The four men at the table in the back of the store started to move and Eagle Eye kept a close watch on them.

One of the four men at the poker table said to him, "Nigger, what you doing wearing gun?"

Another said, "I don't like niggers with guns."

Eagle Eye said, "I ain't looking for no trouble, and there ain't no law 'gainst wearing a gun. You got guns on."

"We is white men."

"You come in here wearing a gun, nigger you asking for trouble."

The third white man at the table stood up and said, "Nigger, I need a new gun."

"Then you should buy one."

"I want the one that you are wearing."

Eagle Eye looked around the store, there was a stairway leading to the rooms on the second floor of the building. He could not see behind the counter where the shopkeeper was standing. However, Eagle Eye was suspicious of the shopkeeper. He suspected that he had a gun behind the counter. His eyes never left him except to watch the four men at the table. He kept his back to the sidewall so that the entrance into the store could be seen from the corner of his eyes. He didn't want to be shot in the back by a white man entering the store and getting the drop on him. He was finally satisfied that he had all of the danger spots located. He was determined that on this day he would not be lynched without taking as many men as he could to the grave with him. He knew that he could drop the four at the table in the blink of an eye. The shopkeeper worried him. He had no idea where he stood in the confrontation-taking place. Mentally he knew that the shopkeeper was white and therefore represented at threat to him.

The shopkeeper began to bend down and Eagle Eye said to him. "Please don't do that. I don't want any harm to come to you."

The shopkeeper stood up with both hands on the counter.

He said, "I was about to git yore shells."

"The shells are there on the shelf."

"You sure right, I plum forgot them shells being there."

All four men at the table in the rear were now standing.

The tall one in the center said, "Nigger you got one minute to hand over that gun or you going to be a dead nigger."

Eagle Eye said, "I don't want no trouble."

"Nigger, you got trouble."

One man suddenly reached for his gun and Eagle Eye waited until it had almost cleared his holster. In flash he drew his revolver and shot the gun out of his hand.

"I could have put that bullet between your eyes as easy as your hand, had I a mind to do it. Don't any of you try that again, if you want to live."

Eagle Eye put his gun back in its holster and faced the shopkeeper.

Mister, "I want two dollars worth of six-shooter ammunition."

The shopkeeper started to bend down again and Eagle Eye said, "Please don't move other than to git the shells for me. I don't want to do you no harm."

At the top of the stair case there was movement and in a flash Eagle Eye had his gun in his hand. The movement of his gun hand was smooth and quick.

One poker player said, "Did you see that?"

Jesse Martin was the gunman who had attempted to draw against Eagle Eye. He was angry and could not believe that he had been outdrawn by anyone, especially a black man. It was all that he could do to contain himself and not hit his poker-playing companion for his remarks.

Jesse said, "Shut up, I aim to kill that nigger when I get the chance."

"That was the fastest draw I ever seed. He's faster than you are."

"Shut up, that nigger didn't beat me to the draw. I just didn't realize that he knew what to do with that gun. There's going to be another time, just wait and see."

Eagle Eye pointed his side arm in the direction of the staircase. A woman emerged and he lowered his weapon and put it in its holster.

Eagle Eye said, "Come down Missy, I don't mean you no harm."

The woman came down the stairs and looked around the room. She looked at Jesse Martin, still holding his gun hand. His gun lay on the floor.

She laughed and said, "What happened here, someone beat you to the draw?"

"Git back upstairs where you belong woman."

The woman picked up her long skirt and started to turn, going back up the stairs.

Eagle Eye said, "Stay where you are, and don't make no quick moves and you wont be hurt."

The woman froze in her position making no move to go up or down.

Jesse Martin, still holding his gun hand said, "I told you to go back up the stairs, now move."

Eagle Eye pointed his gun at Jesse Martin, and told the woman to stay where she was. He didn't risk the chance that she had a companion with her. He was not willing to take the chance that another man would start down the stairway and present another problem for him.

From the stairway came a voice of a man, "What's going on down there?"

The woman said, "Come down and find out for yourself."

A half dressed man appeared at the top of the stairway and Eagle Eye pointed his Colt at him and said, "You come down here."

An unarmed man came down the stairway wearing only his long johns. Eagle Eye knew that he had made the correct decision. He motioned the man to the area where the others were standing and turned his attention to the shopkeeper. He kept his eyes on the men at the poker table.

He said to the shopkeeper, "Put my shells in a sack and I be on my way."

"Doing it right now, what's yore name."

"It don't matter none, I won't be passing this way agin."

He was sure that the shopkeeper had not given him two dollars worth of shells but he did not question him about it. He wanted to get out of the store and on his way before there was more trouble. He did not know how the four men would react to his leaving. He left that decision up to them.

Eagle Eye performed one other act before leaving the store. There was a bottle of whiskey sitting on the poker table between the men. Suddenly Eagle Eye drew his gun and shot the bottle, it was a clean hit, designed to show the men that he meant business. The four startled men jumped to one side and stared open-eyed at Eagle Eye.

He said to the five men at the poker table, "That whiskey bottle could be anyone of you had I a mind to shoot you. Don't make any sudden moves and all of you be all right."

Eagle Eye, for a brief second considered killing Jesse Martin because he had attempted to draw his gun. He decided to let the matter rest. He only wanted to leave unharmed and be on his way.

Eagle Eye addressed the men at the table after picking up his sack of shells.

"I will be leaving now and if you want to live you will stay where you are until I am out of this town. The first one that looks out that door gits a bullet where his right eye ought to be."

He picked up his bag of shells and walked sideways toward the door. He kept his eyes on the shopkeeper and the four men at the table. He knew that he was in little danger while in the store because the fastest of the gunmen had been disarmed and the others knew better than to try anything. He stepped outside and closed the door, mounted Flower and rode out of the town.

Jesse Martin, Gunslinger

The tall man who had drawn his gun was one Jesse Martin, a local gunslinger. Jesse Martin killed his first man when he was twelve. The man he killed was his father who was beating his mother. Since that first killing, he had killed many men, white, black and Indian and to him killing was a way of life. His only regret in life was that he could not have married his mother. He had left when the urge to have sex with her became overpowering. He was a lonely man who often wished for his own death.

Jesse Martin would never experience true happiness. The closest that he ever came to being happy was watching a man that he had shot die. He hated all men, blacks, white and Indian. He was twenty-five years old and had killed eleven men. He took pleasure in killing. To Jesse killing was a pleasant experience. In the end, only his own death would bring the peace Jesse Martin sought.

His companion and sidekick was Jerry Downs. Jerry Downs was a coward; he was attracted to men of strength. He depended upon other men for protection. He was neither fast with his gun nor an accurate shooter. Jesse tolerated him because he obeyed Jesse's commands without question. Jerry Downs was a follower. He was not a leader and he attached himself to men like Jesse. He would do anything that Jesse asked of him. Jesse liked Jerry because he could control him and Jesse Martin needed to control people. They had been traveling together for about two years. The two moved from town to town playing poker and committing small robberies.

The two local men who had joined them in the poker game were John Pater and Thomas Williams. John was the town drunk and avoided trouble whenever possible. He met Jesse and Jerry in the general store. He enjoyed the drinks that were brought for him. John used his considerable skill in poker playing to amass much of the money of the other three. He did not despise or hate other men, Indian, Black, or white. His objective was to use them and obtain as much from them as was possible. John was a parasite, a freeloader and a flunky. John Pater carried no gun and would not have used it to kill anyone if he did carry one. He met Jesse that morning at the poker game in the general store. John Pater was the big winner in the poker game.

Thomas was a fifteen years old, hardly aware of life or its tragedies. He wanted most of all to be accepted and to be considered a man by his peers. He would follow anyone, anyone who assured him that he had worth and value. He had little confidence in his own abilities. Since leaving the farm at thirteen, he had drifted from town to town trying to find his own place in life. Jesse had treated him as a man and he enjoyed this treatment. Jesse was the father he never had. Above all, he wanted to please Jesse and make Jesse proud of him. He considered Jesse a real man's man. He was too young to know any better.

After Eagle Eye left the store and was well on his way, the storekeeper started back to work on his register. The woman on the stairway turned and went back up the stairs; her companion accompanied her.

Jesse Martin was the first to speak after the door closed and Eagle Eye had left. "No nigger is going to shoot at me and live to tell about it."

"Did you see him draw that six shooter, I never seen anyone that fast in my whole life."

"He got the drop on me cause I didn't think he could use that gun. The next time it's going to be different."

"What you planning to do?"

"I am going to track him down and kill him, that's what I am going to do."

John Pater spoke up and said, "Well it ain't none of my business."

Thomas Williams added, "Why don't we just let it be, no real harm was done and we provoked him?"

Jerry said, "Jesse we should hunt that nigger down, kill him and hang him from the nearest tree."

"That is just what I intend to do. If you cowards don't want to help that's all right with me. It wont take more than two of us to do the job, anyway, on that mule he can't go fast and we gonna catch him before high noon."

"Ain't yore hand sore from his shot?"

"His lucky shot hit my gun not my hand."

"Do you 'spose he aimed at yore gun."

"No one shoots that good, it was just a lucky shot.

"Shopkeeper I want the best gun you got, mines got a dent in it."

Jesse Martin went over to the counter and the shopkeeper showed him five guns. He tested each for balance. Finally, he loaded one that he liked and put it in his holster. He spotted a rat in the corner of the store and drew his recently acquired weapon and shot the rat through the head.

"Now that was not a lucky shot."

"That six-shooter will cost you ten dollars."

"You can put it on my bill."

"I can't let you have the gun on credit, you got to pay for it now."

Jesse grabbed the shopkeeper by the collar, pulled him toward him, drew his gun and put it to his forehead. Jesse Martin was not a man that one could reason with and this shopkeeper was beginning to realize it. He wished now that the black man had killed him. He knew that he was out of a gun, ammunition and maybe his life.

Jesse said to the shopkeeper, while still holding the gun to his head, "How much is this gun going to cost me?"

"There is no charge for the gun, that nigger insulted you and me and if that's the gun it takes to kill him, you can have it. I'll throw in some shells to complete the bargain. All you got to do is bring me back that nigger's right hand."

"That right nice of you, don't you men think so. He is doing his part to finish that uppity nigger. I'll bring back both his hands as a gift to you for providing me with the gun."

Jesse released the shopkeeper and collected the box of shells from him.

"He ain't a coward like you two I ought to put a bullet in both of you."

"We didn't mean nothing by what we said."

"I want all the money from that poker game. I'm going to need expense money for hunting down that nigger. Since the two of you decided not to help, you going to pay for this little venture. I might just drag the nigger back here by the heels so that you can see that your money was put to good use."

John Pater emptied his pockets of the money that he had won in the game along with the money that he had started with. Thomas Williams contributed what little he had left. Jesse held out his hat, keeping his gun hand free and collected the money. He never even considered that he was robbing them and he took their money without even saying thank you. Both of the poker players considered themselves lucky to have escaped with their lives. This far from civilization, there was no law to protect them and the man with the fastest gun was law and order. They could always steal more money.

Jesse said to Jerry, "We got a job to do, let's get going."

They went outside, mounted their horses and headed in the direction where Eagle Eye and his mule were last seen.

The Encounter on the Trail

Jesse and Jerry picked up the trail left by the mule. There was no haste in their movement and they were sure that they would overtake the mule and its rider before noon.

Jesse said, "When you are going to kill a man you should take your time and enjoy it."

"He sure ain't trying to hide his tracks. Maybe we should get more men to help us hunt him down."

"You think that nigger can outdraw me?"

"I didn't say that he could but he ain't scared like a nigger outta be."

"That's his problem. Ours is to find him and kill him."

Eagle Eye had about a half hour start on Jesse and Jerry. He was sure that they would come after him. He thought that all four would be in the party tracking him. He was surprised when he looked into the valley and found that only the one that he had shot and one other man were tracking him.

He knew that they were tracking him. He watched as one of them got off his horse and examined the tracks and pointed in the direction that he had gone. He knew that the two were no match for him but he took no pleasure in killing men. He had avenged the death of his wife and children and now he just wanted to be left alone. He planned to head west and find some land, purchase it with his last gold pieces, farm and raise horses and mules.

Eagle Eye stopped his mule beside a tree and waited for the two men to catch up with him. He reasoned that they would catch up to him eventually and the sooner he confronted them, the quicker the matter would be over. Then he could be on his way. He stopped in the middle of the trail in full view of the approaching riders. He had tied Flower some distance away; no use in taking a chance that she might get hit by some stray bullet.

Jesse Martin and Jerry Downs saw their quarry sitting under a lone tree, his back to the sun. Two hundred yards away, Jesse took out his gun and checked to make sure that it was loaded and ready. He then placed it back in its holster and continued toward his target.

"I ain't never seen no black man so ready to die."

"The fool don't know any better."

The two of them approached within twenty yards of Eagle Eye and stopped. They glared at him and neither party spoke.

Jesse finally said, "Nigger we got some unfinished business to tend to."

"I got no business with you, you best turn back the way you came."

"Uppity son of a bitch ain't he"

"Well we got some business with you. Nigger your time has come. You got any last words before I shoot you down."

"If I were you, I would stay on my horse and ride back to the general store and finish my poker game. Ain't no use in you dying out here on the trail."

Both Jesse and Jerry got off their horses and approached Eagle Eye. They showed no sign of fear and confidence was in their every step.

Jesse said, "Make your move nigger."

"I always let a man who is going to die draw first."

Suddenly and without warning Jesse went for his gun. Just before it cleared his holster, Eagle Eye made his move. He drew his gun; it was more a reflex action than a conscious act. He never really held the gun or aimed, he was the gun and he could not miss. His bullet hit Jesse between the eyes and a blank stare of disbelief appeared on his face just before he fell to the ground dead. Jerry Downs stood unable to move. He could not believe what he had just seen, Jesse was the fastest man with a gun that he had ever known and now he was dead, gunned down by this black man who was faster.

Eagle Eye said, "Go for your gun."

Jerry did not move. He remained frozen in his tracks. Eagle Eye repeated his demand. "Draw you gun or I will shoot you with your gun in your holster."

"I wont draw my gun, you gonna kill me anyway, why should I draw."

"You came here to kill me and now it your turn to die."

"I am giving you more of a chance than you were willing to give me."

"I won't draw, you just got to shoot me, I'm dropping my gun and holster, and you gotta shoot an unarmed man."

"Take your friend back to the settlement but don't let me catch you following me again."

He turned to walk away and sensed movement as Jerry started for his gun. He whirled and drew simultaneously and his bullet hit Jerry Downs a little above the right eye and he fell dropping his gun at his side. He had just cleared his holster and would have killed Eagle Eye without a second thought. Eagle Eye realized that he had a close call and vowed that he would never turn his back on a man with a gun no matter how afraid he appeared to be.

He went through their pockets and removed their money and buried them under a pile of stones. Together they had twenty-three dollars and two gold watches. He reasoned that the money was his due for burying the pair of killers. He now had more money than he would need to buy a farm further west. He was looking forward to settling down, finding a wife and life on a farm.

He removed the saddles from the horses and set them free. When he was finished in the area, only two stones covered graves indicated that man had ever passed that way. At the foot of each grave was an empty saddle. He finally mounted his mule and continued his journey west. It had been a day that he would prefer to forget. He was beginning to realize that his life had been filled with violence and he vowed that the future would be different.

Ben Watford

The Beginning of Winter

There was a chill in the air and the first snowfall had started in southern Kansas. The onset of winter had sent most animals into the pattern of life that insured their survival. The bears had retired to their caves and were beginning their long sleep to wait for warmer times. The beavers, in autumn, had stored up a plentiful supply of food for the winter and were now safe in their lodges. Their two room lodges, one room built above the other provide shelter and storage of food for the winter season. Their food, twigs and sticks of willow, birch, poplar and alder trees, would keep them supplied during the cold months ahead. Their food supplies were stored in their lodge and piled on the bottom of the pond. The cold would last five months and would be severe at times.

Wild game became difficult to find and the few supplies that Eagle Eye had were almost diminished. The temperature had dropped well below freezing. Eagle Eye was not properly dressed for the cold Kansas weather. He knew that he would not survive long in the intense cold. He had to find shelter for the winter, some place where he and Flower could spend four or five months protected from the cold weather. It was already difficult to travel and the snow was beginning to fall. In a few days the severe cold and the snow would prevent travel. He was more worried about Flower than himself. He knew that he could find sufficient game to stay alive but food for his mule would be hard to come by.

He had searched most of the day for some cave or abandoned mineshaft in which to spend the winter. He had almost given up hope when he spotted a miner's shack in the distance. It was situated on the side of a small hill giving it some protection from the cold north wind. He had started toward it when he observed smoke coming from the chimney. The shack was occupied. The weather was too harsh and more snow was beginning to fall. He had no choice but to seek shelter with the occupants of the miners shack. He approached the shack with caution. The greeting was unexpected.

He knocked on the door only to find a voice behind him saying.

"Drop yore gun holster and don't try anything. I got a twelve gage shot gun aimed at yore head. I will blow you to kingdom come if you make one wrong move."

It was the first time that anyone had ever gotten the drop on him. He had no idea of the number of men behind him. If it were a lone man he could drop him but was sure that he would be shot in the process. He had no choice but to drop his gun and holster in the snow.

"Turn around slowly and let me see what you look like, don't try nothing if you value yore worthless hide."

Slowly Eagle Eye turned to face his captor. He found himself face to face with a grizzly bearded old man. He was clothed from head to foot in fur. Only his face was visible. He kept both eyes glued to Eagle Eye. In his hands was the twelve gage shot gun that he had alluded to. He was a good foot and a half shorter than Eagle Eye and he was trying to decide whether he could trust this giant of a black man.

Eagle Eye finally said to him. "If you intend to shoot me, get it over with but take care of my mule."

For a few minutes the old man did not speak, and finally he said. "You sure must be cold with no more clothes on than you got. What you want and where you headed. I ain't see many of your people round these parts."

"I was just traveling through and got caught in the storm. I was looking for some place to spend the winter. I'm more worried about my mule, Flower, than I am my self. Food is going to be hard to come by for her."

"I like a man who cares about his animal more than himself. Come on inside and get warm and we can talk about what's going to happen to you. A man's a fool or crazy to be traveling this country dressed as you are. You are lucky to be alive."

The two of them went inside the shack that was almost completely filled with furs. The old man's cabin consisted of a single room with a fireplace on the sidewall. The floor, what could be seen of it, was caked with dirt and debris. The insides of the cabin smelled as if something had died there and had been allowed to decay on the spot. There was a fire in the fireplace and a stack of wood on the hearth.

There was no furniture in the shack except a table and a few broken chairs. Eagle Eye hardly noticed the cabin's interior or the smell. He went directly to the fireplace; he had not realized how cold he really was.

He thought of Flower and said to the old man.

"I have got to go out and take care of my mule. She's the best friend I got."

The old man, still with his shotgun said:

"Stay here and warm some life in that body of yours. I'm going out and put your mule up with my donkey in the shed out back. There's some coffee left in that pot. Hang it on the rack in the fireplace and get it warm and drink some, you will feel better."

Twenty minutes later the old trapper returned to the shack carrying his shotgun and Eagle Eye's six shooter and holster.

"I put your mule in with my donkey and they took to each other like Adam and Eve. She was sure hungry, when did you feed her last. Animals don't last long in this weather without good food and water."

The old trapper's name was John Little Fox. His mother was Indian and his father white. John Little Fox didn't feel totally welcome with either group, Indian or white. He considered himself Indian, but he could not live on the reservation with his people. He found life on the reservation too confining. He preferred living by himself, not responsible to the federal government or any other agency.

He left his tribe after the death of his Indian wife at the hands of the pony soldiers. John Little Fox loved his isolated life, his donkey and the forest. He had trapped in this valley for ten years. He returned to civilization only once a year in the spring to trade his furs for supplies. His life was a simple one. He lived alone with his donkey, his mountain and his trees. He knew every stretch of the valley. The plants and animals and even the insects were his friends. He took from his environment what he needed to survive and no more. The two men talked late into the night.

John Little Fox finally decided that Eagle Eye could spend the winter working for him, helping him set the traps and skin the animals. He knew that left alone, in the wilderness, the man and his mule would perish during the cold Kansas winter. In return he would teach him how to care for himself and his mule.

The Long Winter

Outside the cabin, snow came down in large fluffy flakes turning the world into a blanket of whiteness. An eerie silence filled the air. Only the occasional sound of the snowbirds interrupted the silence. Those few birds that stayed the winter would find lean pickings. A few seeds and the larva of insects were all that they could expect to find. Their thick coat of feathers protected them from the winter cold. Food was their main concern. John Little Fox put out small crust of bread each morning to feed the birds and other animals. It was his contribution to the animals that shared the land with him.

The snow bent the small trees and bushes nearly to the ground. The wind had piled the snow in drifts some as high as the trees themselves. Only those who knew the terrain would be safe venturing into the storm. John Little Fox knew every inch of the terrain. He knew the path to his traps as well as he knew his cabin.

The next day John Little Fox gave Eagle Eye fur clothing, similar to his, and then the two men donned snowshoes and started out to inspect the traps. The snowshoes were about three feet long and foot wide. John little Fox had made them during the Summer months knowing that he would need them during the Winter. As was his habit, he made pairs of everything that he used and the extra pair Eagle eye now wore. He made the snowshoes with a light wooden frame, bent into a long oval. Strings of animal hide stretched across the frame, making the snowshoes look like oversized tennis rackets. Eagle Eye had never worn snowshoes and Little Fox explained to Eagle Eye how one walked using them.

"Move your feet so the snowshoes slide along the surface of the snow. Make an outward motion with the snowshoes with each step. That way we can walk at a rate of one or two miles an hour."

"Suppose you have to run in these snowshoes, how is that done."

"Well, it is more of a dogtrot than a run and that way you can double the time. I didn't make these to run in. They aren't strong enough to run in, anyway, it will be all that you can do to walk in them in this snowstorm. Just walk behind me and watch how I do it until you get the knack of it. Walking through the snow in the snow shoes is difficult and without snow shoes it would not be safe to venture out."

After checking on the two animals, they left the cabin. As Little Fox explained to Eagle Eye, their animals were their most prized possessions. The animals were needed to transport the furs to the settlement when spring arrived. They did not want to leave the care of the mule and donkey to chance. They made sure that the animals were well fed and protected before leaving the cabin. Finally, after making sure that all was well with the animals, the two men decided that it was time to leave and inspect the traps.

They walked about a half-mile and Eagle Eye found walking in snowshoes more difficult than he imagined. It would take them more than an hour to travel a half mile in the deep snow. They went from trap to trap and found nothing. Little Fox removed the old bait and replaced it with fresh bait and then moved on to the next trap. Finally, they approached the last trap, and it too was empty.

"Well it looks like I am going to have little luck this winter. The animals are not hungry or the spirits of the woods are protecting them."

"It could be that you have trapped all the animals in the area. How long did you say you have been trapping in this area? There is a limit to the number of animals occupying a given area."

"Not the way I trap animals. When I see females in my traps, I always set them free. That allows them to have young to replace those that I kill. The winter is just not far along and they are not hungry."

"What happens if you do not trap animals all winter?"

"That has never happened. Eventually there will be animals caught in the traps."

After baiting the last trap, the two men started the long trip back to the cabin. They walked slowly, tired from their long trek, they had covered two miles in snowshoes. What they wanted most was to take them off and sit by the fire with a small glass of warm corn squeezing.

"This weather is not fit for man or beast. Flower would never let me take her out in this snow."

"You treat that mule better than most men treat their children. You should let her know who is in control."

"I am in control but I get more cooperation from her if I treat her with kindness."

They were within sight of the cabin when they heard a loud roar just off the trail. Both men froze as a large Grizzly bear ambled through the deep snow directly toward them. Little Fox raised his rifle and fired at the approaching animal. He was sure that he had hit it, but the bear continued to advance toward them. The bear was ten feet in front of them.

Eagle eye yelled, "Get down! get down! I need a clear shot!"

Little Fox continued trying to reload his rifle. Eagle eye dived to one side drawing his gun simultaneously. He fired twice before hitting the deep snow. Both of the bear's eyes disappeared in a blur of blood. The giant bear let out a roar of pain and fell to the ground. The bear fell three feet in front of Little Fox. Little Fox unable to reload his rifle was just about to use it as a club when the big animal fell. He looked around at Eagle Eye lying in the snow trying to regain his footage.

"Why didn't you get down, when I yelled?"

Little Fox was still stunned and just looked at Eagle Eye.

He finally said, "How did you do that? I have never in my life seen a man shoot a short gun like that. Where did you learn to shoot like that? That was the best shooting that I have ever seen."

"I taught my self to shoot, it is more instinct than anything else."

"Instinct or not, I would not like to face you with a gun of any kind. Did you aim for the eyes or was it an accident?"

"It wasn't an accident. I knew that the only way to kill it was with a shoot it directly in the eyes. Under twenty feet, I hit what I aim at. Beyond that range my gun is not much good. It would be an accident or just luck if I hit my target beyond thirty feet."

"I don't care what you call it, I have never seen a man shoot like that."

"We have to get that bear to the cabin. That is enough meat to last the entire winter."

"We are going to eat that bear?"

"We killed it didn't we. The Great Spirit will be angry if we throw the meat away. Bear meat is good eating too, though it likely to be strong-flavored and tough. It is best if the bear has been living on acorns for sometime."

"What was it doing out in this weather?"

"Bears don't sleep during the entire winter. They leave their caves from time to time in search of food or maybe to look around and to get they muscles working again. I don't know what makes them behave the way they do. It's the way bears are. It is the way of the Great Spirit that decides the way animals behave. Each animal including man behaves in a manner prescribed by the Great Spirit."

"If you say so."

"The bear's fur is thickest in fall and winter. I should get a good bargain for this fur, once I have cleaned and tanned it. I have had very few furs of bear to sell or trade. They are too difficult to come by. Most of the time, the bears destroy my traps and eat the bait. Now we are going to eat him."

John Little Fox cut two small trees and removed the branches. He then tied vines to the poles. The two of them loaded the bear Carcass on the makeshift sled and headed for the cabin. It took the two men the rest of the day to get the bear carcass to the cabin. At times they thought they would have to abandon the effort and give up their kill.

They had to drive off a pack of wolves that wanted to share the kill. Only the skill of Eagle eye and his gun saved the day. He managed to drive the pack off by killing its leader. John Little Fox and Eagle Eye watched as the pack disappeared into the surrounding bush. They kept a continuous lookout for the pack but they did not return. The two men left with their kill, resumed the task of getting it to the cabin.

"Later, I am going to come back for that wolf that you killed. If meat gets scarce during the winter, we can always eat it. The pelt I will trade for supplies when the spring comes."

"I don't know if I could eat wolf meat, it's like eating dog."

"Well, we killed it and it ain't right to see it go to waste. It would not please the Great Spirit. We should not kill and leave the meat to rot, though I suspect that the scavenger would make quick work of it. That dead wolf will not last long with all the animals around. If you get hungry enough, you will find that you will eat just about anything and be glad that it's there."

With much hard work, the two men got the bear carcass to the cabin. It was there that the real work began. It was dark when the two men arrived at the cabin. The light of the moon was all that they had to rely upon. They started the task of skinning the animal. After the skinning, they cut the meat into small portions. They intended to store it in the shed for winter.

Early the next morning, Little Fox got up and left the cabin. When he returned, he had the wolf that they had killed. He started the task of removing the pelt while Eagle Eye watched him. After he removed the skin, Eagle Eye cut the meat into cooking portions. Eagle Eye placed the meat in the shed outside the cabin. He was careful to place it in one corner of the shed. He placed it well away from the bear meat and the small game meat that Little Fox had already stored in the shed. Eagle Eye still did not like the idea of eating wolf meat. Yet, he reasoned if the winter lasted longer than usual he would eat it.

Every part of the bear carcass they used, not even the toenails went to waste. Little fox planned to make a necklace out of them to sell along with his furs.

Outside the cabin was a small shed about the size of an oversized doghouse. It was here that Little Fox kept his store of winter meat and other food. It was a storage unit that depended upon the cold weather. It was sturdy enough to keep out the scavengers. It was made of logs, big logs, planted in the ground. John Little Fox's unique construction of the shed prevented the entry of animals looking for a meal.

In the deep of night, the fox and other animals could smell the meat. They would attempt to get at it. Signs of attempted entry were visible on the sides of the shed. All that had tried had eventually given up in frustration and had walked away empty handed. John Little Fox was proud of his storage shed.

In his many years of experience in living in the wild, Little Fox had learned how to protect his winter meat. He knew that fox and other animals would dig under a structure if they could not enter above ground. He had dug the logs supporting the little shelter more than six feet in the ground and burrowing animals could not go beneath it.

Little Fox taught Eagle eye how to remove the fur without damaging it.

"The meat will remain frozen during the winter months."

"What do you do during the winter for meat if you cannot find a large animal to kill?"

"There are enough small animals like rabbits, winter birds and fish to keep one alive but at times it becomes difficult to survive. With this bear we will have all the meat that we need. I have roots, nuts and dried fruit to provide some winter food. I am sure that we will run out of coffee. We will cross that bridge when we come to it. I am not much good in the morning without a cup of coffee. Yet there have been winters when I have had none and I survived. We don't have to worry about this winter, we will survive."

"What do you do if you get sick during the winter months?"

"What does any animal do, they live or they die? We are no different from the animals that roam the forest. We live and we die when the time comes. The time will come when we will all pass and go to the happy hunting grounds. My time will come and so will yours. Does it matter where or when that time comes? All of us end the same way, to be eaten by worms or other animals. Our spirit becomes a part of the Great Mountain of Life. In some ways I look forward to the long sleep. I want to sit by the campfire with my friends and relatives. Many have passed on before me to become a part of the cycle of life. Remember, a man must die in his own time. I would like to die with honor, if not, so be it."

"Little Fox how do you feel about slavery?"

"I would not be enslaved by any man nor would I have any man as slave of mine."

"How do you feel about killing?"

"I would not like to kill any living human being without cause or good reason. I kill animals but I use all the parts. The furs I sell and the meat I eat. I take no pleasure in the killing of animals. It is the way of the Great Spirit, the strong kills the weak."

"You married a woman once, don't you miss the company of women?"

"That's all behind me now. I had a woman once and the blue coats raided our campsite and killed her and my five children. That was so many moons ago that I have lost track of it and the events surrounding it. I don't like to think of it. It just brings back bad memories. You said you married once, do you miss your woman."

"Yes, I had a woman once and she was also killed by the pony soldiers. I avenged her death by killing as many of them as I could."

"Did it make you feel better, killing the blue coats or did it bring back you woman?"

"No it didn't, but at the time it felt like the right thing to do."

"The way that you handle that six shooter I would say that you killed a fair number of them."

"I killed until I was tired of killing and did not hurt anymore. Maybe what I did was wrong, but the thought of my wife and children was more than I could handle."

"I finally made peace with my self and today I find happiness in the memory of my wife and children."

"I have no need to go on killing. That's enough of this talk of killing. The Great Spirit in the end makes everything all right. It is not the job of men."

"I got a jug of whiskey. It doesn't replace a woman but on cold nights like these it keeps the body warm. It makes one forget the past. Remember that tomorrow will be another day. I just take one day at a time. The end will come soon enough and I will be ready when it comes."

"Where did you learn to speak like you do and to read and write?"

"I went to a mission school after my family was killed in a raid. The white women who ran the school taught me to speak correctly. It was not as difficult. I was only three years of age when I arrived there, learning their language was easy. Especially since the teachers only spoke English. Indian dialects were never spoken at the school."

"I always wanted to learn to read and write. Most slave owners did not allow their slaves to learn reading and writing. The white man knew that learning to read and write would make you equal to him and he did not want that."

"I did not realize that you could not read or write. I just took it for granted that you could. Starting tonight, I am going to teach you to read, write and count. It is the least that I can do for you my friend. If your mind is anything like the way that you handle that short gun, it will not take long."

That very night Eagle Eye went to school for the first time in his life. John Little Fox was a good teacher and he had a willing pupil. The lessons went smoothly, both Eagle Eye and John Little Fox enjoyed them. In three months Eagle Eye could write his name and read in a primitive fashion. John Little Fox took delight in his ability to teach.

The rapid progress that Eagle Eye made surprised even him. Using charcoal and a tanned fur skin, Eagle Eye had a new world open to him. He learned to read and count. He thanked Little Fox repeatedly for his help. Learning to read and write his name was one of Eagle Eye's goals in life. He spent days reading wanted posters that little Fox had collected. He read two-dime novels, with many pages missing. John little Fox pulled them from under a pile of furs.

"Where did you get these books?"

"I really don't recall when but I have read them so often that I could quote them from memory. I always intended to buy more but shopkeepers don't take kindly to half-breeds buying books."

Two Men and a Log Cabin

The long winter days passed slowly and at times the two men were snowbound for weeks. They found that they enjoyed each other's company. They spent many nights talking about the Indian's way of life, the forest and its animals.

Eagle Eye sometimes became moody, thinking of his wife and children. Little Fox always had some tale to tell that would make him forget the past. Little Fox taught him many survival techniques during the long winter. He taught Eagle Eye to ice fish and to trap animals and small snowbirds. He taught him to make a fire without matches and how to enjoy the winter. John Little Fox taught Eagle Eye patience.

He explained that winter was winter and it was followed by spring. He finally told Eagle Eye that the Great Spirit, the Maker of the Universe, decreed that this would happen. No matter how harsh the winter it would pass. One had to wait and survive, spring would come.

Eagle Eye tried to teach Little Fox how to shoot. They practiced both the quick draw and shooting. Though Little Fox improved, he could never quite measure up to Eagle Eye. To Eagle Eye the handgun was an extension of his arm. It was a part of his body to be controlled and used by him. The use of the gun was as natural to Eagle Eye as breathing.

Finally Little Fox said, "I am going to stick to the long gun. I will never be as good as you are with that short one."

"I don't think when I am using the gun. I just shoot. You are thinking of what you are trying to do. You should just shoot the gun. Let the gun become a part of your hand and just point and shoot."

"Some men are born with the ability to use, draw and shoot the short gun. I don't have that ability, and I never will, no matter how hard I try."

"There was a time I could not shoot and draw with speed and accuracy. I worked at it until I got good. Now I fear no man with a gun. I suspect that I can outdraw and out shoot the best of them."

"You wont get no argument from me on that score. You are the best that I have ever seen barring none."

The two men continued the daily lessons until Little Fox put a stop to it. "I am too old to learn to use the short gun like you use it. We have wasted enough ammunition. I shoot well enough with the long gun to satisfy me. No matter how much I practice I will never be any good. It could get me killed eventually. I will stick with what works for me. Thanks for all your patience and help, lets just let it be."

"You are improving each day, give me a few more weeks and I will have you shooting the short gun and well as anyone. Anyway, I want to repay you for teaching me to read and write."

"I know that you are sincere but it's just not for me. I intend to stick with what I know best."

"It's up to you."

"Well, let's quit and get on with more important matters. We have wasted too much time on this already." The long winter was beginning to end and the first signs of spring began to appear. A few birds began returning to the area, in some places one could see the ground as the snow began to disappear. The ice in the nearby river was beginning to melt and large chunks began to move downstream. The water in the river began to rise as the snow from the nearby mountain melted. The melting snow adding its water to the fast moving stream. The water moved more rapidly down the river, heading for the larger lakes. Someday the water would return to the mountain and repeat the cycle.

Little Fox said to Eagle Eye, "Why don't you stay here and help me in the fur trade? There are enough animals here for both of us to make a decent living?"

"No thanks, soon as the weather gets a little better I will be moving on."

"Where will you go?"

"I don't know, someplace."

"I really need someone around that is handy with a gun."

"Last year I had to fight off the fur stealers."

"What fur stealers?"

Eagle Eye at first thought that John Little Fox was making up a story to get him to stay. Then he realized that Little Fox was serious.

"If they come with more than one or two. Then I will be hard pressed to keep them at bay."

"Do you think they will come?"

"As sure as the spring."

"What did you do when they came?"

"Well, there were only two and this cabin is like a fort. You noticed the small gun holes on all sides and the cabin sits in this clearing. I can see anyone who approaches. I just stayed in here and waited them out. They left in a few days. When they found that they couldn't kill me and steal my furs."

"There's no law in these part and its every man for himself. They think nothing of killing a half-breed like me. They wouldn't even stop to bury me. I thought you were one when you first came here. Then I realized that they don't come in the winter and you made too much noise. I figured that you couldn't be them."

"I am going to stay until they come this spring and make sure that they don't bother you again. I owe you that much."

"You don't owe me anything. You are the closest person that I have had as a friend in my whole life. I have even grown fond of that mule of yours. When my donkey passes along, I'm going to try to find a mule like yours to replace her."

The snow melted and the first of the green grasses appeared on the ground. In the warm spring sunshine, plants began to sprout and small animals appeared. The whole world rose from it long sleep. Eagle Eye and Little Fox let their animals graze on the new grass and plant shoots. Eagle Eye took Flower down to the river for water. He patted her and rubbed her with a piece of fur. For his efforts she tried to nip him. He realized that Flower was in the shed all winter and had wanted to get out and walk around. She was really trying to show him that she had not enjoyed her stay in the shed. He talked softly to her and explained that soon they would be on their way. Where they were going, he did not know but they would be leaving soon.

Little Fox was cutting wood for the next winter. He knew that it was early for such a task but it gave him something to do. He did not want to think that his friend would be leaving soon. He did everything that he could think of to entice him to stay. He offered him half the furs taken during the winter.

Eagle eye had refused, stating, "what you taught me about survival and reading more than paid for my small help."

The Visitors

Little Fox was the first to spot the travelers headed toward his cabin. He was in the back yard of the cabin splitting logs for the fireplace. Putting down his ax, he hurried to the front of the cabin where Eagle Eye was. The first time that this happened he had gone inside and bolted the door and windows, load his several guns and waited for the fur stealers. Little Fox would go from gun port to gun port shooting at anyone that came within range of his many shot guns. The confrontation ended in a stalemate. He could not kill them and they could not kill him. They could not get to his furs. Eventually they gave up and left.

He had gone through this routine in the past. It was a tactic similar to that the buffalo used against wolf attacks. The buffalo wouldn't attack the wolves. They would form a circle around the females and the young and protect them until the danger was passed.

This survival technique led to their demise when hunted by men with guns. Their method of survival, against the attack by wolves, was ineffective against men. Men with guns slaughtered buffalo by the thousands. In the end it would have made little difference what technique the buffalo used. They were no match for men with guns on horseback.

Little Fox never understood why the men would shoot the buffalo, not skin them for fur and leave the meat for scavengers. It was not the way of the Great Spirit. He had never in his life killed anything that he was not going to eat and use its fur. Little Fox even used the meat of the animals caught in his traps. He took no pleasure in killing just for the sake of killing.

When he arrived at the front of the cabin he saw that Eagle Eye had his gun strapped to his side. He was standing outside waiting for the arrival of the visitors. Little Fox started for the animals. He was going to bring them inside the cabin but Eagle Eye stopped him.

"What are you doing?"

"I am going to bring the animals inside, bolt the windows and doors and wait for them to leave. We will be safe in there. They can't shoot us in the cabin. They can't see us in the cabin but we can see them through the peepholes. They will not set fire to the cabin because that would destroy the furs that they want. Eventually they will just leave. They know that I am well armed and they will not take a chance on losing their lives for my furs. There are windows on each side of the cabin and holes to shoot from and they are out in the open."

"How long do you plan to stay in the cabin?"

"The last time they forced me to stay inside for two days. They finally gave up and went away. They didn't come back. Had they come back, I would have locked myself in and waited them out."

"We are going to face them out in the open this time. They have no right to claim what is not theirs. They have not worked for the furs as we have. If they start anything, we will take their guns and animals and send them on their way. They have to learn fear. Then they will not return and bother you again."

"There is one big one with a scar on his face he came with another man. Now there are four of them and only two of us. Are you sure that what we are doing is right?"

"Go inside and bolt the windows and the doors if you want to. I prefer to face them in the open."

"I wont have you facing them alone. I will stay here if you think that is what we should do?"

"Don't worry it's going to be all right."

Eagle Eye and John Little Fox waited in front of the cabin for the arrival of the four men. The cabin, built in a clearing, allowed them to see the four men in the distance. Eagle Eye scanned the terrain to make sure there were only four of them. He did not want someone creeping up behind him and getting the drop on him.

"Why don't they scatter and approach the cabin from different directions. That way they would stand more of a chance of getting the drop on us?"

"The one with the scar has been here before and he has nothing to fear from me. He doesn't know that you are with me. If he did, it would make no difference to him. I shot his horse from under him last winter and I think that he wants to kill me for doing it. They will leave their mounts out of range of my guns, if they remember what happened the last time. There were only two of them then and I held them off for two days until they finally gave up and left. They had to ride out on one horse. I didn't want to shoot the horse but I had no choice."

"I would have shot the horse also if that were the only way that I could survive. Why do they have that donkey with them? There must be another trying to circle us?"

"No, that is not their way. The donkey is to carry my furs back with them. This time they mean business."

Eagle Eye was not so sure and he instructed Little Fox to keep his back covered and not to worry about the other four.

"Don't let anyone slip up on us from behind and get the drop on us. I will deal with those four."

He repeated the instructions until Little Fox turned his back to him watching the rear. Little Fox was sure there were only four of them but he was not quite sure that Eagle Eye could handle all of them. He decided that as good as Eagle Eye was with his gun they were in little danger.

It was a clear spring day; only a slight breeze rustled the leaves in the trees. It was the day that John Little Fox and Eagle Eye had decided to clean the cabin. They wanted to put the furs collected during the winter in some order. In a few weeks they planned to leave for the nearest settlement and trade the furs for much needed supplies. They had expected no visitors.

Shootout at the Cabin

Eagle Eye had his back to the sun as the four riders approached the cabin. They tied their mounts at the edge of the clearing. They started walking toward him and stopped about twenty feet in front of him. They showed surprise that Little Fox was outside with the cabin door open.

They looked right through Eagle Eye. They were sure that they had nothing to fear from one lone black man. Scarface waited patiently while one of the men moved their horses further into the woods. He knew that he had plenty of time take care of the John Little Fox and the furs. Scarface said nothing to Eagle Eye. When the man returned from moving the mounts the four men started to advance toward Eagle Eye.

"That's close enough, Mister. State your business."

"What have we got here, an uppity nigger wearing a six shooter? Nigger if you value yore life you will hand over that gun and be on yore way? We got business with that half-bred and you blocking our way."

"Why don't we just kill that nigger and be about our business?"

"That nigger is a good as dead if he don't turn tail and run like a good nigger should."

On a signal from Scar Face the four men started to fan out.

Eagle Eye said, "Stay just where you are.

Don't make any sudden moves. Move and you will get a bullet in the gut. I don't want to have to hurt anyone."

The three men stood where they were, waiting for Scarface to decide what to do.

Scarface said, "Now can you beat that, that nigger is talking about hurting us. What are we going to do about it boys?"

"Let's string that nigger up."

Scarface looked directly at Eagle Eye and said, "I'm going to give you one last chance to high tail it out of here. Nigger, there are four of us and just you and that half-breed. My advice to you is to leave while you got the chance and let us get on with our business. We got no fight with you. We come to see the half-breed."

"I am Mr. Little Fox's partner. Any business you have concerns me."

"We come for the furs. We gonna teach that half-breed a lesson. Shooting a man's horse from under him, we aim to make sure he don't do it agin."

"The furs belong to Mr. Little Fox and me. You must kill me to get them."

"We will do that, nigger."

The first man went for his side arm and in a flash Eagle Eye drew his six-shooter and shot him in the arm. "I could have put that bullet through yore heart as easy your arm, had I a mind to do it. Now if any others of you want the same treatment go for your guns."

Scarface thought for a second and said to the other three. "We are going to draw at the same time, he can't kill all three of us. I want that nigger dead."

Eagle Eye had put his gun in its holster and waited for the three to go for their guns.

Scar Face said, "Now!" The three of them went for their guns.

Eagle Eye cleared leather while they were still in the act of drawing. In a flash each man had a wound in his gun arm. The four would be killers were holding their wounded arms, as John Little Fox gathered their weapons.

He looked Scarface in the eye and said, "It will be a long time before you shoot another gun. You won't be needing these."

"I have two shots left and my partner's got his shot gun. I am going to give you three minutes to clear our of here or the next bullet will not be in the arm. Mr. Little Fox has his shotgun. He don't shoot like I do. I can't be sure of him hitting your arm. He will hit you some place. You can be sure of that."

The four men holding their arms started for their horses and Eagle Eye stopped them.

"I said that you could leave. I didn't say anything about the animals."

"We can't get out of this woods without our horses."

"You should have thought about that before attacking us. You have one minute to start leaving. Now get afore I start shooting."

"Can't you let us have our guns? There are lots of wild animals here about and all of our food and water is on them animals."

"Your one minute is up, get moving or I start shooting."

The four men left the cabin the way that they had come, without their mounts, each holding his gun arm. Eagle Eye watched them until they were out of sight and then walked over to their mounts. He started removing the saddles and other gear. John Little Fox joined him.

"What are your plans for the horses and the donkey?"

"I am going to set them free. I am going to wait awhile and make sure that those men can't get them. We don't need them and they have brands. There is no reason to have people accusing us of horse stealing. Anyway, we would have difficulty finding enough food for the horses and their donkey with our own animals. The animals can fend for themselves. You can keep their long guns and the rest of the gear. I want the six-shooter ammunition. White men don't like selling ammunition to a black man. There is enough here to last me for a long time."

"Why did you call me mister around those bad men? You never called me that before?"

"I just wanted them to know that they were dealing with a man and not a half-breed."

"I will still say that no man is a match for you with that gun. I sure wish that I could shoot like that."

"Sometimes it's good and sometimes it's bad. I have the advantage because I am a black man. It surprises most men to find that I can handle a gun. That will always give me the edge in a gunfight. I will try again to teach you to shoot the short gun if you will let me. We have plenty of ammunition now."

"Forget it, I could never handle that short gun like you."

Near nightfall they released the animals and brought their gear to the cabin. Little Fox made a fire and heated some coffee. The two men sat in silence and drank the coffee. They left the saddles out side the cabin door.

"We have to get rid of those saddles. We don't need them and they are extra baggage. We could bury them in the back or just leave them. I don't think they will return for them."

"That's fine by me. Let's bury them in the back of the cabin. I plan to leave this place when the furs get traded. I'm going further north. Those men have friends in the settlement. They are sure to come looking for us, or me, since you will be leaving soon. I have wanted to move for sometime and now is as good a time as any other. In the morning we will load the furs on the donkey and the mule and search for a settlement further north. I don't want to go to the settlement where those men came from. There is no need for us to go looking for trouble."

"If you think that is what we ought to do, then we will do it. I'm not going to let any man chase me from my home."

"Sometimes it is better to avoid trouble than to look for it. Anyway, I'm ready to move on."

"The beavers around here are not as plentiful as they were a few years ago. It is time to look for a new site."

"I sure wish that I could convince you to stay with me. I know you have decided to leave, so be it."

"It is the will of the Great Spirit."

Little Fox finally convinced Eagle Eye to stay with him until all the furs were ready. Then he wanted Eagle Eye to accompany him to the settlement. Eagle Eye realized that this was Little Fox's way of keeping him with him. He did not mind doing it.

He realized that both he and his mule would have perished during the winter, if it were not for John Little Fox. They had survived because of little Fox's Kindness.

At any rate, he was in no hurry to leave. He had no special place in mind to go so he consented to stay until they had bartered the furs. He knew that John Little Fox would try to think of another way to delay his departure. Yet, he had made up his mind he would leave John Little Fox after they took the furs to the settlement.

Fur Trading in the Settlement

In the morning, the two men loaded the furs on the donkey. Flower would have nothing to do with the furs. She refused to allow Eagle Eye to load them on her. Eagle Eye decided that they would take turns riding her while the donkey loaded with furs trailed behind them. They traveled about ten miles heading due north and then camped for the night.

"There is a settlement and a trading post about ten days ride from here, we can trade the furs there. I'm going to set up a trapping cabin about fifty miles north of here. That should be far enough away so the four and their friends wont bother me."

"What will you do if the same problem occurs there?"

"Then I will just move further into the wilderness."

"There are lands around here where the white man has never been or seen."

"Where will you go when your time of leaving comes?"

"I intend to head west. I want to go where there are no white men. Whenever I meet white men, someone dies."

"The way that you handle that gun, I think that it will not be you that dies."

They traveled by day and each night selected a place to camp. They sat by the campfire at night with a cup of hot coffee and shared their experiences. The weather, except a few rainy days, made the trip a pleasant one.

It took ten days for the two men to reach the outskirts of a small settlement. It was typical of the many settlements that dotted the western section of the newly formed states. There was a hotel, bar, general store, livery stable, jail and about fifty houses. The settlement was prosperous.

John Little Fox watched the settlement from a hilltop about a half-mile away. He was sure that he could exchange his load of furs at the general store. This was his first time bartering his wares in this settlement. He selected it because of its distance. He did not want to encounter Scar Face and his friend, whom he suspected lived in the settlements closer to him.

He never really got what he thought his fur were worth. The white men never treated him as an equal and always cheated him when he tried to trade his furs. Yet, he could get much needed supplies. John Little Fox never took money for his furs, only supplies.

"Sooner or later we have to go down to the settlement. I am as ready as I will ever be. I don't like going into the white man's village but it is the only way that I can trade my furs and get supplies."

Eagle eye loaded his gun and made sure it was clean.

He said to Little Fox, "I hope that our business in the settlement goes peacefully. I don't want use my gun. I am going to be ready if we do have trouble. If I do get into a fight I will need you to cover my back, make sure that no one shoots me from behind."

"I will do my best in case there is trouble. I don't expect any trouble. We are going to trade our furs and get the hell out of there, as quickly as we can. We wont even go near the bar."

"We can get done and leave the place within an hour."

It was a warm spring day. The two men and their animals entered the settlement just as the sun was making its transit across the noon line. They were a strange looking pair, a black man riding a mule and a half-breed leading a donkey loaded with furs. Yet, no one even bother to turn and stare at the two as they entered the settlement. The town's people, accustomed to seeing mountain men, showed no interest as the two entered their settlement. They went directly to the general store and Eagle Eye stood silently as John Little Fox traded his furs for supplies.

The storekeeper paid no attention to Eagle Eye. He examined the furs that the two of them brought into the store. He spoke to Little Fox about the supplies he wanted. The storekeeper took his furs and offered him a few meager supplies. Little Fox complained that the furs were worth more than he was offering.

"The storekeeper said to him, "Take it or leave.""

In the end Little Fox accepted the offer. The two of them left the store.

As they approached the door, the shopkeeper said to Eagle Eye, "Ain't seen many niggers round these parts. I ain't ever seen a nigger wearing a gun. Where you hail from boy?"

"I am not a boy and where I'm from is of no concern of yours."

"Uppity nigger, ain't you. We got laws in this town and one is that no nigger wears a gun."

As the two went out the door Eagle Eye looked back and said, "Your laws don't mean a hill of beans to me. I am on my way out of your town."

As the two men reached their mounts and were loading their supplies on them the town drunk approached them.

He said to Eagle Eye, "Nigger, Bart is over at the saloon and he wants to talk to you. Claims heard of you. He wants to see how fast you are with that six shooter."

"Tell your friend that I got no quarrel with him. I just intend to leave town the way that I came in."

"You can tell him your self he's in the street in front of you and waiting for you."

Eagle Eye saw a man wearing two side arms walk toward him. Wearing two guns did not bother Eagle Eye. Eagle Eye knew that two guns were just for show. They represented a show of force when a lone man is stacked against a crowd. Eagle Eye wasn't worried, though he considered the man dangerous. He would avoid a fight if he could. If he couldn't, someone would die.

The man wore a wide brim hat, white shirt with a black scarf around his neck. He wore knee boots and black trousers. Bart, from what Eagle Eye could see of him, was in his mid-twenties. He walked toward Eagle Eye with confidence. His gait and demeanor suggested that he had done this often and had nothing to fear.

The entire saloon had emptied it customers. Even the poker players had stopped their game to watch. They were waiting to see what was going to happen next. The hotel manager stood in the doorway. The ladies from the brothel stood on the porch waiting to see who would die. Eyes watched from windows all along the dusty street. Word of what was about to happen spread across the little settlement faster than a brush fire across the open plains. Across the street, the Sheriff came out of the jailhouse. He was curious and wanted to see what was about to take place. He made no effort to interfere with the gunfight about to take place.

"Nigger, you wearing a gun, I sure hope that you know how to use it."

107

"I got no argument with you, I just want to leave this town."

"Well, I got an argument with you. Niggers don't supposed to wear guns. I am going make you eat the one that your are wearing and hang your carcass from yonder tree."

"You got one chance to walk out of this town alive. You can drop your gun belt and take off all your clothes and just walk away."

"That I ain't going to do."

"Then you gonna die."

"I ain't going to draw my gun."

"If you don't draw, I'm just gonna shoot you in the legs first and then the arms. You will still be alive, but barely."

Eagle Eye faced Bart. He did not want a gunfight. He was waiting for the sheriff to put a stop to it. The sheriff simply turned and looked the other way.

Someone in the crowd yelled, "Bart, shoot the nigger and get it over. I want to get back to my poker game."

Eagle Eye looked back at Little Fox. True to his word, he was guarding his rear with his shotgun. Eagle Eye knew that he did not have to worry about shots from his rear.

He looked at Bart and said, "You are so intent on dying today. Draw your gun whenever you are ready."

In a second it was all over. Bart went for his gun. He had just cleared leather when Eagle Eye made his move. Then Bart was lying on the ground with a bullet hole between his eyes. Eagle Eye started to mount Flower and stopped as he saw the sheriff move toward him.

"Hold it there nigger, I want to talk to you. I am Sheriff Bob Jones and I keep order in this town."

"What you want with me, you watched what happened. You saw him draw his gun first?"

"I drew after his gun had cleared leather. It was a fair fight and I am leaving this town forever."

"What you are saying is true but I have to have an inquest, according to the law."

"Now nigger you hand over your gun and accompany me to the jail while we get this mess sorted out."

"A man is dead and now the law is involved."

"The judge gets here in a day or so. Then you will be free to leave and be on your way. You have just killed a man and we have to have a hearing to get to the facts."

"I saw him draw first. I know that you were within your rights to kill him. I still have to do my duty."

"Mister Sheriff, the only way you gonna get my gun is over my dead body."

"You can draw your gun when you are ready."

"You and no mob are gonna to lynch me in this town or the next town."

"If anyone in that crowd goes for his gun I'm gonna to shoot you first, just remember that."

"You will be the first to die."

"I'm ready to die. If you feel the same way, go for you gun."

"Now you listen nigger. You listen good to what I am going to say cause I won't repeat it. I promise you a fair hearing. All you got to do is give me your gun, and come with me to the jailhouse and sign some papers. Then you will be free to leave this town and be on your way. I will make sure that no harm comes to you. If you don't give me your gun, that mob is going to tear you apart and hang you from the nearest tree."

"I ain't giving up my gun. If anyone in that crowd attacks me, I am going to shoot you."

"I mean what I say. Unless you are ready to draw yours, get out of our way."

"We intend to leave this town right now."

John Little Fox was already on his donkey. He kept his shotgun ready. If Eagle Eye died today, he was going to die with him. Sitting armed on his donkey he waited for Eagle Eye and the sheriff to finish their conversation.

He looked at Eagle Eye and said, "Don't give up your gun."

"If you give up your gun, we will never leave this place alive."

"I know that and so does the sheriff. Mister Sheriff, we are riding out and if you intend to stop us, do it now or get out of our way."

"If that crowd attacks me, I will draw my gun. I will put a bullet between your eyes, you can be sure of that."

"Then I am going to shoot the leaders of the mob."

"You just remember that I am going to put a bullet between your eyes first."

The jeers from the mob were getting louder and they were about to make a move on the two but the sheriff stopped them. He knew that Eagle Eye intended to shoot him first if the crowd got out of hand. The sheriff held up his hand toward the crowd of men that had gathered.

He said, "It was a fair fight. We got no cause to keep this nigger."

"Let him and the half-bred git out of town."

"The first man that makes a move against the two of them must answer to me."

Eagle Eye mounted Flower and backed her out of the range of the sheriff's gun. As he rode out of the town, he watched over his shoulder. John Little Fox and Eagle Eye finally reached the edge of the town. They did not rush, and rode slowly out of the town. Eagle Eye watched as the crowd moved back into the Bar. No one made a move to stop them and the two left the town and headed northwest.

John Little Fox said, "That was a close call. I didn't think that we would get out alive."

"Most reasonable men think twice about dying, that sheriff came close to making me kill him."

John Little Fox knew that this was not a settlement that he could enter again. He would have to trade his furs some place else. He would have to find a settlement further north that he would use in the future to barter his wares. He decided to avoid as much trouble as possible, since he could not use a gun like Eagle Eye. He had no intentions of ever returning alone to the settlement that they were leaving.

"Will they come looking for us?"

"I doubt it, but we should be on guard tonight. The sheriff was glad to get rid of us."

"He knew that I was in the right. If I had given him my gun, I would be dead by now."

"He did not care who drew first or last."

"He wanted me because a white man had been shot by a black man. That was why the sheriff wanted my gun."

"You are right about that."

"He would have lynched me before sunset if I had been stupid enough to trust him and turn my gun over to him."

"If he didn't do it, then the people in the town would have done the job for him."

"That sheriff would just leave the jail cell open and go have a drink in the bar, that mob would do the rest."

"That crowd would have come to the jail and strung us up within the hour."

"Why did he let us leave town? Surely he could have stopped us with all the town's people to help him?"

"He knew that I would shoot him first if the mob came after us."

"He considered his life. He knew that I meant what I said."

"What would you have done if the mob had attacked us?"

"I would have shot the sheriff first, just like I said I would. Then I would have shot as many leaders of the mob as I could. That would frighten the others into stopping the attack."

"If all else failed, then I would die like a man with my gun in my hand and my boots on."

"No white mob is going to lynch me when I ain't done nothing wrong."

"I tried my best to avoid a fight. Ain't no one going to make me strip naked and then run me out of no town."

"I didn't want to shoot that gunslinger but he gave me no choice. I had the advantage because he didn't expect to find a black man that could handle a six shooter."

"What will we do if they come after us?"

"If they come after us, we will give them the fight that they are looking for. Someone must die, let us hope that it is not us."

"I like you Eagle Eye. You are my brother. I will be sad when the time for parting comes."

"I too will be sad to leave, but like the coming of the seasons, the parting is a time of rejoicing."

"I have gotten to know you Little Fox. I will remember all that you have taught me. May the Great Spirit smile upon you and give you peace."

The two men rode in silence for the rest of the afternoon. They considered themselves lucky to be able leave the town alive. Both men were glad to be on the open trail heading away from the town.

With their mounts, they knew that if the sheriff and the men in the town came after them on horseback, they would soon catch them. Flower and donkey could not match the speed of horses. They hoped that the affair had ended and that the sheriff would forget the matter and let it rest. Yet, both of them knew, that an Indian or black man who kills a white man is hunted down like an animal.

Law and Order

The night after leaving the settlement, they camped by a quiet stream and Eagle Eye took the first watch. The night was quiet, like a sailboat on a calm sea. There were no clouds in the sky. The moon provided little light and the stars were out in all their glory. Camping outdoors suited both men and they enjoyed the mild spring night with its clear sky with stars and moon overhead.

Eagle Eye looked at the sky and tried to find the drinking gourd. He located it low in the northern sky. He remembered the first time that he had attempted to escape by running away from the plantation in South Carolina. He remembered following the drinking gourd. He remembered being caught, the dogs, the overseer and his punishment the next day. Tonight it seemed like a dream, only the three fingers on his left hand told him that it had really happened. It was a long time ago and he was still running, Someday it had to end.

He thought of Aunt Sal, long since dead. He wished her well and hoped that she found the peace in heaven that she always talked about. He wondered what Tom and the other boys that shared the bunkhouse with him were doing. Were they still alive? Were they still in the South? Did they have families and were they happy? He thought of his Indian wife and his children. He said a silent prayer.

There were no sounds from the songbirds and the coyotes were silent. A chorus of frogs, in the nearby stream, occasionally broke the silence of the night. No breeze stirred the leaves of the trees. It was a curious silence, a silence that foretold of impending doom.

Eagle Eye was enjoying the silence of the night. He knew that he could hear any sounds made by approaching men. It made watching and waiting easier. He strained to hear sound that were not there, the sound of horses. The sounds that would indicate the sheriff and his men coming to kill them.

They did not make a fire because they were afraid that the flames and smoke would attract too much attention. They knew how much the white men resented being bested by Indians or blacks and the felt sure that they would be tracked and hunted down like animals.

It was a quiet spring night; the moon and the stars making it seem almost like daytime. Coyotes could be heard in the distance breaking the sound of the breeze as it passed through the trees. Occasionally, a small animal could be heard drinking from the nearby stream. Yet, the sheriff and his men did not come during the night. John Little Fox was sure that they had forgotten about them and would not bother them again. Eagle Eye's feelings were different. He was sure that it was just a matter of time before they came for them.

Eagle Eye spent most of the night awake not wanting to be surprised by the men from the settlement. He was not sure that they would come after them but he took no chances. Late in the night he woke John Little Fox and told him that it was his turn to watch.

Little Fox said to him, "My donkey will alert us if anyone approaches."

"I know that, so will Flower but I don't trust my life to the animals. If someone gets the drop on us my six shooter and your shot gun will not save us."

Little Fox said, "All right, if you think we should do it, we will."

"We should do it."

John Little Fox took his position, shot gun in hand, and watched for the rest of the night. The sheriff and his men did not come during his watch. This gave John Little Fox added confidence that they would not come.

In the morning he said to Eagle Eye, "Both of us could have gotten a good nights rest. With the mule and the donkey, no one is going to slip up on us."

"Well, we are still alive and I don't intend to put my life in the hands of Flower and Donkey."

It was early in the morning when Flower became restless. She could smell the scent of horses in the distance. Flower had no love for horses and whenever they were near she became restless. Her restlessness alerted Eagle Eye and John Little fox.

John Little Fox said, "I think that we have company. The wind is blowing in this direction and Flower smells something."

Eagle Eye said, "I'm going to have a look."

Eagle Eye took his gun and climbed a hill and saw a cloud of dust about one mile away on the open plain. It could have been a party of Indians hunting or blue coats out on a raid. It could be the sheriff and men from the settlement. Eagle Eye would take no chances; he decided to leave the area immediately. He did not want an encounter with that many men. He came back to the camp and told Little Fox what he had seen and that they were leaving when they could get their mounts ready. The two men rapidly broke camp. They headed westward as fast as the mule and donkey could go.

John Little Fox planned to build a cabin about fifty miles from the settlement that they had just passed through. Eagle Eye planned to continue west where he planned to buy some good bottomland as start a small farm. He still had enough of the gold coins left to make his dream come true.

When the sheriff and the men that he had deputized to hunt the two men down reached the campsite where Little Fox and Eagle had spent the night, they were gone.

"They are less than half hour ahead of us, we can catch up to them before noon."

One man spoke up and said, "Why don't we just let them be, they didn't do nothing wrong? My horse is tired and I'm turning back. The rest of you can go on if you want to. I got no quarrel with the half-breed and that black man."

The sheriff said, "What do you mean, they didn't do nothing wrong, that nigger killed a white man right before your eyes?"

"Bart had it coming, all of us saw him draw first. Anyway, Bart was a bully and we should be glad that he is dead, the town is better off with him gone. Let's take a tally and see how many men want to continue to hunt them down and face that nigger's six-shooter. Some of us are bound to die and I for one don't feel like dying for the likes of Bart."

Another spoke and said, "Bart has killed five men in our town in the last two years that I know about, there are probably others. Each time he is allowed to go free and kill again. I am glad that the black man shot him. He got no more than he deserved. Each time he claimed self-defense but all of us knew that the men he killed didn't know how to use their guns and Bart knew it also. If that black man had not shot him, he would have gone on killing. Which one of us would be his next kill?"

A third man spoke, "I agree with you. Sheriff, why didn't you run Bart out of town, then we would be in this mess?"

Someone else said, "I'm for going back home and forgetting that black man and the half-breed. They didn't do nothing wrong anyway."

Another said, "Bart was a bully and he terrorized everyone in the town."

Sheriff Jones hesitated for a few seconds, considering what the men were saying.

Finally, he spoke, "You can't run a man out of town unless he commits a crime."

Someone else said, "Bart always committed crimes and you just looked the other way. I say good riddance to him. I am riding back to town, my horse is plum tuckered out."

Sheriff Jones said, "All the men that Bart killed drew first and all you men know that. What Bart did or didn't do don't make any difference. That is not the issue here. That nigger killed a white man and that's why we have to hunt him down. We can't let that nigger git away with what he done. I say we catch up with them and bring them back and string them up as a lesson to other niggers."

The men that the sheriff had deputized were not gunmen. They knew that in a fight they stood no chance against Eagle Eye. Bart was the fastest and meanest man with a gun that most had ever seen, and he was gunned down by a black man who was faster with his gun. Most were afraid of Bart and were glad to see him killed.

All of them knew that it was a fair fight. They saw Bart draw first. The majority decided to return to town and let the matter drop. Only five of the men elected to go with sheriff Jones. The others rode back in the direction of the town.

"Well, the six of us are going to get that nigger and the half breed, you cowards can return to the town."

It was an hour later when the Sheriff and the five deputies caught sight of the two men. Eagle Eye watched the dust cloud get closer and closer to them. From the size of the dust cloud he knew that the raiding party was smaller than the one that he had seen earlier. He was not sure that it was the same group of men but he was sure that there were no more than five or six of them. They were riding hard.

He reached a point where the little meandering stream that they were following broke into two branches. He dismounted Flower and Little Fox dismounted also. He knew that their mounts were not as fast as the men on horseback and that they would catch them soon. He wanted to be the one to decide the place where they would make their stand. If he were going to die, he could not decide the time but the choice of the place to die was his. He decided upon the place, a point where the stream divided. It was open space with the sun at his back. It would be difficult for them to be surrounded.

Everywhere, there were signs of spring. The trees were just beginning to open their leaf buds. The water rushed down the little stream in torrents, being fueled by melting snow high in the hills. In a few days the stream would overflow it banks and flood the terrain.

It was the time of the year that Eagle Eye and Flower liked best. There were few insects about to pester them and there was plenty to eat. The green grass was a welcome sight to Flower and the donkey.

The air was filled with the songs of birds. Some place nearby a woodpecker was at work on a dead tree near the riverbank. His pecking sounded almost like gunfire. Further downstream, a family of beaver was busy repairing the dam destroyed by the winter. The bears and other creatures that slept out the winter were awake from their long sleep. Soon the struggle for life and death decreed by Mother Nature would again start. Those creatures at the top of the food chain had little to worry about.

It was a good day to be left alone, alone with nature in its entire splendor. It was a day when birds would be mating and building their nests. It was a day when children would be born and the old die. It was a typical warm western spring day. It was day for friendship and a day for peace. Eagle Eye and Little Fox would know friendship this day but they would not find peace. It was not in the cards.

"We will make our stand here. The sun is at our backs and our mounts are not as fast as theirs."

"They will catch us, and this place is as good as any other place to face them."

"I will make sure that your back is covered, I don't want you to get shot from behind."

"How many are there? Are you sure that you can handle them?

"Do you think we should stay together?"

"If there are six of them, how would you know which to shoot if we are both shooting? Your long gun will make no difference. You will be more help if you cover my rear."

"There are no more than four or five of them and my six shooter will take care of them. You just make sure that no one surprises us from behind."

"I can't shoot behind me or something that I can't see. Go over and stand behind that rock with your long gun and make sure that no one comes around it, I will take care of the others."

Little Fox moved to the rock about twenty yards away and took up position with his long gun. He looked back and saw Eagle Eye standing in the open waiting for the arrival of the sheriff and his men. His gun was in his holster. Both Flower and Donkey were grazing some distance away.

Sheriff Jones and his four deputies approached Eagle Eye. They approached slowly as if they had all the time in the world to get their business done. There was no urgency in their movement or their actions. The slow pace worried Eagle Eye and he was positive that there were more of them and that they were waiting for the others to get into position. He also wondered why the five of them didn't fan out so that they would have a better chance. He knew that if they started to fan out he would have to stop them. Shooting the five of them together would be easier than having them spaced far apart. They approached slowly and dismounted when they were about thirty feet from him. The five men started to walk toward Eagle Eye still with their slow pace. Eagle Eye was convinced that there were others and he did not know how many but he had to trust Little Fox to cover his back. It would be all that he could do to handle the five slowly moving toward him.

About twenty yards away, Sheriff Jones spoke to him saying, "Listen up Nigger, you going back to town with us."

"Mister Sheriff we have talked about this before. You and your men know that I didn't do nothing wrong. I am not going any place with you. Please don't make me draw my gun; I don't want to harm you and your men. I got no fight with you. You and your men got no fight with me. 'Cause I ain't done nothing wrong."

"If I were guilty of any crime, I would give you my gun and return to the town to take my punishment whatever it might be. You know within your heart that I haven't done anything wrong. You saw that gunslinger draw his gun first."

"I didn't attempt to draw my gun until he had cleared leather. Why don't you just ride off and leave us be?"

"I told you before boy that I have to hold an inquest. I gotta get the facts of what happened on the record. The circuit judge will be in the town in a week or so. You just have to sit in jail and wait a few days. Then I can let you go free."

"Mister sheriff, I ain't going to give up my gun to you or no one else. If it's a fight you hankering for, you going to get one"

"Boy, you don't understand how the law works. I am the law in this neck of the woods. I intend to see that the letter of the law works for all men, white men, half-breeds and niggers alike. It don't make no difference to us if you come dead or alive but you gonna go back to the town. There are five of us and one of you. Why don't you just be a good boy and hand me your gun? Where is that half-bred that was riding with you? Is that his donkey grazing over yonder?"

"It shore is Mister Sheriff."

"Call him over here, we got to talk to him. He might know more about how the law works than you do."

"You right Mister Sheriff, I don't know the law. I do know right from wrong and I was in the right. What would you have done to that gunslinger if he had killed me? He was a white man killing a black man and you would have done nothing."

"I would have held an inquest and got the facts on what happened and saw that justice was done. If he were found innocent, he would be allowed to go free. If the judge found him guilty, he would pay for his crime. I have to do the same thing for you."

Mister Sheriff, "You saw that man come out of the bar after me and you did nothing about it. You could have stopped him if you had wanted to."

"I see you niggers don't know the law. I go no right to stop a man from walking in the street. I can only interfere when a crime has been committed."

"I can't give up my gun and if you try to draw yours, I will be forced to kill you. With five of you I can't take the chance of shooting your gun arm. Please don't make me kill you."

"Sheriff, that nigger is worried about killing all of us. Why don't we just go for our guns and teach that uppity nigger a lesson?"

"Now just hold on, Ain't no need for gun play. I think this is a reasonable boy we are dealing with and he understands the stakes. I just have to explain to him how the law is involved here."

"Now boy, I am the law and I have to hold an inquest on the killing that took place. Do you understand what an inquest is boy?

"Yes Sir, I understand what an inquest is Mister Sheriff".

"I am asking you boy, one last time, to give me your gun."

"Mister Sheriff, I ain't going to do that."

"Where is that half-bred that came into town with you to fur trade?"

"I wouldn't worry about him Sheriff, he will be here soon enough."

The Sheriff and the four deputies moved a few steps closer still taking their time in approaching Eagle Eye. Eagle Eye knew why they were taking so much time to make their move. He knew that there was another of them coming at him from behind. He did not look around. He trusted Little Fox to cover his rear.

Suddenly, he heard Little Fox's long gun go off, Eagle Eye drew and started shooting; the five men went down in a hail of gunfire from his gun. He drew with lightening speed and fired five times before the other men knew what was happening. Only the gun of Sheriff Jones, the first one he shot, completely cleared leather. The deputies hardly had time to realize what was happening. They were not gunslingers and against Eagle Eye's gun, with his fast draw, they were dead men.

Eagle Eye looked behind him and saw Little Fox coming toward him. He walked over to the Sheriff and kicked his gun from his hand. He noticed that the sheriff was still breathing. He would not live long but he was still alive.

He bent down near the Sheriff's ear to make himself heard and said, "Why did you come after us, we committed no crime?"

With his last breath Sheriff Jones whispered, "Nigger you killed a white man, no nigger can kill a white man and expect to live."

"Their deaths were useless, why would they hunt us down for killing a man is self defense?"

"You got to remember that you are a black man and I am a half-breed. We ain't allowed to best a white man no matter what the conditions. He could not be Sheriff of that town if he had not hunted you down and killed you."

"His death is not your fault or mine, it is just the way things are.

"He had no choice in his actions and you had no choice in yours, but to kill him."

The Burial

It was a pleasant day for the gruesome task facing the two men. They had to dig graves and bury the sheriff and his men. They spent the rest of the day digging shallow graves for the six men. Eagle Eye still had a difficult time deciding why it was necessary to kill the men. He realized that they knew that he had committed no crime. He still wondered why the sheriff was so set upon hunting him down. He wondered what the sheriff would gain by doing it.

In his heart he knew that he was innocent, his only crime was trying to protect himself from a man who was determined to kill him for no reason. The logic of the sheriff in his quest for narrow-minded justice escaped him. How could they hate him so much for just being black?

They buried them side-by-side and covered their graves with large stones to keep away the animals. They erected crude crosses above each grave. When the graves were finished Eagle Eye and Little Fox divided every thing of value that the Sheriff and his men carried. What money and watches the men had were divided among the two of them. The dead men would have no more use for them.

Eagle Eye said, "That Sheriff's gun is one of the prettiest that I have ever seen. Since he has no more use for it I am going to keep it. I think it is the edge that I need."

Eagle Eye picked up the Sheriff's gun and balanced it in his hand. He shifted it quickly from hand-to-hand get the feel of it.

"This gun is beautiful, look at the pearl handle. I want to see what this gun will do, toss some rocks in the air for me will you."

"I will toss the rocks but first let me pick out one of their guns for myself. With what you taught me about the short gun, it might come in handy."

"If I were you I would not draw against any man until you are sure that you are fast enough. You have the same advantage that I have. No man is going to expect a half-breed to be able to use the short gun, and use it well. You should always use that to your advantage. Make sure that the sun is at your back and let the short gun be an extension of your own arm. Just shoot and don't worry so much about aiming."

"That's very easy for you to say, you are the best man with a short gun that I have ever seen. No man in the west is a match for you. If I could use the short gun like you, I would go into any town and fear no man."

"There must always be someone to cover your back. Today, without you, I would have been hard pressed to survive. I don't consider myself a gunfighter or a gunslinger. Gunfighters don't live long lives, there is always someone out there who is faster and shoots straighter. I only use the gun to save my life and to provide me with food. I take no pleasure in killing men."

While Little Fox tossed rocks in the air, Eagle Eye tested the new weapon. He shot six rocks out of the air and then reloaded. Little Fox held a stick in his hand at twenty yards and at each shot the stick became shorter and shorter. Eagle Eye never realized there were handguns superior to his own. His was the only one that he had ever used and he was surprised to find a six shooter that was better crafted than the one that he had become accustom too. He liked the pearl handle but most of all, he liked the way the weapon fired. It was smooth with little or no recoil. Eagle Eye was sure that the gunsmith that made the weapon was a master craftsman.

It was the most beautiful weapon that Eagle Eye had ever seen. He wondered how the sheriff had acquired it and if it was made especially for the sheriff. He continued to hold the weapon and to marvel at its beauty and ease of use. With this weapon, he would be more than a match with any gunslinger. He put the new weapon in his right holster and shifted his old colt revolver to his left side.

He kept the sheriff's holster and found that even that was superior to the one that he used. He practiced with both hands until he was almost as good with is left as he was with his right. He realized that the right hand was his hand of choice because of the absence of fingers on the left hand. Eagle Eye decided to carry both guns. He knew that he shot better with his right hand than his left and he intended to do some practicing to remedy the situation. Anyway, as a lone man facing a mob, two guns would simply be a show of force. No man would attempt to draw two guns simultaneously.

He had no idea if he would ever need two guns but he would be ready if the time came. He found the new gun far superior to his own gun and wondered why a man would carry such a beautiful weapon and not know how to use it properly. With that weapon, the sheriff should have been able to kill him. As he thought about it, he realized that the short gun was only as good as the man who used it. The sheriff had this beautiful gun but he had no knowledge or skill that was necessary to use it effectively. He also realized that the sheriff felt he had an advantage with his gun, especially with the five deputies backing him up.

The horses were set free and shooed from the area with hit on the rump. Most of the men headed back toward the settlement. Eagle Eye wondered what would happen when the horses reached the settlement without their riders. He was sure that out of curiosity, some men in the town would come looking for them. All that they would find would be the graves and the saddles, unless someone came along and took them. Then all that would be left would be the graves.

He suspected that the town people were planning a party for the return of their sheriff and his prisoners. He wondered how long they would have survived in the town had they been captured and taken back. He knew that they planned to make a public hanging of the two to show the entire town what happen to an uppity black man and a half-breed who had killed a white man.

They would not consider that the killing was done in self-defense and that the white man drew his gun first. Their concern would be the punishment for the two of them for besting a white man, something no nigger and a half-breed was supposed to do. They would never consider burying the two of them. Their bodies would be left for the scavengers, not that it mattered, since they would be dead.

After the burial, the two men rode in silence. About noon they stopped to let the animals graze. The grass shoots sprouting after the long winter was a welcome addition to the meals of dried grass that the animals had lived on all winter. Eagle eye decided to allow Flower to eat as much as she wanted, knowing it would be useless to try to mount her while she was still grazing.

They ate a lunch of dried meat and dried fruit. They sat under a lone tree in the open plains of northwest Kansas and talked of the winter that they had just lived through. They talked of past times and avoided discussing the parting that would soon be taking place.

The Parting

After the animals had finished grazing, the two men mounted and continued northwest. It took them two months to reach the Colorado border. Near the Platte river, about ten miles north of Fort Morgan, John little Fox decided that he was far enough from civilization to build his cabin and start a new season of trapping.

He reasoned it would be a lot easier and safer to barter his furs in Fort Morgan than to continue to deal with the small general stores in the settlements. He convinced Eagle Eye to stay and help him build the log cabin and set his traps before departing. John Little Fox was still not convinced that Eagle Eye and Flower would leave him and he was determined to have the two stay.

Eagle Eye agreed to stay and help him and said, "I owe you that much for helping me survive the winter and teaching me to read but once you are settled, me and my mule will be on our way."

They cut logs and used the animals to pull them to the building site. It was hard work for both the men and the animals. After the logs were notched and fitted together, the cracks between them had to be filled with clay. The roof was covered with bark and rough shingles cut from the logs. With the completion of the clay chimney on one side and a heavy log door on the other the structure was almost ready for occupancy. Gun holes were left on all sides just in case they were needed.

At times it was all Eagle Eye could do to convince Flower that this was work befitting a mule. He talked to her, patted her and finally convinced her that it was the right thing to do. John Little Fox looked at the two and was amazed at the way Eagle Eye treated Flower.

Once he said to Eagle Eye, "Why don't you just take a tree branch to her when she doesn't obey you and do what you want her to do?"

"That was what the slave owner used to do to black men and women when they wanted them to do something. I don't think any living creature should be treated that way. I get enough from Flower by treating her as I would like to be treated."

"You have taught me a lot about animals. I have never given my donkey a name."

"You always called her donkey, I thought that was her name."

"No that's what she is, not her name. Come to think of it, I think that she thinks that's her name. Maybe I will leave it at that and just call her donkey. Yes, I am going to make that her official name."

"I am sure that she will be pleased to hear that."

John Little Fox ignored the remark and went on commenting about the name.

"Donkey, that has a good ring to it, plus she already answers to it. That's what I'll call her, Donkey."

It took two months to build the cabin and to finish the shed for Donkey and the storage shed for the winter meat. When it was finally finished, Eagle Eye decided it was time for him and Flower to be on their way.

One late summer morning, Eagle Eye arose after breakfast and went to the makeshift corral and got Flower. He packed his belongings in a bag and told John Little Fox that he was leaving.

The parting was hard and sad for both men. John Little Fox could not hold back the tears as he watched Eagle Eye ride off into the early morning sun. He made Eagle Eye promise to come back this way and to look him up someday. Both men knew, that the farewell was the last time that the two would ever meet; this parting was final.

In the west there were too many things that could happen to a traveling man to hope that their paths would cross again. Someday perhaps, they would again sit around another campfire. That campfire would be in the land of the Great Spirit. It was doubtful that they would meet again in this world.

It was early spring when Eagle Eye crossed the Continental Divide and headed southwest. He intended to go to the Arizona Territory, buy land and start a cattle ranch, with a little farming on the side. In time he could hire other free black men and women to assist him. Perhaps he could even find a wife and have more children. This was the land that dreams are made of.

During his journey, Eagle Eye had encountered many bands of Indians, both on reservations and living in the open plains. His knowledge of the many dialects was an asset. The fact that he was a black man and a kindred spirit allowed him to move more freely than most men in the west. Many Indians knew about the black man and of their treatment by the whites and they regarded them as brothers. Both groups had suffered greatly at the hands of the white men and the Indians left wandering blacks to themselves or took them in as tribal brothers.

Eagle Eye had one other advantage when meeting Indians. He had become a legend among the plains Indians. He was always welcome around the campfires of the Indians that he met. Most wanted him to tell of his exploits with Quanah. During his travels westward he was greeted as a hero by most of the Indians that he encountered.

The Cabin in the Valley

Eagle Eye crossed the Southwestern corner of the Colorado territory and headed south toward Mexico. He spent the winter in an abandoned cabin on the Rio Grande. The mild winter was a pleasant surprise to Eagle Eye and Flower. He caught fish and shot wild game and waited for spring. With the coming of spring, Eagle Eye and Flower were again on the move.

Eagle Eye came upon a log cabin in a valley between two small hills. At first he thought the old farm was deserted. There were holes in the roof and one side of the house. There was a barn and it was in dire need of repairs. Most of the windows in the house were without shutters. The porch was leaning precariously to one side and looked as if it would fall at any minute. The fields were overgrown with weeds. The only signs of life were two scrawny chickens and a half nourished dog lying on the dilapidated porch of the cabin.

There was a well on the side of the house and this caught Eagle Eye's attention. He decided to approach the house with caution. He would ask the occupants if he could have some water for himself and his mule. He cautiously approached the log cabin. He started to tie his mule to the lone pole that was holding up the porch and decide against it. The pole holding up the porch was too fragile and looked as if one slight push would cause the entire porch to come falling down.

He was on the porch when he saw the door start to open. Instinctively, he went for his six-shooter. A woman appeared at the door holding an old rusty rifle that looked as if it had not been used in many years.

She appeared to be about thirty years of age, white, about five feet six inches tall and weighting about one hundred sixty pounds. She was wearing a long dress an apron and no shoes. Around her ample abdomen was a rope belt. She had rolled the sleeves of the dress up to her elbows. Her dress, stained and ragged, looked as if it had been washed many times. She wore an old yellow stained bonnet on her head that framed her round face. Her feet were bare and from the looks of her feet they had never known shoes. Her hair hung in long strands on either side of the bonnet. Her hands were rough and coarse from hard work. She looked scared but was willing to stand her ground. She held an old rusty rifle pointed directly at Eagle Eye.

"What do you want mister? I ain't got no money and there ain't nothing around here that anyone would want to take."

"Ma'am, I don't want no money and I don't take what is not mine. I just want to water my mule and we be on our way."

"Where you from, I ain't seen many men like you around these parts?"

Eagle Eye noted that she referred to him as a man and not a slave, nigger or black man. He did not totally understand her meaning. Of all the white people that he had ever met, none had referred to him as a man. They always referred to him as a nigger or boy.

All the whites that he had ever had contact with either tried to kill him or treated him like he was so much dirt. All of his previous dealings with whites had taught him caution. Only the Indians had treated him as an equal. Yet, here was a white woman referring to him as a man. In all his life he had never met anyone like this overweight white woman.

In her own way, she was still a handsome woman but years of neglect and being overweight made her appear course and rude. Her blue eyes stared straight into Eagle Eye's and he gazed directly back at her. This was something that would never happen if he were still a slave. Whites never wanted blacks to look them in the eyes. On the plantation, severe punishment would be the result of such an insult. In the south, the large plantation owners would have called her white trash. Her appearance was one that would not command their respect. She appeared to have few redeeming qualities.

Yet, there was a certain dignity about her and she carried her weight and bearing with authority. Eagle Eye wondered what she would have looked like ten years ago. He thought that once she must have been a beautiful woman.

"I come from the south and I been traveling for a long time."

"Well, you welcome to the water mister, just go to the well and help yourself."

"Thank you ma'am."

Eagle noted that she addressed him as mister. No white person had ever addressed him in that manner. This was very strange to him. The least offense term that whites had call him was boy. He looked at this strange white woman not knowing what to make of her. He could not believe that there were whites in the world that regarded him as an equal and call him mister.

Eagle Eye put his gun back in its holster. He realized that he had nothing to fear from the woman with the old rusty rifle. His first observation of the rifle told him that it would not fire and that the woman was aiming a useless weapon at him.

Even if the rifle could have been fired, he was not sure that he could shoot a woman. If he were forced he would shoot the rifle out of her hand. That was not necessary since she was holding a useless weapon.

"Why don't you put that rifle down ma'am, it won't shoot anyway?"

Eagle eye turned, his mule and started toward the well.

The lady followed him and said, "How did you know that the rifle wouldn't shoot?"

"I saw that the firing pin was missing, I served in the military during the war. I know that guns don't work without firing pins."

Eagle Eye drew water from the well and poured it in the trough for Flower. Flower smelled the water first and then started to drink and then he drank himself. All the time the woman watched him. She had put the gun barrel on the ground and was leaning on it as if it were a crutch. He looked back at her and then continued drawing water from the well.

Finally, she said to him, " Mister, I need some work done round this place and I got a pot of fat back and collards cooking in the fireplace. You look as if you could use a good home cooked meal such as it is. If you could find it in your heart to help me, I could fix you a good meal. I would offer to pay you, but I ain't got no money to pay you with or anything else of value."

Her tone was one of pleading. The tone was one of a woman who desperately needed help and did not know how to ask for it. Throughout the one-way conservation, she kept her eyes on Eagle Eye. Occasionally, she turned her gaze to Flower. When he had finished drinking and was sure that Flower had all that she wanted, he turned his attention to the woman.

"What do you want done? This place is sure in need of lots of repairs? Where is your man?"

"He went off to the war many years ago and never returned, I ain't seen hide nor hair of him since he left many years ago. I tried to keep the farm going but it is too much for a woman and a young boy, it is all that I can do to keep food on the table."

"Where is the boy now?"

"He went down to the river to catch fish, left early this morning, he will be returning soon. He is only eight years old and can't do man's work. He helps me with food by fishing and trapping rabbits and birds. He is a good boy. You could start by cutting some firewood and then patch the roof of this old cabin. Part of the cabin roof was torn off two years ago by a windstorm. I pile the boards up 'gainst the barn over there."

It appeared to Eagle Eye that she had already made a decision concerning him. She would have him stay and help her put the place in order. He was not sure that he was making the right decision. Yet, he decided to take her up on her offer of food and help her as much as he could. It was the first time that he had ever talked to a white woman as a man and not a slave.

There was something about her that made him feel pity for her. The woman was alone on a little patch of land with a young boy and trying to survive. The way that she talked to him made him feel that he was an equal and not a servant or slave. No white woman had ever treated him like a man. The woman looked like a black aunt Sal. He realized that she was white and he approached the situation with caution.

"You can put your mule in the old corral and you can sleep in the barn tonight. I don't have any money but I am a good cook."

Already she was making plans for him to spend the night, not bothering to ask if he wanted to. Yet, the way she spoke was more of a plea than a demand. He felt that she realized that the choice was up to him.

"I will take you up on your offer. I'll start on the wood and in the morning I will fix the roof on the cabin. Then I will put some posts under that porch cause it isn't going to stand long like it is. You need some land prepared to grow crops but I wont have time for that."

"I really appreciate you helping me mister. I will fix you a dinner that you will never forget. What's your handle?"

Eagle Eye looked puzzled and she smile and said, "What is your name?"

"I have been called by many names but the one that I go by is Eagle Eye."

"I like that, is it an Indian name?"

"Yes, I spent a long time living with an Indian tribe and that was the name that they gave me."

"You must have been very special to them, the Indians that is, cause they don't usually give a person a name unless they are special. Well Mr. Eye, I should go and get dinner ready. The woodpile is over there and there is an ax of sorts that you can use. I still have lots trouble chopping wood. My boy does it most of the time but he isn't much good at it, he just ain't strong enough yet."

"I didn't get your name?"

"My name is Elizabeth Jones, but you can call me Liz, most people do."

"Where are you from, I mean before you and your husband started this farm?"

"My husband and I came here from back east with a wagon train. We were headed for California to the gold mining field. We fell in love with this valley and decided to take up farming. It was good living here for the first few years. We built the log cabin with our own hands and added the second bedroom when Jim was born. Even the Indians left us alone; we used to give them corn during the winter. They used to give us wild game."

"It was a good life for many years. Then the war came and we heard talk about it in the settlement. I never dreamed that my husband would go off to war. The war did not even concern us. Then my husband, like many men just had to go off and fight. Most didn't even know what the war was about. He had no reason to leave; we had just started making the land pay for our hard work. It was a beautiful place; you should have seen it then. We had corn growing, a good garden, two cows and a calf and two horses. Everything was going so well. Then he just up and left. Sometimes I think he just wanted to get away from the farm and me. It was right after our son was born that he left."

"One day he just packed his gear and left for the war and I haven't heard a word from him since. I tried contacting the War Department but they had no record of him ever joining the army. I really don't know what happen to him. It has been so long and lonely here, I just forgot him. I gave up hope long ago that he would return and take care of his son and me. Now it's just Jim and me. He will leave when he is old enough. Then I will be here alone."

"We are off the main road, so very few people pass this way and those that do have their own problems. The only people that I have seen in the past six months were a group of Indian braves that passed this way. They took my last horse and a few chickens but did not harm us. The Indians are not like white men. They will not kill a woman, especially if she has children."

"Yeah, they don't like to harm women and children, that is the way with most Indians that I have met."

They asked me if I wanted to go with them, I said, "no."

"Have they ever returned?"

"No, they left and never returned."

"Is there no settlement nearby where you could get someone to help you run the farm?"

"Mr. Eye, I have no money. My husband took all of our money with him when he left and people don't work for nothing. There is a settlement about ten miles from here. When we had the horse, we went there to sell some of my belongings for food. After we lost the horse, it was just too far away to walk and carry anything. Anyway I don't have anything left that's worth selling."

Eagle Eye could see that she was near tears and he turned back to pour more water for Flower. She turned and walked back to the cabin as Flower and Eagle Eye watched her. She walked away with a peculiar dignity that suggested that she was determined to survive no matter what the costs. She did not look back but headed straight for the cabin. As she entered the door, Eagle Eye stood and watched her go inside.

He felt pity for this lone white woman and her young son left to fend for themselves. They had no work animals and just a few chickens and an old dog. He was not sure of how much help he could be before leaving but he would do as much as he could.

Jim

Eagle Eye waited until Flower had her fill of water and took her to the makeshift corral. He had to talk to her for a few minutes before she would enter. She tried to kick him and it recalled a legend from his slave days about mules and how stubborn they were.

"A mule will work patiently for a man for ten years just for the opportunity of kicking him once."

He finally got her settled and went over to the woodpile.

Eagle Eye picked up the old rusty ax with half the handle missing and started chopping wood. He spent the first hour cutting the wood into blocks and then split it into small pieces. He then started to stack the wood. He turned, and caught a glimpse of someone about ten feet from him. His gun was already in his hand in the blink of an eye. It was a young boy with two fishing poles and a string of fish. After seeing that it was only a boy, he put his gun back into its holster and looked at the boy.

"You should not sneak up on a man with gun. You could have been killed."

"Why would you kill me? You are sure fast with that gun."

"I would not kill you, but you should let someone know that you are coming."

The boy had come up silently. Eagle Eye had no idea that he was there or how long he had been watching him.

"My name is Jim what's yours?"

"People call me Eagle Eye."

"Are you an Indian? I have never seen an Indian that looked like you, but I have not seen very many Indians."

"No, I'm a black man."

"What's a black man, are there many people that look like you?"

"In some parts of the country there are."

"When I grow up I am going to travel all over this country and meet lots of different people. Look at the fish I caught. He held up a string of small perch. He had strung them through the gill openings with a piece of rope. There were about twenty of the small perch and the boy was pleased with his catch. I should get these to ma so that she can cook them for dinner."

Like his mother, the boy wore no shoes. He had on a pair of bibbed overalls and no shirt. The overalls were well worn and had holes at the knees. His overalls were covered with mud and were wet up to his waist from wading in the stream. His hair was blond and his eyes blue. He was small and looked fragile. He showed no fear of Eagle Eye.

In one hand he held the fish and in the other the two poles that he had used to fish the stream. He stared at Eagle Eye out of curiosity. Eagle Eye began to realize that the boy had not seen another person except his mother for a long time.

"You sure know how to chop wood mister. I hate chopping wood but sometimes I have to do it."

Eagle Eye noted for the second time in one day someone had referred to him as mister.

"Your Ma asked me to help her with some chores around this place. This place sure needs a lot work."

"I like to fish, maybe tomorrow I can take you to the stream and we can fish for a few hours."

"That would be good."

"Good, after I give these to ma I am going to dig the worms and we will fish all day."

"Not all day, cause I got work to do, but we can fish for an hour or so."

A few minutes later Jim returned and said, "Ma said that we could fish all day tomorrow and you could do the work the next day. If you fish with me, I will help you do the work and we can spend some time hunting rabbits too. Do you like to hunt? I have a bow that the Indians gave me. I haven't been able to kill rabbits with it yet. Are you any good with that gun?"

Eagle decided to give the boy a demonstration; anyway, he needed the practice. He looked at the corral about twenty feet away.

"Put some stones on that corral posts."

Jim started toward the corral.

Eagle Eye said, "Wait put two stones on two different posts."

Jim set up the two stones on the posts of the corral about twenty five feet away and stepped back.

"Watch this."

Eagle Eye drew his gun and both stones on the posts shattered a fraction of a second of each other. All that was left of the stones were shards on the ground.

Liz rushed out of the cabin to see what the disturbance was about.

Jim said to her, "Ma you should see this man shoot that gun. He shoots better than the men in the dime novels we have.

"Shoot two more stones so that my ma can see how good you are with that gun"

Jim rushed over to the coral posts and placed two small rocks on the posts and stepped back,

"Ma watch him shoot."

Eagle hesitated for a few minutes, he was not sure that he was doing the right thing. To allow the boy to see him shoot was one thing. To allow the woman to see him was different. He did not want to give her the impression that he was a gunslinger or a killer.

Liz said, "I ain't got all day, my dinner is cooking, go on and shoot."

In the blink of an eye both rocks were flying through the air.

"Where did you learn to shoot and draw like that? Are you a gun fighter?"

"No, I'm not a gun fighter, I taught my self to shoot and I only shoot to protect myself and for food.

"Sometimes I hunt wild game to eat but I don't hunt men. I'm not a gunfighter."

"When you came to the door, suppose I had a loaded gun and intended to shoot you, what would you have done?"

"I don't know. I could never shoot a woman no matter what she was doing. Most likely I would have shot the gun out of your hand but I would not have harmed you."

Then she used a strange word, a word that was beyond his vocabulary a word that had never been used in reference to him.

"She said, Mr. Eye you are a gentleman."

"Thank you ma'am, that the finest thing that anyone has ever said to me."

Liz turned and started toward the house, she stopped and said, "Dinner will be ready in a few minutes, and you two should wash up and come inside."

"Ma always makes me wash up before we eat, even when I ain't dirty."

"She even wants me to take baths, when I grow up I ain't going to wash less I want too."

"I think we should do what she says, lets go over to the well and wash up."

"You a grown man, you ain't got to wash up unless you want to."

"It's the right thing to do and when something is right one just does it."

"I'll wash up if you think it's right. Which do you like to do most, fish or hunt?"

"I like to hunt and fish. We will talk about it later."

"Can you read and write, have you ever been to school?"

"Ma taught me my numbers and I can read a little bit, long as the words ain't too long. Have never been to a schoolhouse. Don't suppose I'd like it if did."

"Ma tries to teach me what she knows bout school things, when I grow up and become a man I won't need no schooling."

"A person always needs schooling."

"What fur?"

"So that when you make a business deal, like buying food or land, the other person can't cheat you."

"Can you read?"

"Yes, I learned to read a little while ago."

"'Spose you want to teach me to read and write."

"Only if you want to."

Eagle Eye let the subject drop, he realized that eventually learning to read and write would become more important to Jim.

Jim talked non-stop while they walked toward the well. Eagle Eye just listened; he reasoned that the boy had not had another person other than his mother to talk to for many years. Jim treated him like he was special and not like the white children on the plantation. On the plantation, the white children would make you do things just because they had the authority. They knew that they could push the black slaves around. If the slave did not bend to their wishes, they would tell the master and his day would be made harsher.

"Can you teach me to shoot like that?"

"I bet that no man would stand a chance against you".

"Have you ever killed a man"?

"How many bullets does that gun hold?"

'Will you promise to teach me to shoot like you shoot that gun?"

"Well let's go fishing and hunting first and talk about those things later."

Eagle Eye realized that at the present, just surviving took up most of Jim and his mother's time. He tried to imagine how the two of them had managed to survive alone and so far from civilization. He decided to do what he could for her and then be on his way. He was not sure where he would go. With the money that he had, he planned to buy a piece of land and set up a homestead.

Before entering the cabin, Eagle Eye could smell the food. Liz had put her best cooking into this dinner. Eagle Eye entered the room and saw that the table had been set for three people. Liz put a cloth on the table and there were green plants growing from a pot in the center. Eagle Eye was not sure that he should sit at the table with them, after all they were white and he was black. He had never sat at a table and ate with white people in his entire life. He stood at the door and hesitated, not knowing just what he should do. He was ready to take his plate and eat outside.

Liz finally said, "Mr. Eagle, you sit there at the head of the table. Jim you sit here and I will sit at the other end."

Eagle Eye took his place at the table and ate his first home cooked meal in many moons. He ate collards cooked with fat back and seasoned with wild onions. There were the fish that Jim had caught, corn bread and hot sassafras tea.

"I grew the collards in a patch out back of the cabin, I let some of them go to seed for the next crop."

"I have to spend a lot of time picking the worms off them but it is worth it. Jim don't like collards much. He says that we eat too many of them."

Jim said, "When I grow up I ain't gonna never eat no collards."

"I could never grow tired of eating collards cooked this way. You sure a good cook ma'am."

Jim spoke up and said, "There are some ducks down by the stream, I bet that you could get them with your six shooter and there are lots of rabbits and possum here about. We will go hunting tomorrow and ma can cook a real meal for us."

"Tomorrow I have to fix the roof. It must rain a lot in here with the roof half gone."

"It has been raining in here for two years, so another day won't matter. Why don't the two of you go hunting and get some fresh meat? The roof can be fixed any time. It's just the back room that we can't use because of the roof. It don't rain much during this time of the year, it's the winter when it's really bad".

Again Eagle Eye got the impression that they were trying to get him to stay. Yet, they treated him like a long lost friend and with more kindness than he had known for a long time. He sensed that the longer he stayed, the more difficult it would be to leave when the time came. Yet, he had no place in mind to go and he could use a good nights sleep, even if it was in the barn.

The small barn was more comfortable than the cabin with its gaping hole in the roof. At least the barn had its roof intact, even though there was no clay left between the logs.

Both Liz and Jim were literally starved for information from the outside. They asked him many questions about what was going on in areas outside their environment. Eagle Eye did his best to answer all of their questions.

"When we were last in the settlement, there was talk of the railroad coming out this way."

"Have they started on it?"

"How long will it take before it reaches this area?"

"The rails stop back east of here some place near Missouri. It will be at least ten years before it reaches this far and it will pass north of here. There are not enough towns in this area to pay for the laying of the rails and the hauling of freight."

"Are the Indian wars still going on? It's a shame what they have done to the Indians."

"The Indians wars are still going on, though most of the Indians are on reservations. There are small pockets of resistance all over the west. Their land has been taken and most of the buffalo are gone so the war on the open plains is almost over."

Jim said, "It's a shame the way the Indians are treated. There is enough land for everyone."

Liz looked at Jim and answered, "One would think so, but that isn't the way things are."

"I enjoyed the meal very much. You are really a good cook. Those were the best collards that I have had in a long time. Now I am going to finish cutting the wood. Then I am going to gather the planks for the roof and place them by the house. I can start on the roof early in the morning."

"No, early in the morning we are going fishing and hunting."

Ma said that you could fix the roof the next day. I will help you fix the roof, after we get back.

"Mr. Eye, I am pleased that you like my cooking. You just take your time with the roof. I have lived with it for so long, another couple of days won't matter none."

"Ma'am just call me Eagle or Eagle Eye. I am going to finish my work now. Jim and I will go fishing early in the morning."

"Leave your clothes outside when you go to bed and I will wash them. I am going to give you some more clothes while I wash yours and get them clean. I will leave some blankets by the barn door. It gets cool at night around here."

Eagle Eye left the table and went outside to complete the work that he had started. Jim followed him outside. Liz started to clear the table and put the remaining food away. She took some scraps from the table and went outside to feed the dog. She watched as Eagle Eye effortlessly cut the wood while Jim stacked it. Then she went back into the house to finish her chores.

She marveled at how well the two of them worked together. She was pleased to have a man to help her with her chores and wondered how she could convince him to stay with her and Jim. She realized that with the mule they could farm a portion of the land and all would be well. She liked this big black man.

He was the answer to all her prayers. He was young, strong and beautiful. She was pleased that her son liked him. To Liz, the two of them got along like long lost friends.

Liz said to herself, "There must be someway to get him to stay with us. We could be so happy. With a man around this place, we could again farm the land."

Jim gave no thought to whether Eagle Eye would stay or leave. His goals were short range; he wanted someone to show his favorite fishing hole. He wanted someone to hunt with. Jim wanted someone to talk to, someone other than his mother. Like any eight year old he was full of questions. He found Eagle Eye patient and kind. He considered Eagle Eye a friend, and someone who had seen the entire world as some day he would do.

Eagle Eye had no idea of the plans that Liz had for him. He saw her as a white woman. He was sure that she would never consider him an equal. Although Liz treated him as an equal, Eagle Eye still had his doubts. He would do what he could for the two of them and them be on his way.

A Visit in the Night

One night after Eagle Eye had been there for two months, he went to the barn and prepared for sleep. As was his habit, he was reading a dime novel by candlelight before retiring. He opened the book, "The Escapades of Randy Thomas, Gunfighter." He had just started to read at the point where he had left off the previous night, when he heard someone outside. There was a knock at the barn door. Liz entered carrying a lantern.

"I couldn't sleep and I thought that you might like some company."

Eagle Eye put his book aside and gave her a pillow to sit on. He was not sure why she was there. He thought it had something to do with the work on the farm. The work was progressing well and he was sure that she was satisfied. He knew that she was getting the best of the agreement that the two had entered. His only compensation for his work on the farm was food and clothes. After the first night in the barn, he had never again seen his old garb. Since that first day at the farm, Liz had starting putting out his clothes at night. Each morning he would find clean clothes outside the barn door. Sometime during the day Liz would take his dirty clothes from the barn, wash and return them a few days later.

"Do you like to read?"

"Yes ma'am, but I don't read very well. There are too many words that I don't know. It takes me a long time to completely read one page. It will take me more than six months to finish this small book. The more I read, the easier it gets, so I try to read some every night. It is a new experience for me, that is, being able to read and write. I learned to read and write just a few months ago. I enjoy doing it."

"I wish Jim liked to read. I purchased those dime novels for him but he shows little interest in them. He likes for me to read to him but he won't read by himself."

They talked about, the farm, fishing, hunting and what needed to be done around the cabin. Much of their conversation centered on Jim.

Liz said, "I wish that he had someone his own age to play with."

"I agree that he needs to be around children his own age but he seems to really enjoy life."

"I know he enjoys your company, you have been very good to him since you have been here. He and I appreciate what you have done and your relationship with him. A boy his age needs a man around; it's not good for him to grow up with only a woman. All that he talks about these days is you, hunting and fishing. He wants to grow up to be just like you. I hope that he does."

"He is a easy boy to like. My son would be just a few years younger than Jim, had he lived."

During their long conversation, Liz never asked when he would leave. She seemed to take it for granted that he would stay with them forever. Eagle Eye avoided the subject of leaving. Whenever he hinted at leaving, the look on Liz's face was one of such dismay that he would let the subject drop. It was late when Liz got up to leave. She left the lantern in the barn so he would have more light to read by.

She said to him, "The candles are unsafe and I have another lantern in the house. We are growing short on lamp oil but there is enough to last for a while longer."

She got up slowly and started for the barn door.

At the door she hesitated. She turned and looked back at Eagle Eye.

Liz said, "Do you think that I am ugly?"

"No ma'am, I think that you are a very pretty woman."

Liz closed the barn door and went back to the cabin.

The nightly ritual continued, Eagle Eye would retire to the barn and later Liz would join him. They would talk late into the night. Then Liz would return to the cabin. He would read for a while after she left and then go to sleep. He never read for long periods after Liz left because he knew that they were short on lamp oil.

Eagle Eye enjoyed talking to her and looked forward to her visits. The regular visits to the barn at night had continued for about two weeks. Liz came every night and they would talk, then she would leave for the cabin.

Eagle Eye was puzzled by her visits. Yet, he enjoyed her company and the conversation. However, he did not know what to make of them. Sometimes he thought Liz would make and excellent mate but he dismissed the notion. After all, Liz was white and he was a black man. Yet, both realized that they needed each other.

One night when Liz did not come to the barn, Eagle Eye went to the cabin to see if anything was wrong. He had grown accustomed to her visits and looked forward to them. He went to the cabin and lightly tapped on the door. Liz answered his knock.

He asked, "Ma'am is everything all right?"

She explained that Jim was sick, and she was reluctant to leave him alone. He went into the cabin and stayed near Jim for most of the night. It was almost daybreak when he left for the barn. In the morning Jim was feeling better and by noon he was his usual self and feeling fine.

He said to Eagle Eye, "I 'appreciate you sitting up with me last night, I feel all right now. It must have been something that I ate. It was sure a bad stomach ache I had last night."

"I am glad to see you up an about, I was worried about you."

The visits were innocent and Liz always went back to the cabin to sleep. Eagle Eye continued to sleep in the barn. Their talks usually centered on Jim, the farm and how well it was doing. They spent hours discussing the future and it seemed to Eagle Eye that Liz had made plans for his future.

Eagle Eye knew that she was white and he was black. He was very cautious in his conversation with her. He always played the part of the perfect gentleman. He had never been alone with any white woman until he met Liz. He was not sure that her visits to the barn at night were right for her or him.

One day Jim said to Eagle Eye, "Do you like my ma?"

Eagle felt sure that Liz had planted the question in Jim's mind. Otherwise, why would the young boy ask him if he liked his mother? He answered Jim's question truthfully.

"Yes, I like her, why do you ask?"

"Why don't you marry her and then you could be my pa?"

"What makes you think that your ma would marry me?"

"The way that she talks about you."

"What has she said about me?"

"She said that you were the finest man that she has ever met."

The next day Eagle Eye and Jim went to the stream and made a blind of fir limbs. The sat patiently for five hours until a small herd of deer appeared. Eagle Eye shot a male and with Jim's help took it back to the cabin. There was no salt to preserve the meat. It was more meat than they could eat in two or three meals.

Liz said, "I have never seen so much meat, we are going to put some of it up for later."

Eagle Eye asked her, "How will we keep that much meat without salt?"

"I know what to do, I'm going to smoke some of it and dry the rest."

Liz built a fire and smoked large quantities of the deer meat. The rest she hung in the sun, cut into thin strips, to dry. With the deer meat and the hunting of small game they would have enough for the winter months. The collards and other leafy plants would provide vegetables and the nuts and dried fruit would supplement their diet.

One night Liz made her usual trip to the barn. Eagle Eye noted that she had on a beautiful dress, one that he had never seen before. Eagle Eye had never seen Liz in anything but her work clothes. He did not know that she owned anything as beautiful as the dress that she wore.

Her hair, washed, was piled high on her head. Several small combs kept her hair in place. She wore no shoes. It was obvious that she had spent an inordinate amount of time on her appearance. She sat on a pillow and they talked of Jim, the farm, the coming winter, and their preparations for the year.

"We have more meat stored than we need for the winter. I am not going to hunt more animals until we use up what meat we have. Jim will understand about not hunting, once I explain it to him. He is really a good boy and I am very fond of him."

Eagle Eye you say the most beautiful things. He is a good boy and he wants to become a man just like you. Jim idolizes you. I suppose that you know that, the way he follows you around. I am really happy that the two of you get along so well."

"He is good to have around. I enjoy his company as much as he enjoys mine."

"There have been some winters since I have lived here alone with Jim that I thought we would not make it. We had to live mostly on collards and dried fruit when Jim was very young and could not trap rabbits or fish."

"Well, this winter we don't have to worry about food."

"I know, thanks to you."

"Eagle Eye, I want you to be my man. I want you to move into the cabin with Jim and me. Later we can be married proper and be a real family."

"What does Jim think about it?"

"He was the one that suggested that you move in with me. I believe I put the idea into his head. I know it is what he wants. He desperately wants you to be the pa that he never had."

"I am going to sleep with you tonight here in the barn. In the morning, I want you to move into the cabin with me. You are the nicest and kindest man that I have ever known. I am very fond of you."

"I have wanted you for sometime but I wasn't sure that it was right for both of us."

"Why not?"

"I am a black man and you are a white woman. I am not sure how others would feel about it."

"It's no one's business but yours and mine. No one has anything to do with it. It is what I want. If it is what you want, that is all there is to it."

"It is what I want ma'am."

Liz smiled and said, "Don't ever call me ma'am again call me Liz."

"All right, Liz it is."

That night Liz slept with Eagle Eye. The next morning Jim helped him move his meager possessions into the cabin. His possessions were placed in Liz's room. Jim was all smiles and was overjoyed that at last he had a real pa.

He said to Eagle Eye, "I wish you would teach me to read like you read, and my numbers too."

"We have all winter, when spring comes you will read better than I do, I will see to that."

The smaller room, now with the roof covered was where Jim slept. Eagle Eye and Liz shared the larger bedroom. The three-room cabin radiated with happiness. Jim was happy with the arrangement. He found another dime novel and presented it to Eagle Eye. The book was the only gift that he could find to give to his new pa. The book had no cover and half the pages were gone. That made no difference to Eagle Eye or Jim. It was Jim's way of saying to Eagle Eye, I love you and you are my pa. It was a gift that Eagle Eye would always remember and cherish.

Most of all Jim enjoyed fishing and hunting with Eagle Eye. Now they rarely killed anything because they had all the meat that they needed. They both enjoyed the long walks in the woods and surrounding fields. He was learning to shoot the gun and was as happy as any boy could expect to be. He had his ma and a new pa and to Jim that was all that mattered in the whole world. Jim no longer talked bout leaving the farm and seeing the world. His world was now Eagle Eye, Liz and the farm.

The Trip to Town

They spent the winter as a family. Jim and Eagle Eye spent most of their time hunting and fishing. At night, while Liz puttered around the cabin putting everything in order. Jim and Eagle Eye played school. Liz had some difficulty understanding why Jim was so willing to allow Eagle Eye to teach him. He always resisted her attempts at being a teacher. Yet, with Eagle Eye, he was the perfect scholar. His lessons progressed rapidly and the teaching improved Eagle Eye's ability to comprehend the written page. Liz was called to help from time to time when some difficult word was encountered. She was pleased that Jim was now getting an education and that Eagle Eye was the teacher.

The winter was mild and there was plenty of small game for Eagle Eye's gun. The three, Jim, Liz and Eagle Eye, enjoyed the closeness that winter brought them. They spent long hours together in the cabin enjoying the games they devised and the conversation.

Eagle Eye helped Liz with the cooking and cleaning of the cabin. This surprised Jim and delighted Liz. When Jim mentioned it, Eagle Eye called him his little Indian warrior. He had to spend an hour explaining why Jim reminded him of the Indian warriors and their ways.

The winter passed and spring brought with it the hope and dreams of a new season. Soon they would be preparing the fields for the new planting. They made many plans for the New Year and the years to come.

They had an abundance of food, more than Liz and Jim had since the disappearance of his natural pa. Spring came and Eagle Eye started tilling the land for the spring planting of corn. He wanted enough to share with the Indians, just in case they wondered by the cabin. During his stay he had seen no other living persons except Jim and Liz. He repaired the old horse cart that had sat beside the barn and hitched it to Flower. Flower, unhappy with the cart, did everything possible to prevent being hitched.

He said to Liz, "We need some supplies from the settlement. I would like for you to take Jim and go for them."

"Eagle, I told you long ago that I got no money, not one copper cent. We don't have anything that anyone would want to trade either."

He showed her his gold coins and the rest of the money that he had accumulated.

She said, "Why didn't you tell me you were rich?"

"I am not rich."

"I have never seen that much money in all my life. Where did you get so much money? Why did you never tell me that you had it?"

"The subject of money never came up and I came by it honestly."

Eagle Eye you are sure full of surprises and you never cease to amaze me."

"I want you to go to the settlement with us, you know more about what seeds and other supplies we need. I can buy the food we need but you have to buy all the planting supplies."

"Whenever I go into a white settlement someone tries to kill me and I have to kill them. I want to avoid trouble if I possibly can. My going to town as the husband of a white woman is sure to cause trouble."

"We could pretend that I am your hired hand, rather than your husband. If you think it is all right."

Why should we pretend anything, its no one's business but ours? You are my man and they will just have to get use to the idea."

"Liz, I want to avoid trouble and going to that town as your husband is asking for trouble."

"I don't like this one bit. It is no one's business who I'm married to. You take care of my son and me, not them. No one in that town has anything to do with how I live or who I pick to be my husband."

"I know that but it doesn't make any difference to them. I'm a black man and you are a white woman and that is all they will see."

"All right, all right, we will do it your way, but be sure to wear your guns."

"No, I am not going to wear my guns, that is a sure sign there will be trouble. I will carry one gun in my hat. No one will know that I have it. He tied the gun inside his hat and put it on his head.

Take this ten dollar gold piece and buy as much food and supplies as we need. The rest of the money we will use to buy seeds for planting. I need a new plough also. I think that should be enough to buy everything that we need."

"It is more than enough. I'll bet few people in the settlement have ever seen a ten dollar gold coin."

Early in the morning, Liz dressed in her finest dress and made Jim wash and put on his Sunday clothes. They got in the cart and the trio headed for the settlement about ten miles away. They knew that it would take a full day for them to reach the settlement and buy supplies and return.

Eagle Eye said to Liz, "Give Jim twenty five cents from the change so he can buy something for himself."

"That would be wasting money."

"Give it to him anyway."

"I will give him a dime."

"Please Liz, give him twenty five cents."

"All right, all right, but I don't want him to get the idea that money is easy to come by."

Jim was thrilled; he had never had money in all of his life. Twenty-five cents to him was a small fortune.

There was a trail of sorts that led into the town. In places it was difficult to decide where the trail ended and the terrain began. They had to pick their way between boulders and washouts. They had to ford a small stream that blocked their passage. Eagle Eye wondered how Liz had ever found the town.

The trio entered the settlement. It was not different of the many settlements that Eagle Eye had encountered. It consisted of a general store, a bar, a bank, about sixty houses, a run down church and a brothel. Most of the buildings lined the dusty main street that led through the center of town. Entering the town, they went directly to the general store. They wanted to get their supplies and get back to the cabin before nightfall.

Liz and Jim entered the store, followed by Eagle Eye, hat in hand. His old ragged hat contained his gun with the pearl handle, fully loaded. He did not expect trouble. Yet, just in case he met trouble, he wanted to be ready.

The shopkeeper was Albert Adams. He wore new overalls and
a plaid shirt. His apron, tied around his waist, reached down to his
ankles. He was a tall man with blond hair and a thin mustache. His
blue eyes darted from item to item in his store. Albert Adams was
watching all the items in his store against thieves. He trusted no
one. He kept a shotgun under the counter in easy reach. He did not
intend to allow anyone to take advantage of him. He extended credit
to almost everyone in the town including the self-appointed mayor,
who owned the bar and the brothel. He would not extend credit to
strangers.

He kept accurate records of all purchases made on his buy now,
pay later, plan. He occasionally padded the accounts of those who
could not read. To Albert Adams, it was just interest on the money
that he had paid for the supplies.

"Can I help you ma'am?"

"Yes you can, I want this list filled."

"That's a mighty lot. Ma'am are you sure that you got that
much money? The last time that you were in here you didn't have
any money. I can't let you have these supplies on account. You got
something to trade."

"Just fill the order and I will pay you in cash."

Looking beyond her and Jim, he spotted Eagle Eye and said,
"What do you want nigger? Ain't anything in here going to be
stolen?"

Eagle Eye said nothing, Liz spoke up and said, and "He's with
me He's my hired hand."

"Nigger you wait outside. I can't keep an eye on you and fill this
order too."

"I told you that he was with me and he is not going to steal
anything."

Adams grudgingly allowed Eagle Eye to remain in the store. His
blue eyes watched Eagle Eye's every move.

The shopkeeper filled the order and said, "That's an even eight
dollars."

"Let me add up the prices and then I will pay you."

She added up the price of the purchases.

Liz said, "It comes to six dollars and twenty cents."

"I might have made a mistake. Let me see the list, six dollars and twenty cents it is, by golly, you shore know your figures."

"Liz handed the shopkeeper the ten dollar gold piece. He looked at it and then bit into it. He put it in his mouth and bit into it again and satisfied himself that it was real gold. He gave her a two dollar gold piece in return and the rest of the change in copper.

She stepped over to Jim and handed him a twenty-five cents. He purchased a dime novel for Eagle Eye and brought sweets and pocketed the rest. They loaded the wagon and headed out of the settlement. Jim got in the wagon and sat beside Eagle Eye. He waited until they were out of the settlement before speaking.

He asked Eagle Eye, "Why didn't you just shoot that shopkeeper? He had no business talking to you like that."

"One can't shoot another person because of something that he says."

"I would have shot him dead, if he had talked to me like that."

"The shopkeeper was wrong. I would be wrong if I had shot him. His words can't hurt me."

It was late in the evening when they reached the cabin. Liz handed Eagle Eye the change from the ten dollar gold piece.

"Eagle you are a man of many surprises."

"Why do you say that?"

"Well, you are a rich man and yet, you stay with my son and me."

"I love you both very much."

Liz started crying.

"I have wanted to hear you say that for a long time."

She took his hand and looked into his brown eyes with her blue eyes and said, "I will always love you."

"Why are you crying ma?"

"Be quiet Jim, you are too young to understand."

"He says that he loves us, and you start crying, aren't you happy 'bout that."

"Let it be Jim, yore ma's happy, she just has a different way of showing it."

"It's sure a strange way of showing it."

Eagle Eye changed the subject and asked Jim why he had spent part of his money on a dime novel.

"It ain't for me. I don't even like to read. I got it for you as a present."

It was now Eagle Eye's turn to wipe tears from his eyes.

He pulled Jim close to him and said, "You are really a good boy."

Jim said, "I'll never understand grown-ups."

Shootout in the Town

It was early spring and Eagle Eye started clearing land for the corn planting. He first plowed and prepared the garden for Liz. She wanted to plant her greens and get an early crop in before the summer months. During the summer months, the worms got more of her crop than she could harvest. The more worms that she picked from her collards and other green vegetables, the more appeared. She had found that planting during the early spring and just before the onset of winter produced good worm free crops.

With the help of Jim, Eagle Eye plowed and set rows in four acres of land. It took two weeks to prepare the land for the corn planting. They started planting corn during the last week of February and finished the end of March. Watching the small seedlings come up and begin to grow were the happiest moments in Eagle Eye's stay at the cabin. He went out each morning to inspect his crop. He wanted to make sure that deer and other animals left his small crop of corn alone.

While preparing the land and planting the corn, Eagle Eye didn't take time to fish and hunt. Two months passed and he and Jim had neither hunted nor fished. Jim never complained about this. He helped Eagle Eye as much as he could with the chores.

Finally Jim said to him, we planted the corn and ma's garden is in. Can't we take a day and go hunting?

Eagle Eye realized that he had neglected Jim during the planting season. Jim was always with him and working beside him. He had helped him at each stage of preparing the land and the corn planting. He knew that the boy only worked because he liked him. He was sure that Jim would not work for his mother or any other person. Jim regarded Eagle Eye as special. He was willing to do anything to please him. The least that he could do was to bend to the boy's wishes, and try to please him in return.

"Tomorrow we are going to get up early in the morning and fish until lunch time. Then we are going to hunt the rest of the day. When the hunting is done, I am going to let you practice with the gun."

Jim let out a yell of pure pleasure. He ran into the cabin to tell his ma the good news. They were low on meat but Liz had not complained. There were many days when they had only collard greens for dinner.

No one said, "You should hunt meat for us to eat. No one complained."

They knew that it was important to Eagle Eye to get the land ready and planted. There would be plenty of time to hunt and fish later. It pleased Liz that Jim had gotten her man to stop his work and take time for pleasure. She was also looking forward to them putting some fresh meat on the table.

The next day they went to the stream and fished all morning. Jim was happier than Eagle Eye had seen him in months. They caught thirty small fish, took them back to the cabin and went to the well and cleaned them. He gave them to Liz and she hugged and kissed him. Late in the evening the two of them left for the hunting trip. Jim's mind was not on hunting. He wanted to practice with the gun. After about an hour of walking and stalking rabbits, they had killed two. It was time to return to the cabin and clean them. Liz would cook them that night because there was no way to store them. They would be tomorrow's dinner. That would still leave enough daylight for Jim to practice with the gun.

Jim had accepted Eagle Eye as the father that he had never known. He loved this strong black man. Jim was happy that Eagle Eye and his ma got along so well. He never considered that Eagle Eye was a black man. He knew nothing of color or prejudice. His was just happy that Eagle Eye was there to protect and provide for him and his ma.

They went to the corral and set rocks on the posts about ten yards away. Eagle Eye showed him again how to draw and shoot. Jim put on the holster and the pearl handle gun. Eagle Eye handed him the gun. He drew and shot and hit the post just below the rock.

"That's not bad shooting. This time don't hesitate, just draw and shoot."

"How do I aim, if I don't stop before I shoot?"

"Think of the gun as an extension of your arm. Most of the time you will not have time to aim if you are shooting at a rabbit. The rabbit will run away while you are taking aim. Just draw and shoot. Let the gun do the work."

Jim drew the gun and fired almost when the gun cleared the holster. The rock on the corral post went flying through the air. Jim let out a yell and jumped high in the air waving the gun.

"Be careful with that gun. Remember it's not a toy. You should always handle a gun with care."

"I hit it! I hit it! Did you see that?"

"It really works, I didn't take time between the draw and the shot and it worked. I have watched you for a long time draw and shoot. I never realized that was the way that you did it."

"You just let the gun do what it's made to do."

During that practice session Jim did not hit the rock again but he hit the post often. Hitting the target that one time was enough for Jim. During supper, Jim centered his entire conversation on that one shot. After dinner, they sat around the fireplace and talked until bedtime. Eagle Eye wanted to buy some cloth as a present for Liz. He wanted her to have a new dress. He also intended to buy her some shoes. He used the mule as an excuse.

He said, "I want to go back to that settlement to get some feed for Flower. She has worked hard and needs some good food."

Liz laughed.

She said to him, "Sometimes I think that you love that mule more than me."

Eagle Eye went over to her and held her close and whispered, "You might be right."

They both rolled on the dirt floor of the cabin, laughing together. They finally decided to leave for the settlement early in the morning. Jim was happy. He enjoyed going to the settlement.

"You should wear you gun."

"We went over that before, I don't feel it's a good idea to go into town armed. When a man is armed, he is looking for trouble."

"You would never look for trouble. You are my man and the people in the settlement must get used to the idea."

"Well, maybe you are right. Tomorrow when we go to the settlement, I will wear my gun. I suspect that if we go to town we are not going to have any trouble. We went before with no problems and this time should be no different."

"There are always some bad people around though. I'll bet there are people there that would kill all of us for twenty dollars in gold and think nothing of it.

"There shouldn't be any gunfighters in this part of the country who would want to shoot us."

"I just don't want to have to shoot anyone.

It was late spring. April showers came frequently. It pleased Liz, because the cornfields and her garden needed the rain. She had been pulling water from the well to water her garden. The corn fields were too large to water in that manner, they had to depend upon nature.

Flower was standing under her shed in the corral and refused to come out in the rain. Nothing Eagle Eye could do would make her come out. He decided to wait for an hour. There was a patch of blue in the western sky and he knew that it would soon stop raining.

"When are we leaving for town?"

He said to Liz, "The rain will stop soon."

Half-hour later they had Flower hitched to the cart. They headed for the settlement ten miles away. The trio entered the settlement and passed the little mission church at the entrance to the town. There were boys playing ball in the churchyard, Jim looked at them. The game they were playing was strange to him.

There were five of them and they all wore shoes, pants and shirts. Jim never wore anything but a pair of bibbed overalls. He was sure that they would not let him join them in the game. He looked back at the boys playing their strange game as the cart moved down the dusty trail toward the center of the town. The boys were enjoying their game and Jim had a secret urge to join them. He mustered all his courage to wave at them. The looked at him but did not return the greeting. Only Eagle Eye noticed what had occurred. He wondered how they would react if they knew that Jim called him pa.

They continued into the town and went directly to the general store. The shopkeeper made no comment about Eagle Eye. He acted as if Eagle Eye did not exist. All of his dealings were with Liz because she was the one with the money. Yet, he watched both Eagle Eye and Jim as they moved about the store.

While the shopkeeper filled the order, Eagle Eye picked out cloth for Liz and passed it to her. He then picked out as pair of brogans for himself and Jim. He bought Jim a shirt and one for himself. He told Liz to buy shoes for herself.

When Eagle Eye passed a twenty-dollar gold piece to Liz the shopkeeper looked closely at the two of them but said nothing. They were good customers and they paid cash and that was his only concern. He did not care where the money came from, since it ended in his coffers.

Jim got his twenty-five cents and purchased two dime novels, one for himself and one for Eagle Eye. With one penny he purchased candy the rest he kept. Liz still did not approve of giving Jim money. She considered it wasteful but she knew that Eagle Eye wanted him to have it so she yielded to Eagle Eye's wishes. She intended to talk to him about it when they returned home. There were times when twenty-five cents meant a fortune to her and she just could not see money wasted. She felt that Jim would grow up not understanding the true value of money. She wanted him to understand that one used money to purchase only things that were necessary for survival and never for pleasure.

After purchasing their supplies, Jim and Eagle Eye took them to the cart and loaded them. Jim kept his shoes and shirt close to him. He had never worn store bought shoes and the shirt was his pride and joy. It was made in the western style, embroidered with buffalo designs on the front and back. He wanted to put it on so that the boys in the churchyard could see it. He held it in front of him and showed it to his ma. He was trying to think of some way that he could repay his pa for the shoes and shirt.

He finally said, "Pa, these are the best gifts I have ever received, Thank you."

"You are welcome son, and those things are for helping me around the farm."

Liz was sitting in the front of the cart putting her new shoes on. Liz was all smiles.

Sally, one of the ladies from the brothel came over to her and said, "I see you found yore self a new man. He shore is handsome. How's things going on that farm of yours? You shore looks happy."

"I'm happy, things couldn't be better, and we got the farm going. The corns all planted and my garden's coming long fine. When I come to town next time I'm going to bring you a mess of collards."

"Would shore 'appreciate that, well you take care of that boy of yours and your man."

Sally took another look at Eagle Eye and then started across the street. Liz and Jim were sitting on the back of the cart and Eagle Eye was about to get out of the cart when he heard a voice behind him. He turned to see the sheriff and two of his deputies approaching him. He wondered what they wanted with him and his family.

Sally returned and sat on the cart beside Liz and whispered to her. "I think there is going to be trouble."

"Why? We ain't done nothing wrong?"

Eagle Eye heard the sheriff say, "Nigger, I want to talk to you."

Sally said to the sheriff, "Why don't you leave this family alone? They ain't done nothing wrong."

"Shut up woman before I throw you in jail."

Eagle Eye Said, "What do you want Mister Sheriff?"

"Ain't I heard something bout you boy."

"Don't think so Mister Sheriff, I ain't from round these parts. I come all the way from South Carolina."

"You one of them black soldiers, who fought in the war?"

"Yes Sir Mister Sheriff, I was in the war. Got out when the war ended and headed west."

"I heard bout a gun totting nigger who killed a white man in Arkansas or was it Texas?"

"I want you to hand over that gun and come over to the jail house for a little talk."

Sally said, "I wouldn't do that cause he intends to kill you."

"Another word out of you and I will arrest you for interfering with the law. Now git, before I lose my temper".

Before leaving she whispered to Liz, "Don't let your man give up his gun if you want to see him alive again."

Sally took her time getting of the cart and sauntered over toward the brothel. With no intentions of going very far she stood in the door of the brothel and watched the events about to take place.

Eagle Eye said, "Mister Sheriff, I ain't never been to neither place."

"I want you to hand over that six-shooter and come over to the jail house for a little talk."

"You got no cause to arrest me Mister Sheriff."

"I ain't said anything bout arresting you, I just want you to give me yore gun and come over to the jail for a spell I got some questions to ask you. You new round these parts ain't you?"

"Yes Sir, Mister Sheriff, I am new round here."

Both Liz and Jim had gotten out of the cart and faced the sheriff.

"This man is my husband and we been together for years. You got no call to take him to the jail house."

"This nigger yore husband, huh?"

"That's right, he's my husband."

"He's my pa and you had better leave him alone."

It was the first time that Jim had ever referred to Eagle Eye as his pa away from the farm. He was angry and felt helpless. He did not intend to let the sheriff harm the only man that he had call pa in all his life. Now he didn't care who knew it. Eagle Eye was his pa and he was proud of him. He was not afraid of what would happen. He thought that his pa was the fastest man with a gun in the world.

Liz said, "Eagle Eye don't go with them."

"I ain't going any where with them."

"Nigger, there are three of us and one of you, you coming with us dead or alive, the choice is yours. You got a minute to decide. No nigger comes into my town wearing a six-shooter. Woman, you and the boy move over there. Ain't any need for you to get mixed up in this. We just want the nigger".

"We got no quarrel with you and the boy."

"He's my husband, he ain't done nothing and you ain't taking him to no jail."

"I don't care whose husband he is, he is going to go with me to the jail for a little talk and without that gun."

"We are not going any place, my boy and me are going to stay right here with my husband."

"You best leave my pa alone."

162

Eagle Eye said to Liz and Jim, "Move aside and let the sheriff do what he has to do, don't you worry about me I can take care of myself."

Liz and Jim moved to the side and stood by helpless as the drama took place. Liz was worried, Jim was not; he had all the confidence in the world that Eagle Eye would be able to protect himself.

By this time a large crowd had gathered to watch. Even the banker, the shopkeeper, the ladies from the brothel and the preacher who had been in the brothel were watching to see the event about to unfold. All the town's people were curious about the shootout. They knew that it would not be a fair fight with three against one. The black man was doomed. One man was taking bets and the odds were a hundred to one that the black man would be killed. Even at those odds there were very few takers.

"Nigger, your minute is up. Give up that six-shooter or draw."

"Mister Sheriff, I never draw first on any man. You draw your gun when you are ready."

Someone in the crowd yelled, "Git it over sheriff, I got to git back to my work."

Few gunfights in the town had attracted so much attention.

Someone else in the crowd yelled, "Well sheriff, you going to shoot the boy or just talk to him?"

The shopkeeper was watching from safety of his shop. He was secretly rooting for the black man because he was one of his few paying customers. His concern was losing one of the best customers that he had seen in many years and that was about to end.

The sheriff looked at each of his deputies and said, "This nigger is asking for it. Let's give it to him and go to the saloon and have a drink."

The bartender said, "The drinks are on me, just get it over with."

The sheriff and the deputies went for their guns, two seconds later the three were lying in the dusty street. They died without ever seeing Eagle Eye draw his gun. The crowded that had gathered in the street went over to the sheriff and his deputies.

One man reached down to the necks of the three men and held his hand for a few second and said, "They's done fer."

Some of the men in the crowd grabbed the dead men by the heels unceremoniously dragged them across the street to local undertaker. Eagle eye reloaded his six-shooter and went to the cart.

The only question left was who would get their boots and guns. No one in the town seemed to mind that they were without a sheriff and deputies. After watching Eagle Eye gun the three men down none were willing to take a chance with their lives, not for the likes of the sheriff and his deputies. No one in the entire town cared for or liked them. They were goons and used their authority to bully everyone in the settlement. The townspeople reasoned that the town could always hire a new sheriff and more deputies and they could be no worse than the previous ones. They just watched as Eagle Eye reloaded his six-shooter and got into the cart.

Eagle Eye said to Liz and Jim, "Get in the cart, we are leaving this town."

No one in the crowd tried to stop them. It was a fair fight. Everyone saw the sheriff and his deputies go for their guns first. Anyway, it was one man against three. Those who had bet on the odds were busy collecting their bet. The shopkeeper, pleased with the sequence of events, reopened his store and business went on as usual. Gunfights and death were part of life in the west. They were like the landscape, they were always present but most people did not really notice them or object to them.

Only the part-time undertaker was dismayed by the turn of events. He had started building one box when the black man first entered the town. He would have to build two additional wooden boxes and he would be working late into the night. The undertaker was not pleased with the prospect of additional work. Like most of the town's people, he was sure that one box would have been more than enough. What with the sheriff and two of his deputies facing a lone gunman and a black man at that. Anyway, he figured that the sheriff would decide not to bury the nigger, and he would be out of the fifty cents for the first box anyway. The sheriff would leave the body hanging from some tree for the scavengers. There would be others dead in the town before the end of the week and he could always use that box for someone else.

The three of them left the town and headed for their farm.

Jim was the first to speak, he said, "I never saw you draw your gun and I bet that the sheriff and his men didn't either."

Liz took one of Eagle Eyes hands in her hand as the mule and cart move slowly across the open plains.

She said, "I'm glad that I told you to wear your gun. You would be dead now if you didn't have it on. Sally said that the sheriff hung the last black man who came to town and he had come to the town just for supplies. She said he hates Indians, Blacks and Chinese and kills any that he comes across. You would be dead now if you didn't have your gun with you."

"They would have never let you out of that jail alive if you had gone with them."

"I know that. Liz, where do you know that woman from that you were talking to?"

"Oh, that was Sally, she works in the hotel. When my first husband left, I came to town looking for news of him. Sally helped me send a telegram to the war department. She's a good woman but I don't like the kind of work she does."

Jim asked, "What type work does she do?"

His ma said, "Not your business."

Jim just turned away and then look at his pa but Eagle Eye said nothing.

"She was always kind to me, she even paid for the telegram, cause I didn't have any money. She told me to make sure that you didn't give up your gun. I was sure that you wouldn't do it and I told her so."

Jim said, "One day I am going to shoot like you and then no man will bother me."

"I don't want my son to grow up to be a gun fighter. I am going to spend more time teaching you to be a good farmer and hunter."

"I want to learn to shoot. Someone might want to kill me like that sheriff and his men wanted to kill you. I want to learn to protect myself. Suppose you hadn't been able to draw and shoot, where would you be now?"

"I would have preferred to walk away from there without shooting, if I could have. What I was forced to do ain't right."

Liz said, "You had no choice in the matter. If you had not shot the sheriff and those other men, they would have shot you. He would have put you in jail and killed you later or just waited for the town's people to do it."

"They never intended for you to leave that town alive. They had no cause to take you to the jail, the sheriff said that himself."

"Sally was right, he intended to kill you and no one in the town would have lifted one finger to stop it."

They traveled across the open plains and headed for the farm. They crossed the stream and avoided as many small boulders as possible. It was near nightfall when the cabin came into view. Eagle Eye was in deep thought. He was concerned about the aftermath of the Shootout. He was convinced that the men in the town would come looking for them and he did not want to confront them in the cabin. Eagle Eye was not concerned about himself; he was concerned about Liz and Jim.

He would prefer to face a group of men in the open plains where he would have more of a chance at survival. He had no idea of how many would be coming but he was sure that they would not let the matter rest. Although it was a fair fight, being a black man added another dimension to the shootout. Black men were not supposed to kill white men regardless the circumstances.

When they arrived at the cabin it was late evening. Eagle Eye told them not to unpack the cart. He told them to put everything that was worthwhile on the cart.

He said, "We are leaving."

Liz said, "We can't just leave, we have the corn planted and my garden? Think of all the work that we have done to get this place fit to live in. I won't let anyone run me off."

Eagle Eye said calmly, "I must leave and I want you and Jim to go with me. I love you both. If you force me, I will stay and die with you. It does not have to be that way."

"What about the farm and all the work that we have done around here?"

"We can return in a few weeks if conditions permit us to return. If not, I have enough money for us to get a fresh start farther west. We will buy another farm. I know that at first light all the men in the town are going to come looking for us. It don't matter who is right. Someone is going to die and I don't want it to be you, Jim and me. We can plant more corn, and you can make another garden. No homestead is worth dying for."

"Anyway we can return in a few weeks if the men in the town decide to let the matter rest. I don't think they will."

"I don't want to go back to that town and I am not sure that it is safe for you and Jim to go back there."

Jim said, "I got my shot gun and I can help if they come after us."

"Son, I am not talking about three of four or even five, I am talking about fifteen or twenty men, maybe thirty. We would be no match for them. If I thought that only six would come I would stay, but I know better. While we are standing here arguing about it, the people in the town are making plans. If we leave now, by daylight, we will be too far ahead for them to follow us. We can save our lives but we can't save this farm."

"While we are packing Jim, I want you to feed the mule and give him plenty of water to drink. I know Flower's tired but we have no choice. With the cart packed we will walk and that will cut down on the load. Don't take anything that we can purchase later."

Later Eagle Eye said, "Jim get as much wood from the wood pile as you can and pile it near the fire place."

Jim asked no questions. He did what Eagle Eye requested. He realized that time was important. He didn't waste it by asking useless questions. He piled a large stack of wood near the fireplace. Eagle Eye put as much wood in the fireplace as it would hold. He put kindling at the bottom and wet the upper wood well with water. Just before it was time to leave, he lit the fireplace.

Jim was overcome with curiosity.

He finally asked, "Why are you making a fire?"

"That fire could give us the five or ten minutes that we might need to get away safely. If the men who come see smoke coming from the chimney they will stop and make plans before attacking. We are going to need all the time we can get."

That night about nine o'clock, Eagle Eye, Liz and Jim with their mule and cart headed west. With them were all of their necessary belongings. An old dog followed behind them.

Decision Time in the Settlement

In the town saloon an argument was in progress. The argument was between John Williams and the rest of the town's men folk. John Williams was middle aged man and slightly bald. He pulled his remaining hair over the middle of head to cover his bald spot. He always wore a suit and tie. His trademark was his top hat and cane. He was never seen without them. He carried a small caliber pistol in his vest pocket. He would use his small caliber weapon if conditions necessitated and if he were pushed into a corner but he was no gunfighter. John Williams was overly concerned about his reputation and his standing in the community.

John Williams considered himself the most important citizen of Hapers Gap. He had used his influence to get himself appointed as the mayor of the town. He was the one who convinced the rest of the citizens of the town to hire a sheriff and deputies to maintain order. The sheriff and his deputies owed their jobs to him and always did whatever he asked them to do. He paid their salaries, which was fine with the townsfolk. However, it allowed him to control all activities concerning law and order in the town. He had the controlling interest in the bank, the black smiths shop and owned the only saloon in the town. He was in the process of buying the town's only hotel, the Lucky Star.

John Williams looked more like an eastern lawyer than the owner of a bar. He was determined to take some action against Eagle Eye and his family. He intended to make them pay for disturbing the tranquility of his town. No Black man was going to disturb the peace and quiet of his town and get away with it. He intended to make an example of that black man and the woman.

John Williams had sent for all the able bodied men in the town and they assembled in the bar, all eighty-seven of them. They came because they knew that free drinks would be available. Whenever the mayor called a meeting at the saloon, there were always free drinks and the men in the town knew this. No amount of business would keep them from the meeting and doing their civic duty. Most thought the meeting was about the hiring of a new sheriff and deputies and they had no objections to this as long as John Williams paid the bill.

Even though that gave him control of law and order, so long as he paid for it, they had no objections. They were surprised when they found out what John Williams had in mind.

Most of the men had forgotten what had happened to the town's sheriff and deputies a few hours ago. They knew it was a fair fight or as fair as any fight was in this part of the west. Even though the odds of three to one favored the sheriff and he had lost, they still considered it a fair fight. The matter was closed as far as they were concerned. The only thing left to do was to bury the three men and divide up their belongings. There were strict rules governing the division of property of the dead. In cases, like this one, where no wife and children were involved the process was simple. The undertaker got the men's clothes, and any money that they might have, for his role in the burial. His guns and horses went to men that he was indebted to.

The shopkeeper brought his doctored documents to the saloon to lay claim to the possessions. He knew he would have to compete with John Williams who generally paid most of their salaries. The undertaker had already gotten his share of the prize and only the guns and horses were left.

Most of the men in the town had been drinking in the saloon since the time of the shooting. Many were already intoxicated. They would bury the three in boot hill at the edge of town behind the old mission church and put the matter to rest. In Hapers Gap, many men died in gunfights. Gunfights were nothing new to the inhabitants of the little settlement.

Some of the men had retired to the upper rooms with the ladies that worked the bar. John Williams continued to supply free drinks as he waited for them to return. He knew that the more that the men drank, the more amenable they would be to what he had planned.

Once all the men had gathered, he called for order. Over the noise of the crowd he said, "Gentleman we got a job to do."

Albert Adams said, "What about my bills, those three owed me money?"

John Williams said to him, "I have already considered the matter, you will be given the dead men's guns and horses to cover any bill that they have incurred. The undertaker gets what is left. Now that matter is settled, lets get down to business."

Adams said, "What business in left, 'cept to bury them and hire a new sheriff and deputies."

Over the noise of the crowd John William, the mayor of Hapers Gap said, "Gentlemen we got to hunt that nigger down. We got to kill him. Our sheriff is dead. The two deputies are dead. A nigger killed them. If this town is to grow and prosper, we got to make the name Hapers Gap mean something. We can't let a nigger come into this town and shoot it up and get away with it. We owe it to our sheriff and deputies, we owe it to ourselves, and we got to make that nigger pay for what he did. What we got to do is go out to that farm and burn it to the ground and kill that nigger and hang his carcass from the nearest tree. We got to make our town safe for our women and children. We can't allow a nigger to come to our town and get away with what he did."

Dallas Taylor, gentleman and local gambler, sat at the poker table. In front of him was a stack of money. The money originally belonged to his gambling friends at the table with him. He sat alone and continued shuffling and reshuffling the cards.

Dallas Taylor heard the comments of the mayor and he listened with interest. He had no love for the sheriff and his deputies. A few weeks ago the sheriff had threatened to run him out of town. The sheriff had experienced a streak of bad luck in a poker game with him. He considered the sheriff a poor sport and a bad loser. He considered him a man who would use his office to intimidate other men and to get his way. He was glad that the sheriff got what was coming to him. The fact that it was done by a black man made no difference to him. He was just gratified that it was done.

Dallas Taylor was a tall thin man with dark eyes, long nose and dark hair. He was always impeccably dressed. He opened doors for the ladies and was always the perfect gentleman. He lived at the hotel, paid his bills on time and with his poker winnings, managed to stay one step ahead of poverty. He was wearing brown deerskin pants. He had on a white shirt with a bright red scarf around his neck. His polished boots contained no spurs. Dallas Taylor had an aversion to horses and never rode them. He had come to Hapers

Gap by stagecoach three years ago. He had to leave his previous abode during the dark of night in fear of his life. Rumor had it that there was a lady involved, the wife of the town marshal. He came to Hapers Gap, liked it and he planned to stay. As to the art of poker, he was an expert. He read the players faces as well as he read the cards. Dallas Williams had never had a long losing streak at the poker table.

Dallas Taylor's dark hair lay close to his head. His bright red vest contains a derringer in the upper pocket completely hidden from view. The gold chain from his watch dangled from the lower pocket of his open vest. He had rolled his shirtsleeves up to his elbows. Dallas Taylor looked the part of a professional gambler. It was his trade and he was good at it. The money in front of him attested to that fact.

Dallas Taylor wore no traditional sidearm and he had stated often, "A gambler with a gun has something to hide. I have nothing to hide."

His derringer indicated that he was a cautious man one that was reluctant to use a gun.

He had listened to John Williams's speech and he was appalled at what the mayor had decided to do.

He said to the gathering, "The sheriff and his deputies drew first, all of you saw what happened. The sheriff had no authority under law to arrest that man. The man had committed no crime. Everyone in this town knows that is the truth. The sheriff got what he deserved. All that is left to do now is to bury the sheriff and his deputies and put the matter to rest. We can always get a new sheriff for this town. Hopefully we will find one that is more honest and fairer than the one we have to bury."

The next speaker was Albert Adams, owner of the general store. Adams interest lay in the gold coins that the trio had used to buy supplies from his store. He was convinced that they had more and he wanted to get his hands on them. He was not concerned with the deaths of the sheriff and the deputies. He wanted to kill them, burn the cabin and later return and search the ruins for what gold coins he could find.

He said, "That nigger is living with a white woman and we should do something about it. I heard her tell the sheriff that he was her husband. That boy called him pa. What white preacher would marry those two? They is living in sin. I say that we get a group of men together and go out there and burn that place to the ground and then string that nigger up."

From some place behind him and out of view came a voice that said, "Where I come from, we string niggers up for looking at white women. We shouldn't let a nigger live with a white woman. There ought to be a law 'gainst it. It just ain't right. It just ain't right for that to be happening."

Another man spoke, "You want to go live and farm with that woman, go ahead, I ain't?"

Laughter almost broke the meeting up.

From the head of the stair near the sleeping quarters came the voice of a woman. It was Sally, the bar maid who worked for Mr. Taylor speaking. Sally was about thirty-five and very pretty.

Sally had long blond hair, blue eyes and a small nose. In spite of her looks, she was a coarse woman, a woman who had seen difficulties in her short life. She had no love for men and their ways. She instilled in the working girls that men were no good. All men wanted was booze and women, in any order.

She had arrived in the town twelve years ago and had been head girl at the saloon for six years. She had talked to Liz, when Liz had come to the town looking for her husband. She empathized with Liz and her problems. She knew that Liz had a rough time fending for herself and her young baby. She was pleased that Liz had finally found a man to take care of her and her son. That the man was a black made no difference to her, that he treated Liz and her son well was all that mattered.

It was her task to take care of the other girls that worked in the saloon. It was her job to make sure that the men paid for their services, that they did not beat the girls or mistreat them. She and the other ten girls that worked in the saloon had been sitting on the top stairs. They were listening to the conversation of the men in the bar below. Sally had heard all that she could take; she wanted to protect Liz and her family.

Sally said, "Now the truth comes out, you don't want to kill him for outdrawing the sheriff and the deputies. You don't want to kill him for out drawing the three of them in a fair fight. You want to kill him because he is married to a white woman."

The Mayor, John William, said, "That ain't so. That nigger killed our sheriff and his deputies."

Sally said, "How many of you went out to help her after her husband up and ran off with Mary Jane? She thought he had gone off to fight in the war. She lived a long time by herself and now she has found a good man and you want to kill him. That man did what he had to do. The sheriff would have lynched him as he did that other black man who came to this town bout a year ago. All of you saw what happened, he even let the sheriff and his deputies draw first. Why can't we just let the matter drop and go on about our business?"

Williams said, "You shut up woman, no one asked for your words or your opinion. This is a matter of honor, a matter for the men folk of this town."

Sally said, "All right go out there and try to kill him. The way he handles that six-shooter, many of you won't be coming back. I'll bet on that."

Mayor William took a vote of the assembled group and most were for hunting the black man down and stringing him up. He called for a free round of drinks for the assembled group. Only Dallas Taylor spoke in opposition to the mayor's plans.

Dallas said, "I will have no part in this venture. It is ill conceived and for all the wrong reasons. We as citizens can't take the law in our own hands. If a crime has been committed then we should call the district Marshall and let him handle it. None of you are gunfighters or handy with your six-shooters and some of you are bound to be killed. Think about it, is the sheriff and his deputies worth your life? I am of the opinion that we should let the matter rest. We should hire a new sheriff and deputies and let the matter end. I will not lift one finger against that man or his family."

Mayor Williams said, "Among men of character there will always be cowards. The rest of us have a job to do. In the morning after we bury the sheriff and the deputies we will assemble here at the bar. I will provide ammunition and firearms for all that need them. By noon we are going to put an end to that nigger."

Sally and the ladies retired to their rooms. The Mayor ordered another round of drinks. There was a festive attitude in the bar as the men talked of the coming event. They treated it as a hunt, only this time a black man was the target. Only Dallas Williams did not take part in the round of free drinks. He sat at the poker table alone, and played poker by himself.

Sally's Journey

Late that night when the rest of the town was asleep, Sally got quietly got out of bed and dressed. It was one hour past midnight and Sally checked to make sure that all the ladies were asleep. She then left the sleeping quarters of the saloon and went to the livery stable and woke Charles Peeler, the owner. Charles peeped at Sally through a crack in the door.

"What do you want?"

Sally said to him, "I need a horse and a saddle."

"At this hour of the night?"

"Yes, at this hour of the night."

Charles mumbled something under his breath and started to go back to his bed.

Sally knocked on the door again.

Charles again looked through the crack in the door. For a brief second he thought he was dreaming. No one needed a horse at this hour of the night.

Charles rubbed the sleep from his eyes and said, "Hold your horses."

Charles Peeler was a newcomer to Hapers Gap. Charles had arrived in the settlement five years ago. He had opened the livery stable and had made it a successful operation. Charles had resisted all attempts of the mayor to purchase his business. He was tall and thin with brown eyes and long brown hair. He understood horses and spent an inordinate amount of his time taking care of the fifteen mounts that made up his stock in the livery stable. He lived alone with his animals, kept to himself and had little to do with the rest of the town's people.

Charles Peeler would rent horses, carriages and saddles to anyone for a price. He also rented tools, guns and sundry other items. Charles made a comfortable living and did not waste his money. Next to the mayor, Charles Peeler was the town's most respected citizen. He had no love for Mayor Williams and was one of the few men in the town that did not frequent the bar. He had come to the door of the livery stable dressed only in his long johns.

After ascertaining that it was a woman at the door he said, "Wait till I get some clothes on, be right back."

A few minutes later, dressed in a ragged well-worn robe and no shoes, he opened the door for Sally and allowed her to enter the stable.

"What do you want with a horse at this hour of the night?"

"I got some place to go."

"Shore looks like it, you wouldn't be going out to that farm to warn that black man and his woman would you?"

"What if I am?"

"Ain't any of my business, that sheriff and his deputies had no business trying to kill him."

"I remember when that last black man came to town bout a year ago. The sheriff just up and killed him for nothing. The he hung his remains in front of the bar for three days, that was not right."

"That black man had done nothing but come to the town for some supplies."

"You wont say nothing bout this will you."

"You don't have to worry yore pretty head bout me talking to the mayor, I wouldn't give Williams the time of day. He is still smarting cause I won't sell him my business. He owns half the town and wants to own it all. Comes round every day trying to buy my business. Wouldn't know what to do with it if he owned it."

"I 'appreciate your help."

"I ain't helping you do nothing, I'm just renting you a horse and saddle and keeping my mouth shut. Where you go and what you do is your business. I got nothing to do with it. Long as you take care of my horse and pay me, that's all that I'm concerned about."

Charles smiled and said, "Still, I am going to give you the best and fastest horse I got. I got a lantern that you can use at no charge. You be sure to take a gun with you, you might need it. I got all sorts of guns and ammunition for rent if you need one."

"I got a gun."

"Good, now let's get that horse saddled and get you on your way quick as we can. You sure you don't want me to go with you? It's a long ride out to that farm, 'specially at night?"

"Ain't no need for both of us to go looking for trouble, If Mayor Williams ever found out that you went with me he would make sure that no one in town ever used your business again. I got nothing to lose, and I don't owe him anything. I thank you for asking though."

"Jist a thought."

"I'll bring your horse and gear back in the morning."

"Don't worry bout it, jist take yore time and git back safely."

It was long past midnight when Sally rode quietly out of Hapers Gap. Once at the edge of town she rode as fast as the horse would go. She had been to Liz's farm twice but that was many years ago. She was not sure that she could find her way there again. She wanted to get there well ahead of the towns men folk and give Liz and her family as much of a head start as possible.

It still saddened her to think of what had happened to Liz and her son. She had never gotten the courage to tell Liz what her husband had really done and why he went away. She did not have the heart to tell her that he had run off with another woman. Sally had dared the other ladies to ever tell Liz the truth. All of the ladies went along with the charade about him joining the army.

Sally had even gone so far as to help Liz contact the United States Military about the matter. Liz's husband running off with another woman finally convinced her that all men were no good. To Sally, even the father that she had never known, who had left her mother before she was born was not worth the time of day. To Sally, all men were of no value and should be taken advantage of before they took advantage of you. In her lifetime she had never known a good man. Dallas, the gambler, was as close to being a good man as Sally had ever come to know. At least he treated the ladies with a measure of respect. That was more than she could say for Mayor Williams. To the mayor, the working girls were so much property not distinguishable from his horses, his bar or his bank.

Sally was thankful for the full moon. She saw this as a sign that she was doing the right thing. She would not need the lantern.

In spite of her occupation, Sally was a kind and thoughtful person. She would help anyone in need and she was convinced that Liz and her family had no idea of what was in store for them. She was determined to warn them of the impending raid by the town's men folk. She was going to stop Mayor Williams and his men from harming Liz and her family.

The sun was just starting to rise when Sally spotted the cabin. There was smoke coming from the chimney. She put the horse into a fast gallop and headed toward the cabin. She said a silent prayer as she reached the outskirts of the farm. She knew that Liz and her family would be given the time that they needed to escape. At any rate she would have done all that she could to help them. If they decided to stay and fight, at least the men from the town would not surprise them.

The first thing that Sally noticed about the farm was the absence of the dog. She knew that Sally owned one and had seen it in town with them that very day. She wondered silently why the dog did not greet her or at least bark a warning. She also noticed that the corral was empty but she reasoned that the mule could be in the barn.

She tied the horse to the porch post and went to the door. She knocked and no one answered. She knocked again and still no one answered. When no one answered her third series of knocks on the door, She opened the door and went inside. There was a fire smoldering in the fireplace but the cabin was empty. Sally went into all three rooms and found no one. She went back outside and looked around for signs of life and saw none. Sally finally went to the barn and looked in, it too was empty. She went out to the back of the house and surveyed the landscape. She saw Liz's garden and the cornfield. Everything was as it should be, but family was nowhere to be found.

Sally went back to the cabin and looked around and saw that there were some things gone. There were no clothes and all the food was gone. The beds contained no blankets and most of the cooking utensils were absent. It suddenly dawned on her that Liz and her family had left the farm.

She said, "I'll be damned. That black man is not only, handsome and good with a gun, he's smart. Somehow he knew that the men in the town would come looking for him. He even made a fire to make them think that they were still here."

Before leaving the farm Sally put more wood on the fire in the fireplace. She was determined to help as much as she could. It was daylight when Sally mounted her horse and started back toward the settlement. She knew that soon the men from the town would be on their way to the farm and she did not want them to know that she had been there. Sally was not sure what Mayor Williams would do to her if he found out that she had rode out to the farm to warn the family.

On the trip back to the town she kept a sharp lookout for the riders that she knew would be headed her way. She was half way back to the settlement when she spotted them in the distance. She and her mount hid in the woods off the trail until they had passed her. She counted about thirty of them. She smiled as she realized that they would find nothing when they reached the farm. She also knew that the fire in the fireplace would slow them down and make them approach the cabin with caution.

Sally arrived at the livery stable just before noon and returned the horse, saddle and lantern to Charles Peeler. He did not ask her any questions about her mission. He acted as if Sally were just another customer returning one of his rented mounts. While Sally waited patiently, Charles Peeler examined the horse, fed and watered it and then put the lantern away. Finally, he turned his attention to Sally; he had almost forgotten that she was still there.

Sally looked at him and said, "I'm sorry I had to get you up so late last night."

"It don't matter none."

Sally was starting to take out her money to pay him.

She said, "How much do I owe you?"

He said to her, "There won't be no charge for this, what you did was the right thing to do, I'm glad that I could help. I just hope that Mayor Williams doesn't find out about your little trip. If he finds out about it, it wont goes well for you. I hope that family managed to get away safely. Most all the men in the town left for the farm a few hours ago."

"I passed them on my way back."

Sally did not explain what she had found at the farm and Charles Peeler, though curious, did not inquire further about the trip.

"Thank you Mr. Peeler, you make me feel like life is worth living after all."

"You been living round Williams too long, all people ain't as bad as he is."

"Thanks again for your help."

"Think nothing of it."

Sally left the livery stable and went to the saloon. She went directly upstairs took off her clothes and got in bed. She had not slept during the entire night. She intended to get some well deserved rest. In a few minutes she was sound asleep.

The other saloon girls suspected that Sally had rode out to the farm. They knew what Sally had done but none asked any questions and Sally did not volunteer any information. They let her sleep and only woke her when the men folk were returning to town from their mission to the farm.

The Chase

The mayor ended the meeting by informing the men that it was their civic duty to hunt the nigger down.

He said to the assembled group of men "I want thirty five men to meet me tomorrow morning right after we bury the sheriff. We are going to put and end to that nigger loving white woman and her man. When we finish with them, we are going to burn the place to the ground."

There were many among the assembled group that were not sad at the sheriff's demise. They considered him overbearing and accused him of taking the law into his own hands. Most of those who had attended the meeting came for the free whiskey. They thought that Mayor Williams was going to talk of hiring a new sheriff. Many were surprised by the mayor's remarks. Few thought he was serious about killing the black man.

The next morning the town's people gathered at boot hill on the outskirts of the town. Three wooden boxes containing the bodies of the sheriff and his deputies were placed in the ground. There were no songs sung, and there were no prayers said. The town's people simply bowed their heads and removed their hats as they placed the boxes, containing the three men, in the ground. When the burial was finished they left boot hill and headed for the saloon and the free whiskey.

The ceremony over, the men once again gathered at the saloon. Williams gave all of them free whiskey. With the whiskey under their belts, they were more determined than ever to hunt the sheriff's killer down and kill him. All the men in the town were present except Dallas Taylor, the gambler and Charles Peeler, the livery stable owner. They both felt that the whole idea of killing the black man was stupid. They reasoned that it was a fair fight. The sheriff had gotten what he deserved; both knew that the sheriff intended to lynch the black man. Dallas did not intend to put his life on line for a sheriff who was a lousy poker player and Charles Peeler did not number the mayor among his friends. Charles secretly hoped that the mayor would be one of those who did not return. Dallas Taylor had no intentions of fighting for a sheriff who wanted to run him out of town.

The mayor was saying, "We need only about twenty or thirty men. It is only fair that those men without families go on this hunt. If all goes well, we should be back before nightfall."

Thirty men checked their guns, picked their mounts and headed west toward the cabin. They carried extra ammunition, water, food and whiskey. They expected to arrive at the cabin within about three or four hours.

They had no definite plans about what they would do once they reached the cabin. With thirty men against one, they felt that no plans were necessary. They would call him out and if he did not come out they would burn the cabin and force him out. Once he was out in the open they would shoot him down and hang his body from the nearest tree.

The group stopped and allowed their mounts to rest about two miles from the cabin. They ate and a few of them pulled out bottles of whiskey, drank, and then passed the bottles around. After resting for about twenty minutes, they continued toward the cabin.

When the group reached within one half mile of the cabin, they spotted smoke coming from the fireplace. They dismounted and made their first plans for an assault on the homestead. They spent about twenty minutes deciding what to do. They were sure that the occupants were not expecting them. They would have the element of surprise.

The group approached the cabin from three sides. About one hundred yards from the cabin they dismounted and left their mounts.

The mayor said, "There ain't no need of losing a good mount in a hail of gunfire. No nigger is worth a good mount, dead or alive."

As they approached the cabin on foot, they were sure that the black man and his family were inside. They made torches using the long grass from the hillside. They approached the cabin and called for the occupants to come out and talk.

No one came out of the cabin and three men crept up to the back of the cabin and set it afire. Still no one came out of the cabin. When the cabin had half burned to the ground the men realized that no one was in the cabin.

At first they were elated that they had burned the cabin and the barn and that no shots were fired. Then they became angry. They realized that Eagle Eye and his family had cheated them and had left during the night.

There were those who wanted to follow their trail immediately. Others wanted to return to town and get supplies and then take up the hunt. Mayor Williams, the leader of the group, called the men together to discuss what should be done.

Mayor Williams said to the men, "With that mule pulling a loaded cart, they can't travel fast."

"Yes, and we have plenty of time to go back to the town and get supplies and fresh mounts and still catch them before tomorrow noon."

They finally decide to return to the town for supplies. They would get fresh mounts and the entire group would return the next day.

The Journey West

Liz, Jim and Eagle Eye headed west toward Arizona and though Flower was tired, the urgency in Eagle Eye's voice told her the journey was necessary. They traveled all night with Flower pulling the cart with their belongings. The three of them walked. Liz and Jim walked behind the cart while Eagle Eye held the reins. He urged Flower to move as fast as possible. At intervals he allowed them the stop and rest for five or ten minutes. During those rest stops, he looked for signs of anyone following them. The only sounds that he heard were those of animals. During one of their rest periods Liz came up to Eagle Eye.

She said, "Are you sure that it was necessary for us to leave our farm?"

"We would be dead by now, if we had stayed."

They were about eight miles from the cabin and he took her to a nearby hill as showed her the smoke from the burning cabin. She was still not convinced.

"She said, that smoke could be the smoke from a range fire."

"No, if it were a range fire it would cover a wide area, that is our cabin burning. I am sure there are more than twenty men coming after us."

"What will we do if they come after us?"

"I have given it some thought and the next town that we pass near I want you to buy me a rifle and ammunition. With the short gun I am only good at close range. With a rifle I can keep them away from us. Eventually they will come for us. I want to be ready for them."

Five miles later they came to their first settlement. Eagle Eye allowed Flower to graze after giving her water and Liz prepared to enter the settlement. While Jim and Eagle Eye waited, Liz went in to buy the rifle. She entered to general store and explained to the shopkeeper that she wanted a rifle to shoot wolves. The wolves were after her cattle. He asked her where her farm was and Liz told him it was about twenty miles east of his store. He looked skeptical but he did not question her further about it. They talked for a few minutes about the problems of wolves in the west. They discussed the ways to get rid of them. He tried to sell her poison but Liz explained that her husband wanted a rifle.

Eagle Eye had given her a ten dollar gold piece. He told her that the rifle should cost between four and five dollars for a very good one. She should pay no more than six for the best in the shop.

The shopkeeper showed her his finest rifle.

He said to her, "I can let you have it for ten dollars."

She looked at him and said, "I want a rifle, not the man who is going to shoot it."

"How much you willing to pay for it?"

"Four dollars, remember I have to buy the ammunition also."

"Make it six dollars then."

"No, five dollars."

"Five seventy five in cash."

"Five fifty in cash and fifty rounds of ammunition and not a cent more."

"Lady you drive a hard bargain, but you got yourself a deal."

Liz purchased the rifle after a demonstration by the shopkeeper. She then joined Eagle Eye and Jim. She gave Eagle Eye the rifle and the ammunition. She told Eagle Eye what had occurred in the general store.

Eagle Eye was pleased with the rifle. He said to her, "That rifle might make the difference in whether we live or die."

The trio continued heading west. Eagle Eye waited for the attack that he knew was sure to come. He intended to be ready for it.

The hunters would not track a lone man so far. They would track a man and his family with a mule and cart. They realized the three of them could not travel fast with the mule and cart and eventually they were sure to catch them.

They finally had to stop. The mule was tired. They decided to stop near a lake where Flower could graze and drink. Camping by the lake allowed attack only from their front. It would prevent the attackers from getting behind them.

There were large boulders near the lake. Eagle Eye decided this would be a good place to make a stand if the men caught up with them. Eagle Eye walked back up the trail and climbed a hill to see if they were followed, but saw nothing. Liz was convinced that the town's people had given up after burning the cabin and had decided to let them leave in peace. Eagle Eye knew that this was not true and that eventually he would have to face them.

He went back to the lake and answered the many questions that Liz and Jim had about the hunters. He told them that he had seen nothing but they were less than twenty miles away and that sooner of later they would catch up with them.

"Flower is not as fast as horses and pulling the cart makes her even slower. If they are set on hunting us down, they will catch us before dark."

"What will we do if they catch up with us?"

"You and Jim will continue with the cart. I will remain behind and try to stop them. Take the money that I have left just in case I don't return and join you."

"No, that is giving up.

"I know that you will join us. I don't want to live without you."

"We must take what precautions are necessary. Don't worry, I love you and will do everything within my power to survive. If I die, many of them will die with me."

Jim spoke up and said, "If they catch up with us, I am going to stay and fight with you."

"No, you would just get in the way. I would worry about you and not be able do what I have to do. I want you to take care of your mother just in case something happens to me."

"Maybe we should all stay and fight them."

"No, that is what they expect us to do. The two of you must take Flower and keep going. I will make sure that they never reach you."

They rested for about thirty minutes and then started their journey, continuing to head west. If they got far enough away, the hunters would give up hope of catching them and return to the settlement. They were all very tired but couldn't afford a long rest period. They wanted to put as much distance between themselves and the hunters as possible. Every mile covered, gave them additional protection.

Finally, Flower would go no farther. She had been hitched to the cart and traveling most of the night and the day following. They were ready for a rest break anyway; Flower was not the only one that was tired.

Eagle Eye allowed Flower to rest without unhitching the cart. He fed Flower and gave her water. Liz prepared food for them. The trio sat and ate while Flower grazed nearby. After he had finished eating, Jim went over to Flower and gave her another bag of grain. When she finished the grain, he gave her more water. The food and water put new life in Flower and she was ready to continue the journey. While Flower pulled the cart, the three weary travelers walked along side. They headed southwest toward the California border.

The Fight

Twenty-two miles away from the cabin, Jim spotted a group of riders headed in their direction. He called Eagle Eye and showed him the cloud of dust. They were about a half-mile behind the three of them and riding fast. Jim wondered how long their horses could keep up that pace. Eagle Eye told them to continue the way they were going. He was going to stay and stop them.

Liz said, "You are only one person against twenty or thirty of them. Let us help you. We can shoot from behind the cart. If you intend to die for us, I want to die by your side."

"I have no intention of dying and I will join you farther down the trail. I know what to do; we don't have much time to discuss it. Take the mule and move as fast as you can. Leave the rest to me. I have a plan and I just hope that it works. If it doesn't work, continue west and buy a new farm and remember that I love you both."

Liz was in tears as she started moving the mule and cart westward. She knew that she would never see the man that she loved again. Jim wanted to stay with him but Eagle Eye would not have it. Jim pleaded with him to allow him to fight by his side.

"Please pa, let ma take the cart and let me stay with you. I know how to use a gun."

"No Jim, as I told you before, I would be worried about you and not be able to do what has to be done. You must go on with yore ma. I will be along shortly."

Eagle Eye was firm in his decision to have Jim stay with his mother. In the end Jim and Liz continued the journey westward.

Eagle Eye took the rifle and some ammunition and climbed a hill overlooking the trail. He watched the mule and cart as it slowly made its way along the trail followed by Liz and Jim. Jim still had his rifle in his hand. He looked back over his shoulder to see if he could see Eagle Eye but there was no sign of him.

Eagle Eye was well hidden behind two large boulders on the side of the hill. He waited until the riders were within about fifty yards of him and opened fire. Six men fell from their horses and the rest scattered. He reloaded the rifle and shot two more who ventured out to check the conditions of their comrades.

Though he did not want to do it, he dropped six of the horses and the rest scattered across the open plain. He reloaded and continued shooting after the horses until they were out of sight. He was sure that most of the horses were running away. The group of hunters would have no more than four or five horses among them.

Eagle Eye heard shots coming from the men on the other side of the hill. A few shots came very close to him. He was sure that some men had rifles. Their six shooters would do little or no harm; he had to worry about a lucky shot from a rifle.

He spotted a man moving among the rocks and dropped him in his tracks. The rest of the men stayed where they were hiding, not willing to risk being party to Eagle Eye's marksmanship. Eagle Eye placed his hat on a stick and held it high in the air. A shot rang out and Eagle Eye shot the rifleman before he could duck back down into his hiding place. He was sure that he had shot about one half the men hunting him. Without horses they would bury their dead, and turn back and try to recruit more men. He doubted that they would find others in the town willing to risk their lives. They would not return for one black man, a white woman and a young boy.

He started to move from rock to rock being careful not to remain in the open for any length of time. No shots were fired at him. The remaining men were too afraid to risk moving from their hiding places. They were not gunfighters. They were men with guns; yet, they did not know how to use them effectively. He moved quickly from rock to rock. When he was out of range he started to run in the direction that the mule and cart had gone.

A mile down the road he caught up with the mule and cart. Liz and Jim ran to meet him.

"Are you hurt? We heard gunshots?"

Liz grabbed him and hugged him after making sure that he was all right. Jim ran up and Eagle Eye offered his hand. Jim took it and held it tight for a few moments and then hugged him. There were tears of joy in the eyes of both Liz and Jim. They knew that they were safe. Nothing could happen to them since they had Eagle Eye to protect them.

"I'm fine and we are safe for a while but we must keep a sharp look out because they might come for us again."

Liz again told him that they had made the right decision in leaving the cabin. After the incident in the settlement, they would never live there in peace. She still regretted having to leave after putting so much work and effort in getting the place fit to live in. She thought of the corn growing in the fields and hoped that the Indian braves would return and harvest it. She felt that it was a shame to see all the corn wasted.

She knew that her garden would be overgrown with weeds in a few weeks. Her saddest thoughts were of having to leave that place that she had called home for such a long time. She knew that now there was no turning back.

Jim was glad to be on the move. Yet, he liked life at the cabin, especially since Eagle Eye had joined them. Most of all Jim liked the hunting and fishing trips. Like most young boys of his age, he wanted to see more of the world. Jim wanted to experience what the world had to offer.

Of the three travelers, Jim was the only one that was happy. He was glad to leave the little homestead behind and the thought of adventure filled him with happiness. At last he was going to see more of the world than just the little homestead.

Even Flower was happy to see Eagle Eye. She tried to nip him when he went to pat her. He knew that she was tired and he fed her and gave her water. He allowed her to graze for a few minutes. He did not unhitch her and within a few minutes they were on their way. They would have to cross many hazards and meet more danger before they reached their destination but they were on their way. Soon the sun would set and they would camp for the night. He would not sleep that night even though he knew that Flower would warn him of impending danger. The task of protecting his family was left to him and him alone.

The Return to the Settlement

The men from the town waited almost an hour before moving from their hiding place. They were not sure that Eagle Eye was not there waiting for them to show their faces. They realized that they had misjudged him and his marksmanship. There were fifteen men of the thirty men still alive and unhurt. There were three mounts left and they were twenty-one miles from the settlement. They buried the dead where they were. They removed all the valuables found on the dead men and divided them among them.

John Williams said, "Take anything you want, they ain't got no further use for them. Lets bury them and get out of here."

They collected their gear and headed back to the settlement. With only a few horses, most of the men had to make the trip back on foot. It took them four days to reach the outskirts of the settlement. When the ragged bunch of men entered the town, no one would have believed that one man could have caused so much damage.

The men told town's people they were attacked by Indians when they had their man cornered. That they were just about to get him when the Indians showed up and entered the fray. The men were embarrassed by the turn of events. They did not want to tell the people in the town what had really happened. They did not want them to know that one lone black man had defeated them.

Sally and the rest of the girls, who worked for the mayor at the saloon, were standing in the doorway of the bar when the men entered the town. Sally, like many people in the town, did not believe the tales spread by the men about the Indian attack. She had her own idea of what had happened.

She said to the ladies, "I don't believe they were attacked by Indians. That black man beat the shit out of them and they turned tail and ran. I just hope that the three of them got away. If he were a white man, they would have given him a medal for killing that stupid sheriff and his deputies. They went after him was because of that fat white woman. None of them wanted her and they just couldn't live with the idea that he did. I hope that they find the happiness that they deserve. When her husband ran off, not one of them ever went out there to see if she were alive or dead. Now they are all concerned about her, and it's all because of that black man she married."

When John Williams entered the bar she asked him about the black man and his family.

"Did you kill him?"

"No, after the Indians attacked, the nigger got away."

Sally smiled, and said, "I'm glad that they got away, you men had no right going after them."

John Williams hit her with the back of his hand and sent her flying across the room.

She sat in a corner nursing her bleeding nose and said to him, "That don't change nothing. The black man and his family have gotten away and I am happy that they did. You had no business hunting them down. You knew they didn't do nothing wrong. It was a fair fight."

When John Williams started toward her. Dallas Taylor the gambler was sitting at the poker table alone, playing poker by himself. He had not taken part in the hunt.

He had said to men when they asked why he was not joining them, "For my own personal reasons."

He blocked Williams's way and would not let him get to Sally.

"Go take it out on the black man, if you want to, but leave her alone."

"You stay out of this, she works for me."

"That don't give you the right to beat the woman up. She has a right to her opinion and I agree with her."

"You are a coward, Taylor, and the town will not forget that you did not go with us."

"Well, I am still alive and there are many dead men out there. That black did nothing wrong and hunting him down like a dog was a bad idea. You and your men learned the hard way."

He looked at Sally, who was now standing and winked his eye.

He said, "It was fortunate for him that those invisible Indians came along when they did."

"I'm going to see that you are thrown out of this town. Men like you don't deserve to live around decent men."

"You have just got a half dozen men killed for no reason and now you want to put the blame on someone. I doubt that the citizens of this fair city will buy what you are trying to sell."

John Williams walked up the stairway.

At the top he looked down and said, "I am going to put a hundred dollar reward on that niggers head."

"You mean you and your boys aren't going to go after him again."

John did not answer but left the stairway and disappeared into his room.

The next day the men of the town gathered at the saloon and a discussion followed concerning what to about Eagle Eye, Liz and the young boy. John Williams opened his bar to the men and gave them all they wanted to drink. He did not want to accept the blame for the deaths of the men that he had convinced to help him. He was sure that the free drinks would help the men forget his part in the misadventure.

John Williams, acting in the capacity of self-appointed mayor, conducted the meeting. He wanted to get fresh supplies and go after the trio. He even offered to supply fresh mounts and more ammunition. He informed the gathering of about twenty-eight men that he would give any man, who shoots the nigger, fifty dollars.

Dallas Taylor spoke up and said, "I thought the amount would be more like a hundred."

"Ain't no nigger worth a hundred dollars dead or alive."

"Count me out, fifty dollars ain't worth going after a black man that shoots like that one."

"How many of you are willing to come with me in the morning and hunt that nigger down."

No one in the room raised their hand. Those that had been on the previous hunt knew what could happen and wanted no part of it. John Williams called them cowards and said that he would go alone if no one wanted to go with him. Everyone knew that he would not and the meeting broke up. Most of the men decided that they had enough of the entire affair.

Calm came to the little settlement and in a few weeks the events were almost forgotten. A new sheriff and deputies were hired.

Business in the town went on as usual with the loss of a few of its residents. It became one of those events in the old west from which legends are made. Sally and the ladies remembered the strong black man and his woman. They wondered why the men they knew were not like him. The women hoped that the three would find happiness.

Sally remembered the time Liz had come to town trying to find out what had happened to her husband. She did not have the courage to tell her that he had run of with another woman. She had told Liz that sometimes the army gets the records mixed up and that someday her husband would return from the war. She felt sorry for Liz and the baby. She was glad that Liz had found another man to care for her and her boy. She wished Liz all the happiness that was her due. She knew that Liz had a difficult time trying to survive until her present husband came along.

One morning, the ladies gathered in the bar before the first customers arrived. As usual, Sally was talking to the ladies about the men that frequented the saloon.

Sally said to the ladies, "If I could find a man like that black man I would leave with him and get out of this God forsaken town. If I ever found one like him, I would gladly marry him and go away with him."

Encounter with the Indians

They followed the Gila River while crossing Arizona. They avoided mountains and high hills whenever possible. They did not want to add to Flower's burden. They made sure not to go near any of the few settlements scattered across the open expanse of land.

They had to lighten the load on the cart by removing some things that Liz had packed. Eagle Eye explained that once they reached their new home, they would purchase all the supplies that they needed. By traveling south they avoided the onset of cold weather. The climate in the region was warm and there was little rainfall.

They camped near a small settlement. Liz went to the general store and brought new shoes for all of them. She also bought new shirts for Jim and Eagle Eye. She replenished their dwindling food supplies. She bought more coffee for Eagle Eye and more ammunition for his six-shooter. They continued their journey southwest. Flower was pulling the cart and the three of them walking along side.

At night they slept under the cart. Eagle Eye avoided making fires at night. He did not want to attract unwanted visitors. All three of them took turns on watch during the night. They wanted to make sure that no one slipped up and got the drop on them. With Flower always there to warn them of impending danger, the standing watches were just an extra precaution. The going was rough especially since they had no mounts.

Eagle Eye insisted that Liz sit on the back of the cart for a few hours at the time. He and Jim continued to walk and Flower continued to complain. Once she stopped and refused to go any further. No amount of coaxing would force her onward. Eagle Eye decided to unhitch her from the cart take her down to the river and wash her down and feed her. They spent more than four hours by the river. Jim tried his hand at fishing. He had no luck. Finally, Eagle Eye hitched Flower to the cart and they started on their way to California, the last leg of their journey.

They were about twenty miles from the settlement of Globe when they spotted riders in the distance. There were about thirty of them. At first they thought they were the men from the settlement.

Eagle Eye figured the men were still on their trail and still trying to hunt them down. He thought they were finally catching up with them. They knew that this time they would be better prepared and would bring many long guns. There was no hope of outrunning the riders. Flower was pulling the cart. She could not match the speed of the horses that the riders were using. Pulling the cart Flower's speed was no match for mounted horsemen. They would use the same plan as before. They would allow the mule and cart to continue with Liz and Jim. Eagle Eye would wait and ambush the riders.

Eagle Eye told Liz and Jim to continue and that he would join them farther down the trail. This time there was no argument about their leaving. Liz and Jim knew that it was the only way that they could survive. They trusted Eagle Eye to protect them as before. Eagle Eye climbed a hill and hid behind a boulder and waited for the riders to appear. Unlike before, the riders did not advance in one group. They moved out in a wide circle to surround the mule and cart and its occupants. Eagle Eye knew that it was he that they wanted. He was willing to allow them to take him back and kill him if Liz and Jim were allowed to go free. He tied a white cloth to his rifle and held it high in the air.

He was surprised when three Indians warriors started riding toward him. He spoke to them in three different Indian dialects. It was when he started speaking Apache that they understood who he was.

An older warrior came out of the group and called to him and asked, "Eagle Eye?"

Eagle Eye was the name that the plains Indians had given him. Indians all over the plains told stories to their young of the black Indian warrior named Eagle Eye. The one who rode at the side of Quanah. Among most of the Indians of the open plains the name Eagle Eye was almost a legend. Indians who had never seen this strong black man knew of him. They knew of his exploits with the plains Indians.

Eagle Eye knew that he was among friends. He explained that his wife and son were on the trail ahead of them. He wanted to catch up with them. Eagle Eye wanted to tell them that everything was all right. The old Chief, of the group, Little Big Fox, sent the two warriors to tell the braves not to harm the woman and the boy. He continued to talk to Eagle Eye about his stay with the plains Indians.

The warriors wanted him to return to their camp with them. The stories of his uncanny ability with the gun had spread across the plains. They considered it an honor to be riding with the one that the Indians called Eagle Eye. They hoped that in the end they would have Eagle Eye ride the range with them.

He told them to wait there for him. He wanted to go for his wife and son; he wanted to assure them that everything was all right. The old chief agreed and offered him a pony and a warrior to accompany him. Eagle Eye took the pony that the old warrior had offered and as a show of good faith left his rifle with the chief. He retained his six-shooters.

He and the Indian warrior caught up with Liz and Jim. They were delighted that he had survived and was again with them. Indian warriors surrounded them. They were sure that Eagle Eye was dead. He would never allow the Indians to come near them if he were alive. They had almost given up hope of ever seeing him again.

Eagle Eye told them about his conversation with the Indian chief. He explained that they wanted him to go with them to their camp. The camp was about ten miles east on a tributary of the Gila River. Liz was not sure that it was such a good idea and had to be convinced by Eagle Eye that it was all right. Jim wanted to go. He wanted to meet other people besides his immediate family. He had never been around people other than his mother and Eagle Eye.

They turned the mule and cart around and headed eastward to join the Indian warriors. When they arrived, the Indian warriors met and surrounded them. Eagle Eye carried on a conversation with them in the Apache language.

Liz said to him, "I didn't know that you could speak Indian talk."

"I learned many Indian languages a long time ago."

Liz also noticed that the Indians treated Eagle Eye almost as a God. He rode at the apex of the triangle formed by the warriors. They listened intently to his every word. The treated him like a long lost warrior and offered water, food and their mounts. Liz suspected that their feelings would have been hurt had he not accepted the offerings.

This was strange behavior for Indian warriors and Liz was determined to get to the bottom of it. She realized that for the time being, they were safe from any pursuers and for that she was grateful. Jim, who could not speak the Indian language, was left alone to walk along the side of the mule and cart. He was a young boy and the Indian warriors regarded him as such. They ignored him in their adoration of Eagle Eye.

When they were in sight of the Indian Camp, three of the warriors rode ahead and entered the campsite. The campsite was situated beside a small stream. There were about fifty teepees. From some distance away Eagle Eye could smell cooking food and burning wood. The smells coming from the camp brought back fond memories to Eagle Eye. He thought of Tree Flower and his children. Tears came to his eyes and sadness came over him.

He remembered his stay with the Indians and above all he remembered Tree Flower and his children. When they reached the camp, Eagle Eye was almost emotionally overwhelmed by his memories. He had thought that all the memories of his former wife and children gone. Again he was feeling angry at what had happened to them. He wondered if he would ever get over the death of Tree Flower and his children.

Well over two hundred Indians lived in the camp. It was a hunting camp; there were no cultivated plots of land within view of the campsite. They subsisted upon what they could hunt and the fruits, nuts and vegetables that grew naturally in nature.

When Eagle Eye entered, the whole camp was waiting for him. The children called his name and the rest of the camp treated him like a long lost chief. Even Jim did not understand why his adopted father was treated this way. Since Liz was with Eagle Eye, the women treated her with a certain amount of dignity and respect. She did not understand the reasons for this but she was happy.

The warriors took Eagle Eye away from the camp to watch him shoot his gun. There were many among them that had only heard tales of this black warrior. The wanted to make sure that the tales were true. He shot rocks and sticks thrown in the air. Finally at twenty paces his shot sticks from the hands of the warriors. One even offered to hold a stick in his mouth for Eagle Eye to shoot but he declined.

All the Indian children followed the warriors and Eagle Eye. No one told them that they could not follow. The warriors knew that someday they would tell their children and their grand children about this black Indian warrior. They would tell them that they had met the black man that was known as "Eagle Eye" to all plains Indians. He was the black man who had fought with Quanah for the freedom of all Indians.

Liz stayed in the camp with the Indian women and helped them prepare the feast that would take place that night. She provided her last five pounds of sugar to make sweet water for the children. She shared all the food supplies that were in the cart. She even gave two of her blankets to Indian mothers with young children. She was fast becoming a favorite of the Indian women.

Jim joined the Indian boys in his own age group, though he could not speak their language. He went down to the stream to spear fish with them. He had never seen anyone spear fish before and was surprise that they caught catch fish in this manner. He intended to show them how he and Eagle Eye fished before they departed the camp.

Flower was the unhappiest of the lot. She refused to go into the corral with the Indian ponies. No matter how he tried, Eagle Eye could not get her to enter. He finally let her graze just outside the camp. The Indian children laughed at the strange pony with the long ears. They followed Flower everywhere she went, but kept a respectful distance from her. Flower simply ignored them and continued grazing. Finally their parents had to tell them to come away and to leave the strange pony alone.

That evening, the very young Indian children were fed and sent to their teepees. The rest of the group gathered around a large fire in the center of the camp. They passed the smoking pipe around the assembled group. The Chief of the clan, Little Big Fox, sat beside Eagle Eye. The shared the pipe and ate from the same bowl.

Then the long night of singing and dancing began. The warriors did a dance that had become a favorite of the Plains Indians; they called it, "Dance of the Eagle." From the gestures of the dancing Indians it was obvious the dance had it origins in the legends surrounding Eagle Eye. The warriors danced in a circle with one warrior in the center. The Indian warrior in the center, with his face painted black with dye of the blackberry bush, would point a finger. One by one the warriors would stop dancing and fall. This dance was repeated often during the ceremony.

Many Indian maidens came and sat by Eagle Eye. They were more than just respectful; they kept their eyes on him. They touched his hair and his hands and brought him nuts and dried fruit. It would have been impolite for him not to accept their gifts. For the first time since Liz had met Eagle Eye, she felt the pangs of jealousy.

It was late in the night when the feast ended. Eagle Eye and his family were given a tent near the center of the camp. It was a place of honor. When they started toward the tent, the warriors motioned Jim toward the long house, where the young unmarried braves slept. Liz and Eagle Eye went to their teepee alone.

Once inside the tent, Liz joked with Eagle Eye about the treatment of the Indian maidens.

"I thought that they would attack you on the spot."

"They were just being kind and friendly, it is the Indian way."

"I'm not sure that I like the Indian way when it comes to my husband."

"They meant no harm."

Liz smiled and said, "I'm sure they didn't, but those Indian girls were all over you."

"It's just their way, they meant no harm. They were just being friendly."

"Very friendly."

He realized that it was her way of letting him know that he was her man. She just wanted assurances that no Indian maiden was going to take him from her. Liz had so many questions to ask him and she could hardly wait.

"Why do they treat you the way that do? Where do they know you from? When did you learn to speak Indian?"

"Wait a minute, one question at a time. We have all night and the rest of our lives. What is it that you want to know?"

Liz realized that they were many things about Eagle Eye she did not know or understand. She had only picked up bits and pieces about his former life. He was now her man and she wanted to know everything about him. Though she realized that his former life would not affect their future, she still wanted to know all about it. Eagle Eye told her his life story. He started with his life in Africa, what he could remember about it and then his life as a slave. He told her of his life among the Indians. How he came upon the money and the gun that he carried and ended with his meeting her and Jim.

"Why didn't you tell me these things before?"

"I didn't think they were important."

"Not important, you are a hero among these people and you don't think that is important."

"I don't feel like a hero, I am just me."

"You are just you, and you are a very special man. I knew there was something special about you the first time that I met you. I love you more than life itself. You are going to be my husband forever."

Liz now understood why the Indians treated him with so much respect. She understood that they had found a champion when life for them was so bleak. She realized that he was a legend among the Indians. She loved him and was proud of this strong black man.

"I wish Jim could know about these things."

"He is too young to understand and I don't want him to grow up to be a gunfighter. I don't want him to think that I am a gunfighter, because I'm not. I draw my gun only when necessary, to defend myself. I don't want to be known as a gunfighter. Gunfighters don't live very long lives; there is always someone out there who is faster. Someone who shoots straighter."

The Departure

They spent ten months with the Indians. To Liz, life among them was an interesting and pleasant adventure. The Indian maidens continued to pester Eagle Eye but no one in the camp considered it serious. It was mostly those below the age of marriage. All of the other maidens had braves of their own.

They were all too fond of Liz to consider trying to take Eagle Eye from her. She had become indispensable to the day-to-day operations of the women. She had taught them to plant collards and how to cook them. Liz always helped them prepare their meals and wash clothes.

There was one thing that she did for the women that won her their hearts. She gave them as many of her long iron sewing needles as she could find. She had only one left and it was given to Red Rose, Chief Little Big Fox's mate. With the long iron needles they could mend the teepees and their clothing easier than they could with the bone needles that they were accustomed to using.

Eagle Eye often went hunting with the Indian braves and he always shot game. At night, around the campfire, the braves would relate the events surrounding the hunting trip. They had to tell the tale often for the young children. In the camp, the children played a game called Eagle. They would draw their wooden guns from their belts and make the sound of gunshots; the other children would fall over and play dead. Every Indian boy in the camp wanted to be like Eagle Eye when they became men.

Being young Jim was soon speaking the language of the Indians fluently. Liz had more of a problem with the language of the tribe but she was slowly learning. Jim was treated as a special young warrior. The warriors of the tribe taught him many things about the Indian way of life. After all, he was the son of Eagle Eye. He would someday grow up to be a strong warrior like his father.

Flower had finally grown accustomed to the other ponies. She decided to enter the corral about two weeks into the stay at the camp. She made friends with the ponies and they treated her like one of them. The children still stared and pointed at the ugly pony with the long ears but Flower didn't mind.

Jim enjoyed life in the Indian Camp. He was rarely seen with his mother or Eagle Eye. He spent his time with the boys his own age. There was always something to do, fishing, hunting and swimming in the stream. He had even taken the attitude of the other boys toward the Indian girls. They would not allow girls to follow them. When they went to fish, or to hunt small game or just play in the river, the girls were not allowed to go with them.

They were boys and would some day be warriors. The girls were just that, girls. They could never become warriors. Jim and the Indian boys let the young girls know it at every turn.

One day Chief Little Big Fox announced that it was time to move further south. There, the hunting would be more productive. Eagle Eye spent an hour in the Chief's teepee. When he came out he told Liz and Jim that it was time for them to be on their way. Chief Little Big Fox had tried desperately to convince him to stay with the group but he was determined to move on.

"Is that why you spent so long in his teepee, he was trying to convince you to stay with them?"

"Yes, somehow, I don't want to leave, but I owe it to you and Jim. We are going to California and buy that farm and have a good life."

Jim spoke up and said, "I don't want to leave. I like it here."

"I like it here too but it is not the life for us. You will find another place that you will like even better."

"Can we stay for another week or two? I am just beginning to learn to shoot the bow and track game."

"We will journey southwest with the group for a week. Then we must be on our way."

During the conversation between the man and the boy, Liz was silent. She knew that Jim respected Eagle Eye and would bend to his wishes. Anyway, Eagle Eye knew what was best for them and she would follow him to the end of the world.

Liz knew it was time to be moving on. Yet, she was reluctant to leave. She had made many friends. She would miss the many friends she had made. She knew there would be time to make more friends. Liz agreed with Eagle Eye, it was time to be moving on. They wanted to get to California before spring. They would plant more corn and

Liz would start a new garden. Eagle Eye would purchase a farm and everything would be as planned.

Liz said to Eagle Eye, "I hate to leave, but I know that it is time for us to go."

"If we leave now we can be in our home on our own farm by spring."

The next morning the Indian Camp was busy packing their wares for the trip south to the new hunting grounds. The women did most of the work. They dismantled the teepees and loaded the packhorses. The Indian braves spent most of their time making sure that their mounts were in good condition. Eagle Eye and Jim packed the mule cart and hitched Flower to it. Flower sensed that they were leaving. Flower was more cooperative than Eagle Eye had ever seen her. He knew she was anxious to leave this place and its ponies.

It was noon when the band started on their way Southwest.

They moved at a very slow pace. The braves rode their horses up front while the women and children brought up the rear. Eagle Eye and Flower were in the front of the group of travelers, beside Chief Little Big Fox. They did not unpack their gear when night arrived. The braves would build a makeshift corral for their ponies. After eating they would bed down under the stars with a big fire. No teepees were raised for short stays.

Usually, before retiring, the older men would recite their history for the children. They told stories that were passed down for many generations by word of mouth. Always, the stories ended with the exploits of Quanah and Eagle Eye.

A week later they passed the Mescal Mountains and followed the Gila River south. It was at this point that Eagle Eye, Liz and Jim said their good-byes. There was sadness in their parting. It seemed to Eagle Eye that he was always leaving the people that loved him.

Chief Little Big Fox tried to convince them to stay with them for a while longer. Eagle Eye just wanted to be on his way. The Chief gave Eagle Eye a necklace and Eagle Eye gave him his old six-shooter and fifty rounds of ammunition. It was the first six-shooter that Eagle Eye had acquired. He remembered the time he had first come upon the weapon. He told the Chief that it was the gun that he had used when he rode at the side of Quanah.

The gift pleased the old Chief. He would pass it down his line for many generations; after all, it was the gun that Eagle Eye had used. The women gave Liz gifts and the boys gave Jim a new bow and a pair of deer skinned moccasins. The parting was a sad affair. The young maidens presented Eagle Eye with a reed basket filled with nuts and dried fruits. Liz and Eagle Eye thanked them for their gifts and the three of them headed west on their way to California. They expected to reach the end of their journey within about four months. There was no rush, no one was following them, and so the trio took their time. The Indians had given them enough dried meat and other food so hunting would not be necessary. With their load, they would have to stop frequently and let Flower rest.

During this time of the year there were few wagon trains moving west and fewer still as far south as the trio was traveling. They avoided the towns and small settlements by going around them. They wanted as little contact with the settlements and the white man as possible.

Once, when they spotted a wagon train, it was a small one with only five wagons. Liz suggested that they join them. Eagle Eye did not think that it was a good idea. It was Jim who finally convinced them. He wanted to meet new people. They decided join the wagon train. He volunteered to approach the man in the lead wagon to ask if they could join then as far as the California border. The wagon master looked at the young boy. He told him to tell his family that they were welcome to join them in their trek to California.

"We can always use two more guns."

Jim went back to Eagle Eye and Liz and told them what the wagon master had said. So the three of them crossed the dusty trail toward the five wagons. They got within twenty feet of the wagons and the wagon master said, "Hold it right there. We don't want any niggers in this wagon train."

Jim could not believe what he was hearing, he said, "You told me that we could join you."

"You didn't say that there was a nigger with you."

"He's my pa."

"I don't care whose pa he is, he ain't going to travel with us. Now git on yore way before I have my men start shooting."

Eagle Eye turned Flower around and started back the way they had come.

Liz was pensive, "They don't want us with them and they don't even know us. Maybe we should have stayed with the Indians."

Jim asked, "What do they have against black men and Indians?"

"With the Indians they want their land. Black men have nothing that they want. Black men are just different."

"All men are different."

"Men fear and hate men who are different from them. We don't need him or his wagon train. He will need us if he runs into a group of Indian braves."

They headed west and continued along the Gila River. The first night they camped along the bank of the river. Eagle Eye told Liz and Jim, "Camping on the bank of the river will offer us a small measure of protection."

This would allow them to defend themselves in only one direction if attacked. He did not expect trouble from anyone but he took the necessary precautions. They made a fire and Liz warmed food and hot coffee for their dinner. That night they slept under the stars, each taking turns at watch.

The next morning they continued their way. It was the most pleasant time of their trek. There was no one following them. There was no one out to hunt them or kill them. They stopped frequently to allow the mule to graze. At night under the stars by the campfire they spent some time making plans for the future. Plans to be put into practice when they reached their destination. Liz wanted a large garden and a cabin where she could grow flowers. Jim wanted to visit nearby settlements. Eagle Eye wanted good farmland; he talked about buying a cow and raising chickens. Most of all he wanted to settle down. Eagle Eye wanted to live his life the way that he wanted, without interference from anyone.

The trip to California brought the trio closer together. They enjoyed their journey; it was a time of happiness for the three of them. One month after the encounter with the wagon train they reached the California border.

They crossed the border and entered the flat lands of southern California and camped about a mile from a large mining settlement. Eagle Eye wanted to buy land. He wanted to build a cabin or to find one they could purchase. By the beginning of spring, he wanted to be ready to start farming. With so many mining villages around he was sure that the extra food grown, could be sold or bartered. All of them were looking forward to their new home.

The New Farm

He explained to Liz that as a black man, it would be difficult for him to purchase land. He had the money but she would have to make the purchase. She would have to select the site and conduct all the necessary business. He wanted a farm as far away from any settlements as possible. He told her to try to find a farm that had a house or cabin, one that had been previously farmed. He wanted a farm at least ten to twenty miles from the nearest settlement. He wanted to avoid contact with people that might lead to trouble for him and his family.

They left while Eagle Eye stayed at the camp and took care of the supplies. Jim and Liz went to the settlement to buy the Land. Eagle Eye had told her that the land should sell for no more than one or two dollars and acre. If there were a house or cabin located on the land, it should not increase the price by very much.

"How much land do we need?"

"About twenty or thirty acres are as much as we can farm."

"You have to make sure that it is not sandy or desert land because that would not be good for farming. Try to buy land with a stream nearby so we will not have to worry about water. Don't worry about the house or cabin that we can build ourselves. The most important thing is that it must be good farming land."

Liz and Jim took the mule and cart and headed for the settlement. Eagle Eye watched them until they were out of sight. It was noon when they reached the mining town. It was a large town with two general stores, a bank and more than a hundred houses. The town even had a hotel and livery stable with a blacksmith attending.

The only experience that Liz had in purchasing land was the farm that she and her husband had purchased a long time ago. That farm was purchased from a bank.

The bank was the only adobe structure in the settlement. It was more of a fortress than a bank. Armed guards flanked the doorway. The jailhouse and the sheriff's office were directly across the street. Liz tied the mule and cart to the hitching post in front of the bank. Jim stayed with the mule and cart. Liz went directly into the bank. She passed the armed guards who tipped their hats to her. She represented no threat to them or the bank. She was just a customer doing business. It was about twenty minutes after noon when she entered the bank. Going directly to the one teller in the bank, Liz stated her business.

The teller was an overweight white man. He wore glasses that were perched precariously on his nose. He wore a spotless white shirt and tie. He sat on a stool behind the bank window, working on the bank's books. He looked up as Liz entered the bank, then continued working on his books. He got up from his seat when Liz came to the counter and addressed him.

"Sir, I would like to buy some farm land, do you have any foreclosures for sale?"

"How much land are we talking about?"

"Twenty or thirty acres."

"The bank has several plots of land that size for sale, but they require cash settlement."

"I have the money to pay for the land."

"I am here alone, Mr. Jenkins, the owner, is at lunch and should be returning with a few minutes. Why don't you have a seat over there and wait for him to return? He handles the land sales and foreclosures."

Liz took a seat in a chair near the entrance of the bank. The walls inside the bank were bare. There were no pictures or tapestries on them. There were two windows on the sides and the two in the front of the bank. Heavy iron bars were on all the windows. The double door was solid oak. The little light that entered through the windows left the inside in a sort of twilight. Inside the teller's window was a lamp that provided light for him to conduct his business. After about ten minutes, one of the guards came inside.

He asked the teller, "Is everything was all right?"

He answered, "Everything is fine, that lady is waiting for the return of Mr. Jenkins to conduct her business."

It was about fifteen minutes before Mr. Jenkins arrived at the bank.

Mr. Jenkins was a tall thin man with a receding hairline. He had deep brown eyes and a hawk-like nose. His ears were the largest that Liz had ever seen. He wore a tweed suit, white shirt and a bright red tie. He was an important man in the town and his every movement let everyone who met him know it. He went to the teller and exchanged a few words with him. He then walked over to Liz and asked how he could be of service to her. He did not smile and was all business.

"Are you interested in purchasing a foreclosure? I have a farm just out side of town that might suit your needs."

"How far outside of town?"

"About two miles."

"I want to purchase a place further from the town, about ten or twenty miles."

"You will have difficulty getting supplies that far from town and there are no schools or churches to attend that far away. There are also Mexicans and Indians to be avoided. Being close to the town would offer you some protection. We have a sheriff and deputies to maintain law and order."

"This town is growing and I don't want the town growing up around me, I would prefer a place further from the town."

"I see."

"Do you have a farm farther from town that is for sale?"

"Well, I have to make contact with some land owners further south. You should come back in two days and I will have what you are looking for."

Liz went back to the camp that Eagle Eye had set up and explained to him all that had occurred. They decided to camp where they were and wait two days. Then Liz would return to the bank and try again to purchase the land.

That evening Eagle Eye and Jim went hunting. There were lots of small deer in the area but they never got close enough to shoot them. They had to settle for the two rabbits they managed to kill. They returned to the campsite and skinned and cleaned the two rabbits and gave them to Liz to cook for dinner. While Liz cooked dinner, Jim and his pa went fishing. They sat on the bank of the stream and fished for a few hours and talked.

"Why can't you buy the land, it's your money?"

"I am a black man."

"I know that you are a black man. What has that got to do with spending money and buying land?"

"White men don't like selling land to Indians and blacks."

"I am beginning to understand why the Indians hate the white man. White men want everything for themselves and they don't want others to have anything. If they could get to know you and the Indians, they would feel different about you and them."

"They don't want to know anything about anyone who is different from them."

"There just isn't enough land for the Indians, blacks and white men. The white men have the guns and in the end there will be few Indians left. Even today, most of the Indians are on reservations."

"Ma and me would have had nothing if it wasn't for you. When I grow up I am going to help the Indians get their land back."

They talked until Liz came for them. She had prepared their supper and they sat around the fire and ate. After the repast, Liz and Eagle Eye went down to the stream to bathe. Jim stayed at the camp and took care of Flower. He tried to talk to her as he had seen Eagle Eye do. She nuzzled him to show him that she liked him. He fed her, gave her water and tied her to a long rope so she could graze. When Eagle Eye and Liz returned, they spread the blankets and slept under the stars. Jim took the first watch. Nothing disturbed the night or their sleep; the coyote calls in the distance only disturbed Flower. The trio had one of their most pleasant nights, sleeping under the stars.

On the second morning, Eagle Eye got up while it was still dark, went down to the stream and washed up. He returned early and prepared breakfast while Liz and Jim slept. He made his cooking fire about thirty yards away from the camp; Eagle Eye didn't want to disturb the sleeping pair. The fresh smell of burning wood and coffee finally reached Liz. She sat up and watched as Eagle Eye removed the meat from the pan and added wild tubers.

She went over to him and said, "Why didn't you wake me to fix the meal?"

"Why should I?"

"I can do it."

"That's not what I meant, I should be the one preparing the meal."

Eagle Eye smiled and said, "You lived with the Indians too long. They consider some jobs, as woman's work and unbecoming of a warrior. I am not an Indian and I am not a warrior. Why shouldn't I cook a meal for you? You have cooked many meals for me."

Liz could only shake her head. She loved this strong, gentle black man. She wrapped a blanket around herself and went down to the stream to wash up. When she returned the meal was almost ready to eat. Jim finally got up and ambled down to the stream. When he returned, the three of them had their breakfast.

After breakfast, Eagle Eye hitched Flower to the cart. Liz and Jim headed for the settlement. Jim was to make sure that the land they brought was good farmland.

Eagle Eye wanted a second six-shooter to replace the one given to Chief Big Fox. He explained to Liz in detail, just the type six-shooter he wanted. He told Liz that it should cost no more than five or ten dollars for the weapon. It was high noon when Liz and Jim they reached the town.

Again, Liz went to the bank. She went to the teller and asked for Mr. Jenkins. The teller went into the next room. He came back a few seconds later. He told her that Mr. Jenkins would see her in a few minutes. Liz was thinking to herself that Mr. Jenkins had nothing to do and no pressing business. He would make her wait just to show how important he was. If the town had two banks she would have left, but she waited patiently until he came out. Mr. Jenkins did not smile but bowed politely to her.

He said to her, "I think that I have found just what you are looking for. The farm is about ten miles outside town. It also contains a three-room cabin and a barn of sorts. The cabin and the barn are in need of repair. I will have someone meet you at your camp and take you there to see it tomorrow."

"It will not be necessary for you to have someone escort me there if you could just give me directions I could meet you there at noon tomorrow."

He gave her a strange look and shrugged his shoulder, and said, "If you wish."

He went over the directions many times with her and was finally satisfied that she could find the farm. He told her that the farm

213

belonged to a young couple. They had intended to farm the land but got caught up in gold fever. They were now trying to sell the land and the house to settle their gold digging debts.

"Are you serious about the purchase, it is a long way for me to travel without some assurance that you are going to buy?"

"I will give you five dollars now and meet you there at noon tomorrow."

"We will discuss the price after you have inspected the farm. I assure you it is exactly what you are looking for."

"I would like a receipt for my five dollar deposit."

"As you wish, I will have my teller prepare one for you."

They shook hands and Liz left the bank. Mr. Jenkins followed her to the door of the bank. He watched as she unhitched the mule and got in the cart with Jim. The two guards were still at their post. They did not so much as glance at her as she left. Liz wondered if they slept there at night.

Liz went to the general store and purchased the side arm that Eagle Eye had described. It was not as good as the one that he had taken from the dead sheriff but it was usable. She paid four dollars for the weapon. She also bought additional ammunition.

Liz and Jim returned to the camp and Eagle Eye began talking to Flower. He had started rubbing her down with a piece of fur. Both were as content as man and beast would ever be. Early the next morning, Liz and Jim, following the directions given to her by Mr. Jenkins, set out for the farm.

The farm was about six miles from their camp and they reached it just before noon. Mr. Jenkins and a man that she had never seen before were waiting for them. Mr. Jenkins introduced him as Melvin. Mr. Jenkins had arrived in a buggy and she assumed that the man was his driver. Liz thought only the rich could afford to have a driver. This Mr. Jenkins must be a very rich man.

The little farm was all that she could have asked for. The land was good farmland. It was inspected thoroughly by Jim. The house, in need of minor repairs, was made of adobe brick. It contained three rooms, a kitchen and a small porch. There was a corral and a barn of sorts that was also in need of repairs. An outhouse and shed made up the rest of the buildings on the farm. The house was sturdy but was badly in need repairs. It needed window shutters and doors. Yet, being about fifteen miles from the town, it was an ideal location.

"There is a stream about fifty yards from here but in time, I suppose that you will be digging a well. Shouldn't be too difficult, the water table is not that deep around here."

Liz wondered how Mr. Jenkins would know about the water table but she said nothing. She allowed him to show her the boundaries of the little twenty-five acre farm. Jim tested the soil as Eagle Eye had taught him to do. Liz went into the house and inspected it. Sagebrush greeted her at the door. The roof was intact and the foundation appeared sturdy. She left the house and inspected the shed, the barn and the outhouse.

Finally, she satisfied herself that everything was in reasonable order. She knew it was a place that would meet the approval of Eagle Eye. She told Mr. Jenkins that she was ready to discuss the price of the farm.

"There aren't many farms around here as good as this one. The farm has been on the market for only a few months. I have had lots of people looking at it."

"Yes, and there are lots of people willing to buy farms this far from town," countered Liz.

"I, that is, my client will let you have the farm for four dollars an acre. Let's see, that comes to one hundred twenty dollars, plus twenty - five for the buildings."

"I am ready and willing to pay you two dollars an acre and the buildings come with the price of the land."

"I can't give you the farm."

"No, but you can charge a fair price."

Liz repeated her offer, two dollars an acre."

"Two dollars fifty an acre."

Liz countered with, "Two dollars twenty five an acre."

"My last offer is two dollars forty per acre."

Liz said,   "That must include the price of the buildings also."

"Lady you drive one hard bargain, but you got yourself a deal. We will meet at the bank tomorrow and I will have the necessary papers for you to sign. In two days you should be in your new home."

They shook hands again. Liz gave him a deposit of another five dollars and received a receipt. After the transaction, they again shook hands and each went their separate ways. Mr. Jenkins, went back to the bank to start working on the paper related to the farm, Liz and Jim, went back to the campsite to explain to Eagle Eye what transpired at the farm.

She said to Eagle Eye, "I don't think he would have gone any lower on the price."

"That's a fair price, considering we got the buildings in the bargain."

Liz began to relate to Eagle Eye the particulars concerning the purchase. Liz was so excited that she had difficulty describing the farm. Jim told Eagle Eye about the corral and the stream. He even described the plant life. Eagle Eye was interested in the soil.

He asked Jim, "Was the land rocky or sandy? Was it good farming land and was there water available?"

Jim said to his pa, "The land is like the land on our other farm, I checked it myself. The land is good and we can grow good crops on it."

The next day Liz went to the bank and signed all the documents related to the purchase. She paid Mr. Jenkins in cash for the farm and received a deed and a receipt for her purchase. She went back to the campsite and explained to Eagle Eye that they were now the owners of their own farm. They were all excited about the acquisition.

Eagle Eye was satisfied; he trusted Jim's judgment. He could hardly wait to see the farm. Liz convinced him that it would be there the next day and they should leave for it in the morning. Eagle Eye wanted to leave for the farm that night.

Jim said, "Lets pack all of our things in the cart tonight, that way we can get an early start in the morning. We should be able to leave for the farm by first light."

They packed all of their wares on the cart, leaving out only their sleeping gear. They got little sleep during the night. Most of the night, they spent under the stars discussing the new farm. Eagle Eye had what he wanted most; he had a family and a farm.

When the small family reached the farm two days later, the site pleased Eagle Eye. He tested the soil and found it satisfactory. He went down to the stream and sampled the water while allowing Flower to drink. He found the fast moving stream adequate and not to far away from the house. He examined the house and the barn and though he found them in need of many repairs, Eagle Eye was pleased with it. He was certain that within a month he could have the little homestead as good as the one that they had left many months ago.

After an examination of the farm, he decided that the first repairs that he would make would be to the house. The house was in need of two doors and wood shutters for all of its windows. Liz had already started cleaning the house. She removed the current residents, several lizards and a small snake, from the premises. She was busy making a fire in the fireplace when Eagle Eye returned.

"I will need some lumber, nails and a small saw. Tomorrow I would like for you and Jim to take Flower and go to the town and buy them."

"I have lots of work to do around this place. Why don't you and Jim go and get the timber and supplies?"

"I'll do what has to be done. You and Jim just go and get the supplies."

Liz did not comment further but said, "All right, we will leave early in the morning. I want to get back early and finish my work."

The following morning Liz awoke before sunrise and quietly went outside and hitched Flower to the cart. She then got Jim up and told him it was time for them to leave for the town. Eagle Eye discussed what she was to purchase. Without breakfast, Jim and Liz headed for the settlement. It still dark when they started their trip to the town. While they were away, Eagle Eye planned to work on the barn and shed.

They returned late the same day with the supplies. Eagle Eye immediately started to work on the doors and the windows. It took him three days to complete the tasks. He made crude tables and chairs and beds for both rooms. He gathered pine straw and Liz made mattresses for them. When the work on the house was complete, he finished the barn. In three weeks the little farm looked as if people lived on it.

On her next trip to the town, Liz returned with three chickens. She had purchased a rooster and two hens. Eagle Eye and Jim were hard at work digging the new well. Eagle Eye was doing the digging while Jim removed the dirt with a bucket and pulley system rigged by Eagle Eye.

Liz came home and ran to the well and said, "Look at what I've got."

She wanted Eagle Eye and Jim to quit what they were doing and build a hut and a fenced area for the new acquisitions. Both told her that they could not stop their work. The well was almost finished. They had struck water and were just beginning to get the well working properly. Liz could not understand their concern but let the matter drop. She would allow the chickens to sleep in the house tonight. Tomorrow she would get Eagle Eye and Jim to build a place for them.

The next day Eagle Eye and Jim headed directly for the unfinished well, immediately after breakfast. Again Eagle Eye climbed down into the well and Jim prepared to haul up the debris. Liz came over and insisted that the two of them build her chicken hut and pen. They again explained that the project would have to wait.

Liz said, "I will go into the well and dig. I need that chicken pen today."

Eagle Eye looked at Jim and said, "We will never see any peace until it is done. So we may as well stop now and do it. Anyway, she treats those chickens better that she treats us."

"That's not true."

"Yes it is ma."

"You always side with your pa."

"I only side with him when he is right and this time he is right, we ought to finish the well first."

The two of them stopped working on the well and spent the rest of the day on the chicken pen and hut. Liz supervised every aspect of their work. She wanted to make sure that they built the enclosure correctly. She did not want to leave her chickens to the mercy of the foxes that she had seen roaming the countryside.

She said to them, "In a few months I will have a yard full of chickens. You just wait and see what happens."

A week later one hen laid the first egg. Liz ran to show it to Eagle Eye and Jim. Eagle Eye shared her excitement about the egg. Jim pretended not to even notice it. Finally, he came over and held it for a few seconds.

"This egg is not for eating, I am going to put it back and let the hen raise some baby chicks."

Three months later, Liz had her first twelve chicks. The entire household stood and watched them for an hour. The two hens strutted around the pen with the chicks and the rooster would not allow anyone in the pen.

Even Jim's dog ran around the pen excited about the newcomers. It was a day of celebration, when Liz told them that they could now have eggs for breakfast. No one believed her.

Eagle Eye and Jim entered the cabin after removing their shoes as Liz insisted upon. Eagle Eye announced that they had finished working on the well. They all left the cabin to allow Liz to inspect their work. They hauled up a bucket of water and Liz sampled it and declared that it was the best water that she had ever had. A few days later, Liz went to get water from the well and returned with an empty bucket. Eagle Eye asked her why she had no water.

"There are frogs in the well."

Eagle I said, "I know that, what wrong with frogs in the well?"

"But how can we drink water from the well with the frogs in it?"

Patiently Eagle Eye explained to Liz the relationship between frogs in a well and clean water.

"Liz, all good wells have frogs in them sooner or later. When the frogs abandoned a well it means that the water is no longer fit to drink. You should thank God that our well has frogs in it."

Liz was not sure that this was true but the tone of Eagle Eye's voice told her that everything was all right. She trusted his judgment. She loved him and if he said that the water was fit to drink, then it was all right to do so. She filled her bucket with water and Eagle drank from it and so did Jim. Liz never had any more questions about the water from the well.

Eagle Eye was out at the corral with Flower. Liz approached and took his hand.

She looked into his eyes and said, "I love you very much. You are the best thing that has happened to me in my lifetime."

Eagle Eye smiled and said, "I love you too, now what is it that you want me to do, build you another chicken pen or a new outhouse."

"Eagle, I am going to have your baby?"

Eagle eye pulled her close to him and said, "When?"

"In about seven months, I guess."

He held her close and whispered, "This is good news. I had hoped that we would have children. Don't work in the garden anymore. Jim and I will do it."

"Eagle, I didn't say that I was sick, I am just going to have a baby. Women have had babies since the beginning of time. It doesn't mean that I can't continue to work."

"I don't want you to lose the baby, just take care of yourself."

She kissed him and said, "I promise."

"Should we tell Jim?"

"I don't see why not, he will know in a few months anyway."

That evening at the diner table Liz said to Jim, "You are going to have a new brother or sister."

"How do you know?"

"I just know."

"Where do babies come from?"

"Your father will explain it to you."

"I will?"

"Yes dear, you will explain to Jim where babies come from."

It wasn't that Eagle Eye did not want to explain where babies came from to Jim. He had just never thought about it. That night in bed he said to Liz, "What should I tell him?"

"Tell him the truth, he is eleven years of age and someone should have told him before now. It's your job as his pa to explain it to him."

The next day while they were sitting on the bank fishing, Eagle Eye explained to Jim where babies come from. The telling formed a strong bond between father and son.

Liz needed supplies to complete her garden. She spent most of her spare time digging and planting. She was reluctant to take time out of her busy schedule to go to the town.

She said to Eagle Eye, "I need a few more seed and a new hoe. Would you mind going to town in the morning and getting them for me?"

"Why don't you go and get them?"

"I have too much work to do."

"Then ask Jim if he will go. I think that he would like to take the mule and cart into town by himself for a change."

"Don't you think he is a bit young to be going to town by himself?"

"Just prepare a list of the supplies that you want and give it to him. He knows the way and he is old enough to go alone."

During their entire stay at the farm, Eagle Eye had not once gone to the town. Liz had thought about this a lot. At first she felt that he did not want to leave the work on the farm for a trip into town. As time passed and most of the initial work needed to get the farm in some semblance of order was done, Eagle Eye still refused to go to the town. Jim and his ma took all trips to the little town. Eagle Eye never left the farm.

Liz was sure that it was not because he was afraid of the people in the town. She had seen him use his six-shooter and knew that no man could out draw or out shoot him. It finally dawned upon her, that Eagle Eye would go to any lengths to avoid trouble.

Yet, this was a mining town and much different from the frontier towns that they passed on their trip west. The people in the town had always treated her with kindness. She was even given a measure of respect by the men that she encountered. Often they tipped their hat to her.

Liz saw nothing to fear in the town. She thought that Eagle Eye's fear of the town was unreasonable, after all he was her husband. This far west there were no flyers concerning him or his past. Yet, Eagle Eye resisted all of her attempts to lure him into the town with her and Jim.

Liz decided to confront Eagle Eye about going to town. He was her husband and she wanted the whole world to know it.

"I am your wife and you need not be ashamed of me. I am not as pretty as those girls in the bars but I am the one that loves you. Why don't you want to be seen with me?"

"My not going to town has nothing to do with you."

"What then?"

"Every time I go around a white man there is trouble. Most don't like to see black men with white women."

"You are my man and I don't care who likes it or don't like it."

"Let it be Liz, we are happy here and there is no need to go looking for trouble."

The next morning Liz asked Jim if he would like to go town.

"Sure."

"I mean by yourself. I need some supplies and Eagle and I are too busy to go. Do you think that you could go into town alone if I gave you a list of supplies to buy at the general store?"

"I'm grown-up now ma, even pa says so. I can take flower to town by myself."

Liz prepared a list of the supplies that she needed, tomatoes, collards, beans and other seeds. Included in the list was a hoe and a dime novel for Eagle Eye. She gave Jim last minute instructions about what he was to purchase. Liz told him that she expected him back before sundown. She told him to make sure that the shopkeeper wrote the items purchased on a piece of paper. She wanted the amount of purchase next to each item. This list she would check when he got back.

"Be sure to check behind him and make sure that he does not overcharge us. I will check the list when you return. You can have a dime for yourself."

Eagle Eye explained to him the necessity of making sure that Flower had her fill of water before leaving the town. He gave Jim a bag of feed for her and told him to be careful.

"Thanks ma and you too pa, I'll be back before sundown and I will take care of Flower." On a bright summer day they saw him off. Jim was making his first trip to town alone. It reminded Eagle Eye of the first time he had taken the goats of his father to graze in the valley. Eagle Eye understood Jim's excitement in ways the only he could understand.

Liz said to Eagle Eye, "Our little boy has become a man."

From three o'clock on, Liz would stop what she was doing and look down the trail for signs of Jim. Eagle Eye went about his work and showed no signs of worry. Only once did Liz catch him with his hand shading his eyes looking down the trail. She smiled, she knew that Jim meant as much to Eagle Eye as he did to her.

It was nearly noon when Jim entered the town. Again he saw boys playing their strange game. He ignored their insults about Flower, realizing that most had never seen a mule. Horses were the animals of choice in most of the west. He went straight to the general store. He handed the shopkeeper the list. The shopkeeper looked at Jim and then at the list. He finally inquired about his mother.

"My ma and pa are working on the farm. I came to buy these supplies for them."

"Never seen yore pa."

"Mostly he works on the farm."

"I reckon there must be lots of work to do there. Well, give me about twenty minutes and I will have yore order ready for you."

The shopkeeper brought Jim a bag containing the supplies that he ordered. Jim checked the bag carefully as the shopkeeper observed. Assured that everything was in order, he paid the shopkeeper. He then went over to the counter and pointed to a penknife.

"How much is that knife."

"Twenty five cents."

"Ain't got that much. Got any cheaper."

"How much you got."

"Ten cents."

"All right take it for ten cents."

"Thanks mister. I got to be going now, got to get back home fore sundown."

Jim left the store and took Flower to the water trough in front of the bank and let her drink. He fed her the bag of feed that Eagle Eye had given him. Only then did he start the long journey home. It was dark when he arrived at the cabin. Both parents were overjoyed to see him. He gave Liz the bag of supplies, which she inspected. He handed her the list prepared by the shopkeeper and he showed his new penknife to Eagle Eye.

"I can use this on the fish we catch and the rabbits too."

That night in bed, Liz and Eagle Eye talked of their happiness and of the coming baby. They both agreed that the act of fate that had brought them together was the best thing that had ever happened in their lives.

The Encounter at the Farm

It was a late summer day and the corn in the field was almost ripe. Liz's garden yielded a good crop of vegetables. There had been plenty of rainfall and the good soil produced an abundance of wealth.

Eagle Eye had built a new storage shed for the corn that they would harvest. The woodland around the farm contained an abundance of wild game so there was always fresh meat on the table. Since the winters in Southern California were not severe, there was little need to kill more game than they could eat in one or two meals. Sometimes when they killed deer, they would Salt the meat and store it for later.

Eagle Eye explained to Liz and Jim, that there was no need to save the excess meat. He could always kill fresh game. Yet they continued to do it. Liz and Eagle Eye never wasted any of the produce from the garden or the surrounding land. The woods and fields around the farm were teeming with animal life. Eagle Eye and Jim never went hunting and returned home without game.

The lives of the three had settled into a routine that was familiar to all three of them. In the morning Jim would water Flower and take her to the nearby meadow for grazing and then return for breakfast. The rest of the day he would spend helping Eagle Eye do tasks around the farm. Jim was happiest when they took a day off to fish or hunt. It was on those trips that Eagle Eye was teaching him to use the gun with limited success. Eagle Eye continued with Jim's education and each night they spent hours reading and going over numbers.

Liz would make a fire in the fireplace and prepare the morning meal. After the morning meal, she would clean the cabin and then go to her garden. Liz's garden was her pride and joy. It brought her almost as much pleasure as her chickens. Even Flower avoided going near Liz's garden. Jim once commented at the dinner table that his ma cared more for her garden than anything else in the world.

Liz responded, "That garden keeps us from having to eat only fish and rabbits that you delight in bringing home."

Eagle Eye was not pleased that Liz continued to work in the garden. He tried to prevent her from doing it, but she insisted that it was all right and that no harm would come to her unborn child. Finally, Eagle Eye hid her hoe and the rest of her garden tools. When she asked where they were, he told her that if work need to be done in the garden, he and Jim would do it.

Instead of Liz becoming angry as he expected she would, she walked over to him and kissed him.

She said to him, "You are the kindest and most gentle man that I have ever known. Eagle Eye, I love you."

Eagle Eye said to her, "I love you very much and I don't want anything to happen to you are our unborn son."

"How do you know it's going to be a boy?"

"I just know it."

Liz smiled and held him close to her. She vowed that she would never let anything come between her and her man. She loved Eagle Eye because he was good to her and Jim. She loved him because he always looked out for their welfare. Liz was happier than she had been in a very long time.

Eagle Eye would get up in the morning feed the chickens. Then make a quick inspection of the farm to make sure that everything was in order before coming to the morning meal. After his morning meal, Eagle Eye would do farm work with Jim, unless Jim could convince him to fish or hunt. It was always a game with Jim, hoping that it would rain, or that Eagle Eye would find nothing to do. Then the two of them would take their fishing poles or guns and go fishing or hunting.

On the day that the visitors came, Liz was in the house making dinner. She planned to make a very special dinner for her two men. She was preparing fresh bread and baking a cake. That day, they would eat fish, rabbit stew and collard greens. She had just finished making a large pitcher of sassafras tea and had placed it in the sunshine coming through the kitchen window. It promised to be one of their special meals.

It wasn't a holiday or any special occasion, it was just that Liz felt like cooking. She wanted to make this meal special. She even planned to cut wild flowers that grew on the hill to grace the dinner table. She thought about candles and then decided against them. She knew that Eagle Eye and Jim would laugh at that gesture.

Jim was out at the corral feeding Flower. Flower had become his special friend. She had even replaced his dog in his affection. He tried to talk to her as he had seen his pa do. Even Eagle Eye had noticed and commented on the fact that Flower never tried to kick or nick him. Flower would even allow Jim to ride her around the corral. Flower and Jim had developed a special relationship.

Eagle Eye was working in the cornfield. He had a large basket and was collecting ears of corn. Some he planned to feed to the chickens and the rest were to be turned into corn meal for Liz to use to make bread. Eagle Eye came to the end of the row with the basket of corn. He almost collided with the horse of one of the riders. He sat the basket down and looked at the three men on horseback. Two were older men in their forties and the third appeared to Eagle Eye to be about twenty. The younger man spoke first.

"Our horses need water."

Eagle Eye said, "The well is right over there help yourself."

The youngest of the three repeated his demand.

"Our horses need water."

"You are welcome to all the water you want mister, for yourselves or your horses."

Eagle Eye knew there was going to be trouble. He regretted that he was unarmed. Not knowing what to expect from the three men, Eagle Eye reached for his basket of corn. The other two men had said nothing; they followed the lead of the younger man. They were waiting to see what Eagle Eye would do.

The young man said, "Nigger I want you to get some water for our horses."

Eagle Eye hesitated.

Jim came over to where Eagle Eye was standing, still holding a basket of corn.

"What's wrong pa?"

One of the older men spoke, "He yore pa?"

"Yeah."

"Don't look much like yore pa, you sure that he's yore pa?"

"Pa what's wrong?"

"Nothing, go to the cabin."

The young man spoke again, "I don't care whose pa he is he is going to get some water for our horses."

Liz walked out the cabin door. Holding Eagle Eye's rifle with both hands. She walked with determination and pointed the rifle at the youngest of the three men. Around her right arm she had Eagle Eye's six shooter and holster. Jim removed the gun and holster from her arm and handed them to Eagle Eye. Eagle Eye put the gun and holster around his waist and adjusted it. Eagle Eye was again a man and ready to face the world.

Liz said to the three, "What's your business here? Who are you?"

The young man spoke, "My pa owns five thousand acres east of here. If you don't want trouble you had better put that rifle down and do what I say."

Liz replied, "Your pa don't own these few acres, we do and you got no business disturbing us, if you want water or food you are welcome to it. The well is right over there and there is food in the house."

The young man started to get off his horse.

One of the older men said to him, "Let it be Tommy, we got no quarrel with these people."

"I want that nigger to water my horse, and he is going to do it like a good boy."

Tommy dismounted and faced Eagle Eye. "Are you ready to water my horse or you want to go for your gun?"

"I don't want to do either. I will go for my gun if you force me to."

"Nigger I am going to count to three. When I finish, you had better be headed for that well to get some water for our horses, or going for your six-shooter."

"I don't want any trouble, why don't you just go and get the water yourself."

One of the older men spoke again, "Lets get out of here Tommy, before something happens that we will all regret."

The second man who had been silent until now spoke to the younger man.

"Tommy, I'll water your horse. Leave those people alone."

"You shut up Bill, remember you work for my father."

"Lady you can put that rifle away, this is going to be a fair fight. Nigger I am going to start counting. When I get to three you had better be going for your gun."

Tommy counted to three and started drawing his gun. A split second before he cleared leather. Eagle Eye's gun was in his hand. Tommy looked surprised but continued to draw his weapon. Eagle Eye hesitated and then shot the gun from Tommy's hand.

Tommy clutched his gun hand with his left hand and yelled, "Shoot him Bill, shoot that nigger."

"I ain't got no quarrel with you nigger, and I ain't going for my gun. We are going to ride out of here. Tommy, I'll get your gun you get on your horse and let's go. We had no business here in the first place."

"You will get yours when I tell my father. You are fired."

"I'm still alive and I can get another job. You were asking for it and you got it. Now get on that horse and let's go home and tend to your hand."

Tommy mounted his horse, and as the three rode away, he looked back at Eagle Eye and said, "I will be back and you can bet on that. Nigger you are going to get what's coming to you when I come back."

Eagle Eye made no reply, he watched as the three men rode off. He was wondering if he had done the right thing. He suspected that he should have killed all three of them and just buried them somewhere on the farm.

The Dinner

As the three rode off, Eagle Eye picked up his basket of corn and started toward the cabin. Liz and Jim followed behind him. None of them spoke of the event that had just occurred. They walked in silence to the cabin. Eagle Eye went inside and sat the basket on the table. He removed his gun belt and hung it on a rack near the door.

Liz moved the basket to the floor and started setting the table for the evening meal. Jim was perplexed. He had not had the time to digest what had happened. He believed that his pa was the strongest man and the fastest man with a gun in the whole world. He was not worried about the gunfight that had taken place. He did not want to leave and look for another farm.

He wondered how men, white men, could be so bad. Indians never did things like that to each other or to other men. He did not understand why they could not live their lives and allow others to live theirs. He wanted to grow up to be just like Eagle Eye. He resolved to make the world safe for all men, Indians, white men and black men.

The three, Liz, Jim and Eagle Eye, sat to the special dinner that Liz had prepared. Midway through the dinner, Jim brought up the subject of the three visitors. He introduced it in the normal routine of conversation. It was more of a question than a comment on the event that had taken place.

" I wonder why those bad men came here?"

Eagle Eye said, "They were looking for trouble. Not the older men but the young man hates for the sake of hating."

Liz asked, "Will they come back, maybe we should go to town and tell the sheriff what happened? The sheriff could put a stop to whatever they plan to do."

"The sheriff might protect you and Jim but as long as I am with you he will do nothing. I am sure of that."

"It wont hurt to go to town and inform the sheriff about it. We didn't break the law, they did. This is our farm and they were trespassing."

"Pa, let's go early in the morning and tell the sheriff what happened. He will know how to deal with those bad men. If I had been you, I would have killed them anyway."

"You can't kill a man over a bucket of water, it just ain't right."

"He would have killed you."

"Maybe."

After the dinner Eagle Eye and Jim washed and put away the eating utensils and unconsumed food. Liz watched making sure that everything went into its proper place. When they had finished, Liz hugged them both and told them that no woman had two men who were so thoughtful and caring.

Jim left to feed the dog some of the bones and scraps left from the dinner. He then went to the corral and talked to Flower. He rode her down to the stream for water. When he returned it was almost dark. Jim put Flower in the corral and then joined his ma and pa in the cabin.

That night in bed, Liz confronted Eagle Eye about going to the town and speaking to the sheriff. She would go, even if Eagle Eye did not. She explained to him that they had left one farm. She did not want to leave this one. She finally convinced him that going to the town and informing the sheriff of the events that had transpired was the best course of action.

She was concerned about having to leave their farm after having spent so much time making the place into a home. She was sure that the sheriff would use his office to protect them and that would be the end of the matter. Liz wanted to live her life in peace with Jim and Eagle Eye. If that meant going to the sheriff for help, then she would do it.

She said to him, "Where can we go? Is there no place that is safe for us?"

"Tomorrow we will leave early in the morning. I will go to the town with you. I will not wear my guns. We will speak to the sheriff and show him our deed for the land. I hope that he can do something about it before someone gets killed."

"I am sure that is the right thing to do and it is what we should do. We should report it to the sheriff before they do. That way, we will be sure that he hears the truth."

"Most white men side with other white men against blacks and Indians. I just hope that this sheriff is different. We will give it a try anyway. We leave for town early in the morning. We should be there before noon."

The Sheriff of Salton Creek

The little town of Salton Creek was built as a result of the California gold rush of 1849. It reached its zenith during the late fifties and was now on the road to decline. Mining for iron and farming were now the chief occupations of the inhabitants of the town. The gold mines in the area were closing. Many of the townspeople had moved to the gold mining fields farther north, there locating the mother lode was still a possibility.

There was still enough gold left in the overworked mines to support a few prospectors. The towns bar and brothel still did a booming business. So did the general store, where pick axes, shovels and other gear used by prospectors and farmers were still in demand.

When the town was in its heyday, some time in the past, the respectable citizens had formed a committee to provide for law and order. They hired Willard Johnson to be the town marshal at the unheard of price of twenty dollars a month. No one was sure of where Willard Johnson came from. All that they knew about him was that he had been marshal of Salton Creek for more than twenty years. His entire life was centered on the job of law enforcement. No one in the town questioned his authority. There were few honest marshals in the towns of the west. Marshal Willard Johnson was one of those few. In his younger days, he was fast on the draw with his gun and no man dared oppose him. In the last few years he relied more on his shotgun than his side arm. Willard Johnson knew his limitations.

He often said to his deputies, "I intend to die in bed with my boots off."

The citizens of Salton Creek respected Marshal Johnson and they were proud of him. Two deputies, Jack Thomas and Ben Goodman, were paid ten dollars a month. It was their job to patrol the town. They arrested drunks, broke up fights and apprehended enough people so the fines collected covered their salaries. The citizens had built a jail and a sheriff's office just opposite the bank. The jail was the show place of the little town. It had iron bars and two cells. It

233

was a rude reminder to all the town's people that lawbreakers would receive swift justice.

Everyone for miles around the little town knew Marshal Johnson. He was sixty years of age and wise in the ways of frontier law. His hair was beginning to turn gray, but his mustache and eyebrows were still jet-black. His brown eyes no longer carried the stern look that had stared many gunmen down. Yet, he was still a force to be reckoned with and not to be taken casually. He could still hold his own against most gunmen and he had his deputies to back him up.

Marshal Johnson had the look of a peaceful man, a father or grandfather. He had never married and all his adult life had been spent as a town marshal. He was known to be fair but rigid where the law was concerned. He was just what the town of Salton Creek needed. Someone who would guarantee that justice would prevail in the small town of Salton Creek.

Marshal Johnson was always neatly dressed and was never without his ten-gallon hat, his side arm and rifle. He stood about six feet five inches tall and had a commanding appearance. He looked as if he were born to lead men. No one in the town questioned his authority. He ran his town, as he called it, with an iron fist.

No one broke the law of the land and went free. Marshal Johnson saw that all lawbreakers were brought to justice. The marshal was fair but firm in his dealings with the people of the town. No one in the town of Salton Creek could find anything derogatory about him.

Always on Saturday, he could depend upon collecting enough money in fines to cover the week's work. All the miners and farmers came to town looking for a good time. A few came to buy the weeks supplies and to shop for bargains. Some came to town to drink and for the pleasures offered by the ladies of the town brothel. A few came looking for trouble. Those that came looking for trouble ended their quest in Marshal Johnson's jail.

Marshal Johnson's jail usually contained from seven to ten men by Sunday noon. Marshal Johnson would take them one by one to the Justice of the Peace. The two of them would collect the fines that paid their salaries. His treatment of the town's habitual drunks was a little different. He did not arrest them. Deputies took them to the shed in the back of the jail to sleep it off.

Marshal Johnson's cells were reserved for paying customers. He knew that the town drunks had no money for fines. He did not even bother to try to collect from them. He considered them so much trash. He realized that they had no money or other valuables; he allowed them to sober up and just put them on the street with a stern warning. He knew that the next weekend, the same drunks would once again be in custody, yet, he never mistreated them; he did what he had to do to protect the citizens of Salton Creek. It was good work and he enjoyed his role in protecting the good citizens of Salton Creek.

It was early Saturday morning when Liz got out of bed and made a fire in the fireplace. It was still dark outside. She slept very little during the night for fear that the men would return and burn the cabin down.

Eagle Eye slept even less than she did. Eagle Eye sat in a chair with his two six shooters and the rifle across his legs. He decided that if the men came he was going to die defending his home, his wife and his son.

Jim had sat up most of the night with his pa. Eagle Eye finally insisted that he go to bed. Jim, at his young age, was determined that no one was going to hurt the man that he called pa or his ma and he was ready to give his life for them. He had some difficulty understanding why anyone would want to hurt his family. He knew that they had committed no crime and would help anyone in need.

In the morning, the three ate a hastily prepared breakfast. Flower was watered and fed and then hooked to the cart. Liz and Jim drove the mule and cart and Eagle Eye sat in the rear.

Eagle instructed Jim not to call him pa while they were in town. Jim resented this; Eagle Eye pulled him close to him. He held him for a few brief minutes and Jim consented to Eagle Eye's wishes. He explained to Jim that it would go better if he appeared to work for him and his Ma. Jim had lots of trouble with this idea. To Jim, Eagle Eye was his pa and he loved him, and that was all that mattered. In his young mind, he somehow felt that if others could get to know his pa, they would love his as much as he did.

Liz had to intervene and explain to him that people didn't like to see differences in each other and that there might be people in the town that would object to Eagle Eye being her husband and his pa. Jim could not understand what the people in town had to do with who his ma and pa were. No amount of explaining would pacify him.

Jim could only utter, "Why? What they got to do with who my ma and pa is?"

"That's just the way some people are, although it's none of their business. They will make an issue out of it. It wont hurt us to pretend just this time."

"All right, but I don't like it."

Liz was now about seven months pregnant. Eagle Eye was more than concerned about her making the trip. Yet, he realized how necessary it was. It would be Liz who would approach the sheriff and explain their predicament to him. Eagle Eye had little experience with law officials and all of that experience ended in the death of someone. He would leave the negotiations to Liz. Liz would have to explain to the sheriff what had occurred at the farm.

Eagle Eye insisted that she sit on pillows to cushion the bumpy ride. Liz was sure it was unnecessary, that she would be all right. Liz reminded him again that women have had babies since the beginning of time and that it was no big deal.

She said to him, "It nothing really special about having a baby and nothing will go wrong, I will be just fine."

To Eagle Eye, it was a big deal, he said to her, "If anything happens to you or the baby I will never forgive myself.

"Nothing is going to happen, just stop worrying about me, I will be all right."

They packed a lunch and extra food and water for Flower. The sun had not made its appearance in the sky when the three left for the town of Salton Creek. Eagle Eye pointed out the drinking gourd to Jim and told him that it always showed the north direction. Jim wanted to know how his pa knew such things about the night sky. Eagle Eye thought it best not to explain further. He was not sure of how much of his former life his young son would be able to understand.

The trip to the town would take them about four hours. They stopped frequently and allowed Flower to graze. At one grazing stop, Liz came over to Eagle Eye and handed him his gun.

"I remember the last time that we encountered a sheriff. I don't want to take any chances that this one is like the last one that we met. You can keep it out of sight. I insist that you take it with you. We are not looking for trouble. There is always the chance that we will find it or it will find us."

Eagle Eye took the gun and put it in his hat.

"I was just thinking that I made a mistake, not taking my gun to town. I always feel naked with out my gun. You think of everything."

"No, I just think of you."

Eagle Eye smiled and held her close. After Flower had grazed for a while, Eagle Eye decided it was time to leave. Flower did not object and was ready to continue the journey. Eagle Eye gave her some water and they continued their trip to the town.

The absence of rain left the trail to town easy to negotiate. The stream that they had to cross gave them no problems. It was almost ten o'clock when they arrived at the town. The day was typical of the warm days of southern California. There were no rain clouds in the sky. The weather was in their favor and Liz considered this an omen of good tidings. She was sure that all would go well.

The day was Saturday and the main street was packed with people of all sorts. Eagle Eye was not sure that they had made the right decision to enter the town on the weekend. The people that they passed in the street gave them strange looks. A few stared and the children pointed at them. They ignored all the stares and went straight to the sheriff's office opposite the bank. Liz pointed out items of interest to Jim in a voice loud enough for Eagle Eye, in the back of the cart, to hear.

"Over there is the general store. The bank where I purchased the farm is on my right. The saloon is on the left with the big sign. The sheriff's office is on the right across from the bank."

The three arrived at the jail and tied flower to the hitching post. Liz and Jim entered the jailhouse with Eagle Eye following and holding his hat.

Marshal Johnson sat behind a large desk filled with papers. He was alone; both his deputies were out patrolling the town, keeping order on the busy weekend. The doors leading to the jail cells were closed. A large wooded bar across the door prevented entry and protected the occupants of the jail.

One wall was covered with wanted posters. Most offered rewards for the individual's capture or return. A few posters read dead or alive. Near the door was a gun rack containing about ten rifles. The small wood stove in one corner contained a coffee pot and several mugs. The floor needed sweeping and the windows with their bars barely allowed sunlight to enter they were very small windows.

The sheriff's desk, a few chairs and a stool were all the furniture in the office. On the sheriff's desk was a kerosene lamp that provided light even during the day. Marshal Johnson was going through the papers on his desk when they entered. He was wearing spectacles but took them off as the three entered the jail.

Marshal Johnson looked at them and said, "What can I do for you people?"

Liz said, "Mr. Marshall, we live on a farm few miles outside the town."

Marshal Johnson said, "I know where you live, out on the old Simmons place about ten or fifteen miles from my town. You come to town regularly for supplies, usually about once a month. You brought your land from Mister Jenkins, the banker, some time ago. You paid cash for your farm. You have one child, a son I believe. Your husband never comes to town and I don't think anyone around here has ever seen him. You can see that I try to learn as much about people who come to my town as I can. After all I am in the law and order business. Is he your husband?"

Liz hesitated for a split second and said in a firm voice, "Yes, he is my husband."

Marshall Johnson did not look surprised; he showed no reaction at all to the disclosure.

He looks at Eagle Eye and at Jim and asked Liz, "Is that your boy?"

"Yes, he is my son."

Jim spoke and said, "He's my pa."

"What's your name son?"

"My name is Jim and I come to town sometimes by my self. Ain't that right pa?"

Eagle Eye said, "That's right son, you sure do."

The marshal looked at the three of them and then said to Liz. "I'm Marshal Johnson, and who might you be?"

"I am Liz and this is my husband Eagle Eye and my son Jim."

The marshal did not offer his hand and Eagle Eye did not offer his. They stared at each other for a few seconds. The Marshal said to Eagle Eye, "Why don't you take that gun out of your hat, if you intended to use it, you would have done so by now. There ain't no law against a man wearing a gun in this town, unless he uses it to break the law."

Eagle Eye removed the gun and tucked it in his belt. He wanted to ask the sheriff how he knew that he had a gun in his hat but thought it better to just let it be.

The Marshal said to Liz, "Now suppose you have a seat and explain your problem to me."

Liz sat on a stool in front of the desk and faced Marshal Johnson.

She said, "Mr. Marshal, we are farmers and all we want to do is to live on our farm in peace. We got no problem with any of our neighbors cause we don't even know them. We will give water and food to anyone who passes our way. My family will help anyone and we turn no one away, all are welcome to share what we have. Yesterday, three men came to our farm. They were looking for trouble; at least one of them was looking for trouble. We treated them like we would any stranger passing our way. We offered to allow them to water their animals at our well. I would have given them food had they asked for it."

"How many men did you say?"

"Three men, they asked for water and my husband told them that they could use the well for as much water as they wanted for themselves and their horses. The youngest of the three men insisted that my husband water his horse for him. He had no reason for this. He won't ailing and he could have gotten all the water he wanted by himself and I would have given them food if they had asked. He insisted that my husband water his horse and my husband refused. He forced my husband to into a gun fight."

"He wanted your husband to water their horses with the water that you were giving him, water from your well?"

"That's right Mr. marshal, he called my husband bad names. Then he told my husband that he was going to count to three and draw his gun and shoot him. My husband waited until the man had finished counting to three. He waited until he had gone for his gun. My husband waited until his hand was on his gun before he even started to draw his gun. He shot the gun out of the man's hand. My husband had his gun in his hand, all that he had to do was not continue to draw his gun and my husband would not have fired. He could have as easily shot him, had he a mind to do so. My husband didn't try to kill him. He only protected himself. The man, I think that they called him Tommy, left. He said that he would return and do harm to us. We decided to come to you and . . . "

The marshal interrupted her and asked, "What did you say they called him?"

"Tommy, I think."

"A young man about twenty, slim, with brown hair, large scar over his left eye?"

"Yes, that's the one."

The marshal was standing now; his hand went to his chin. It was a habit developed in his early childhood, when he had a problem to solve.

He looked at Eagle Eye and said, "If you outdrew Tommy you must be real handy with that gun. He is the fastest that I have ever seen around these parts. I'm not sure that I would want to draw against him. His pa owns a large spread about twenty or twenty five miles east of here. I can't imagine Tommy forgetting what happened to him. He just can't bear the thought that someone is faster with a gun than he is. Shot a man down right outside about six months ago. He even allowed the man to go for his gun first, so that it would be considered a fair fight. Not that any fight with Tommy is fair.

He has killed at least six men and he is not twenty-five years of age yet. His father is a powerful man hereabouts and it doesn't do to get on his bad side. Tommy is a dangerous man and not one to make angry."

"Mr. Marshal he would have gunned my husband down if he had not shot that gun from his hand."

"I believe what you say lady. Tommy is a spoiled kid, who thinks he is the best in the west with a gun."

He looked at Eagle Eye and said, "Mister, you really outdrew Tommy, now that's something special. Did the other men go for their guns?"

Liz said, "No, Mister Sheriff, they knew that the man, Tommy, was in the wrong, they even said so."

Eagle Eye noted that the marshal had called him mister. That was a first for Eagle Eye; white men always called him boy or nigger. No white man had called him mister in his entire life. He was rapidly developing a new respect for this observant white marshal.

Eagle Eye still wondered how the marshal knew that he had his gun in his hat. He wanted to ask him about it but again he decided not to press the issue. He knew that this sheriff was different from all the other Sheriffs that he had met. He knew that this man was fair and honest.

Eagle Eye spoke, "Mr. Marshal, we don't want no trouble. We just don't know what we should do. We came to you to explain what happened. We want you to help us before someone gets killed."

"I understand your problem, and I would really like to help you and your family. My jurisdiction does not extend beyond the limits of this town. Unless a crime is committed in the town and the lawbreaker leaves the town, then I can go after him otherwise I can't interfere. Tommy committed no crime in this town there is nothing that I can do. I am sure that Tommy and his father know that. I assure you that my talking to him would do no good. I am not unsympathetic to your problem, it just that my hands are tied. I really have no authority to act in this matter."

Liz asked, "Is there no other law officer that we can talk to?"

"Not in these parts, there is no other peace officer within fifty miles of here."

The marshal hesitated for a few seconds, as if trying to think of a solution to the problem of Liz and her family. He looked at

241

the three of them and continued to speak. His tone was serious, not demeaning. The impression that Liz got was that he was really going to try to help them.

"I have some good advice that I can give you, take your belongings and leave the farm. Go as far away as you can. That farm is not worth your lives. You can always find another farm. I assure you that Tommy will not let the matter rest, he will come back to your farm and he will not be alone."

Eagle Eye said, "Mr. Marshal we have spent a lot of money and time on that farm, it just ain't right."

The marshal expressed genuine concern for the three of them as he searched for a solution to their problem.

He said to them, "There is one other solution to your problem, move into my town and I will see that Tommy or no one else harms you. If you move into town you will be safe, that I can guarantee. I will allow no one to bother you in my town. That Tommy is bad news. He will come looking for you mister, and he will not rest until you are dead or he is dead. I don't think that he can live with the idea that a man is faster with a gun than he is, but here in my town I can protect you and your family. I can make sure that no one bothers you or your family."

Mister Marshal, I don't want to harm him but I can't let him do harm to my family or run us off our farm. We put a lot of work in that farm. It ain't right to let someone run us off."

"I understand how you feel. Tommy's father is one of the largest landowners in this state and he has lots of hired hands. He has no control over Tommy. Sometimes I think he is afraid of him. Leave while you still got the chance."

Marshal Johnson looked at Jim. There was sadness in his eyes. Liz noticed this but she did not know if was for the three of them or what might happen to Jim.

The Marshal said, "I am going to ride out to the Stanton ranch and see if I can get his father to exert some control over young Tommy. I don't guarantee anything and my best advice to you is the same. Leave the farm while you still have the chance. My deputies will protect you while you move."

Eagle Eye said, "Thank you Mr. Marshal for your advice, we are going back to our farm now."

"I still find it hard to believe that you outdrew Tommy. That man is good with a gun, and he doesn't mind using it. It might have been better if you had killed him then and there. The law would have been on your side. You still have time to get away. I will send my deputies with you to help you pack your things. They will make sure that no one harms you until you have a chance to leave."

Eagle Eye said, "Thank you Mister Marshal but we are going back to the farm. We intend to stay there. We put a lot of work in that place."

"The decision is yours. I can only advise you what I think is best. Tommy has a lot of ranch hands on that spread and I am sure that he will use them against you."

Liz thanked the marshal for his advice and they started to leave the office.

Marshal Johnson looked at Jim and said, "How old are you son."

"I'm almost twelve, and my pa is going to buy me a horse and saddle for my birthday. Ain't that right pa?"

"Yes, son you are going to have your own horse."

Marshal Johnson patted Jim on the head and said, "You are proud of your pa, ain't you?"

"Yes, my pa is the strongest and fastest man with a gun in the whole world."

Marshal Johnson held out his hand to Eagle Eye. Eagle Eye took his hand and with a firm grasp and shook it. It was another first for Eagle Eye. No white man had offered to shake hands with him before. It made him realize that not all white men were bad men.

Marshal Johnson said, "I wish I could make you take my advice and leave that farm. I know Tommy and his kind very well. There is going to be trouble sooner or later. Tommy can't put a thing like that to rest. He will come back to your farm after you when his hand heals."

Marshal Johnson patted Jim on the head, said his good-byes to Eagle Eye, Liz and Jim. The three of them left the sheriff's office.

Marshal Johnson went back to his paper work. When the two deputies arrived at the office he told them the story that Liz had told him.

"Can you imagine that big black man outdrawing Tommy? I would love to have seen the look on his face when that happened."

He told one of his deputies that he wanted him to go to the farm in a few days or so to make sure that everything was all right. He would like to do more for that family but it was outside his jurisdiction. Talking to Tommy's father was as much as he could do for them and he was sure that would do no good.

One morning a week later Marshal Johnson called his Deputy Thomas and said, "Go down to the livery stable. Ask old man Dawson if I can borrow his hired man for a day or so. I want you and him to ride out to that black man's farm and make sure that everything is all right."

"Ben, I want you to mind the jail for a few days, I'm going to take a ride out to the Stanton ranch and talk to Tommy's father. His hand should be getting better now and I expect trouble. I am going to try to head it off before it happens. I am going to try to talk to Tommy's father he is a reasonable man. I want him to talk some sense in that boy's hard head."

The Second Encounter With Tommy

It was almost dark when they arrived back at the farm. The farm was just as they had left it. The trip back was a quiet one. No one talked about the Marshal or his warning. Eagle Eye was trying to find a way to get Liz and Jim to leave the farm for a few weeks, until the entire affair passed. He decided to use the baby as the vehicle to get Liz and Jim away from the farm. It was the only solution that he could come up with to get his family safely away from the impending disaster. He was sure that the sheriff was right in his assessment and that Tommy would return. In a fair fight he knew that he would win but if he brought men with him that would change the equation. He was not sure of what would happen but he wanted to protect Liz and Jim. He had to convince them to leave the farm for a few weeks or at least until the baby was born.

That night as they lay in bed Eagle Eye said to Liz, "The baby is due soon and I think that you and Jim should stay in town until the baby is born. There is a doctor there that will look after you. You could return to the farm when the baby comes."

"Eagle, I ain't going any place without you. You can stop making plans to get rid of me. This is our farm and no one is going to run us off it."

"It would be only till the baby comes."

"Eagle, I know that you are concerned about that man, Tommy, coming back. I leave only if you leave. There is nothing else to be said about it."

"What about Jim, couldn't we send him to the town, the sheriff would help us and protect him? We could say that we are sending him to school."

"Eagle, we could ask him, but I don't believe that he will leave his ma and the only pa that he has ever known. He would know why we are asking him to leave. He would know that it is not to go to school in that town. He knows all about what has taken place. He wants to stand by you. You are closer to him than I am. Don't you realize this?"

"I know but it would be better if we could convince him to stay in the town until this blows over."

"In the morning I will to ask him to go, if that is what you want, but I can tell you now what his answer will be."

"Just try to talk some sense into him, maybe he will understand."

"We have to try, that's the least that we can do."

"If he refuses, then we have to live with that but I think it would be better if both of you went to the town until the baby gets here."

"You are my husband and my family, the only family that I have and I am not going to leave you here alone."

"If you really loved me you would do as I wish."

"Now that is a low blow and you know it, my husband, you will stoop to anything to get rid of me, and to protect me, but you can forget it. I intend to stick by you until the very end."

O.K. but you can't say I didn't try."

"You tried, you really did."

The next morning Liz was up early preparing breakfast. Eagle Eye and Jim tended to their respective tasks. Jim went to the corral to feed and water Flower. Eagle Eye put both his six-shooters on and checked the farm to make sure everything was all right. When Liz called them to breakfast, the two went to the well and washed up.

They said grace and then started to enjoy their meal.

Liz surprised them with eggs from her hens, corn bread, thick slices of deer meat and coffee.

Jim said, "we are eating ma's hen eggs what is this a holiday."

"Don't eat them if you don't like them".

" I like them fine I just can't believe it."

"Believe it."

This day was like any other day on the farm and all was going well. It was during breakfast that Liz spoke to Jim about attending school in the town. Like Eagle Eye, she hoped that Jim would consent to go to the town school.

Liz said to Jim, "Your father and I think that you should attend a proper school like the one in the town."

"Ma, you know that pa is teaching me to read and write and my numbers. He is getting me a horse and saddle for my birthday. We are going to town to get them when the corn is all in the shed. I don't want to stay in town away from you and my pa."

"But you would learn many other things in the town school. Things that we don't know about, you would learn things that we can't teach you."

"Ma, you just want me to leave because you think that those bad men will come back. I am not leaving. I am going to stay here with you and pa."

"All right, all right, you can stay, if that is what you want to do."

"It's what I want to do."

They spent the next week getting the corn in the shed. Eagle Eye wore both his six shooters and carried his rifle to the cornfield with him. As the days went by, they almost forgot the three visitors. They were busy working on the farm and trying to prepare for the winter.

Liz now had twenty chickens. They had eggs each day for breakfast. Liz still refused to eat any of the chickens.

Jim and Eagle Eye called them, "Ma's pets."

She had promised to cook one once the number reached forty. She had said the same thing about twenty.

Jim reminded her that she had said it and stated, "We are never going to eat one of your chickens."

"One of these days I am going to surprise you and your pa with a nice chicken dinner."

"I will believe it when I see the chicken in one of your pots."

Eagle Eye had discussed the need for another mule or horse at their evening meal. This would be an addition to the one that they were going to purchase for Jim on his birthday. They had already decided that they would purchase a horse so Jim could learn to ride. They planned to go to town in a few days to make the purchase. They were waiting until all the corn was picked and in the shed.

Eagle Eye no longer feared going to town. It pleased him that the sheriff was not like the other sheriffs that he had known. He felt sure that no one in the town would bother him and his family since Marshal Johnson was around.   Eagle Eye promised, "When the rest of the corn was in the shed, we will make the trip."

Jim worked with Eagle Eye each day trying to get the corn picked as soon as possible. He could think of nothing but the horse his pa was going to purchase for him. He didn't try to entice Eagle Eye down to the stream to fish. He just wanted to get the corn in the shed and go get that horse and saddle.

At breakfast Eagle Eye and Liz teased him about his new interest in the cornfield.

Liz said, "Why don't the two of you take the day off and go fishing?"

Eagle Eye countered with, "That a good idea, after breakfast I will get the poles out of the barn and we will fish all day. We have plenty of time to get the rest of the corn in the storage shed."

"Tomorrow the two of you can go hunting."

Jim stopped eating and said, "We have to get the corn in, and it might start to rain."

Both Eagle Eye and Liz almost doubled over with laughter. Jim suddenly realized that they were teasing him.

He knew that the last of the corn would be in the shed by nightfall. Tomorrow they would go and get his horse. He was happy. He started to laugh with them.

Eagle Eye said to him, "Tomorrow we are going to get you that horse. We will get best and fastest horse in Southern California. Tears formed in Jim's eyes. Eagle Eye pulled him close to him and told him that of all the boys in the world he was the best, that he deserved the best horse that they could find."

"I even plan to buy you a saddle. Have you forgotten, tomorrow is your birthday."

Eagle Eye and Jim were in the fields when Jim spotted the group of riders headed toward the cabin.

Eagle Eye said to him, "Go to the cabin and no matter what happens stay there!"

"Lock the door and stay inside!"

Jim went to the cabin but he did not intend to stay there. He said nothing to Liz when he entered. He went to his room and got his shotgun and stood at the door.

Liz said, "What's wrong?"

"Those bad men are coming."

"Oh, my God no."

"Yes, it's them, and they intend to hurt pa. I ain't going to let them hurt him."

Liz went to the bedroom and got a shotgun and stood at the door with Jim. They watched from the cabin door as the riders approached the farm. Liz was praying.

The Shootout

Fourteen horsemen rode up and faced the lone gunmen in the yard by the big tree. Eagle Eye was wearing both of his six-shooters; his rifle was leaning against the tree next to him. The other men sat on their horses and Tommy dismounted. They stayed on their horses and watched Tommy as he approached Eagle Eye.

As he advanced toward Eagle Eye He said, "I wont misjudge you this time nigger. Take my horse and water it."

Eagle Eye said, "Any stranger who enters my farm is allowed have as much water he wants. He has to get it himself. If he is sick or ailing then I will get it for him".

'You aren't ailing and you aren't sick, if you want water for your horse you will have to get it yourself'. "If you or your men need food, my wife will get you some."

Eagle Eye realized that if he took Tommy's horse and watered it, it would make no difference. Tommy was looking for a fight.

"Nigger, I am going to put and end to you today. You ready to die."

Tommy walked closer and face Eagle Eye.

"I know that your men are going to kill me but you will die first."

"My men got nothing to do with it, it's just you and me."

"Then why are they here?"

"They are here to see that no nigger can outdraw me, you want to draw your gun or talk nigger."

"I'm going to count to three and you can go for your gun if you want to it makes no difference to me."

"I am going to kill you".

"Ain't no need for this, I don't want to kill you. Why don't you just ride out and leave us be?"

"Nigger I'm through talking, you got to the count of three to go for your gun or take my horse and water it."

"Whenever you are ready."

The two men were ten feet apart when Tommy confidently went for his gun. He never saw Eagle Eye draw. The gun just appeared in his hand. Tommy was still trying to clear leather.

Eagle Eye hoped that Tommy would not continue. He hoped that Tommy would see that he had the drop on him, and that Tommy would concede. Tommy continued to pull his gun from its holster. Eagle Eye fired. Tommy went down with a bullet between his eyes.

Tommy's foreman started drawing his gun, but the horses were rearing from the gunshot and this gave Eagle Eye the edge that he needed. The foreman fell with a bullet above his right eye. Eagle watched and another man started for his gun and he too died. Six of the men fell in rapid secession as they went for their guns on bucking horses.

Eagle Eye drew his second six-shooter. Four more of the men went down. He heard Liz scream in the background and looked back to see what was wrong. When he turned to check on Liz and the boy the first bullets hit him. He heard Liz's shotgun go off and then Jim's. Then darkness came.

The Aftermath

Deputy Jack Thomas and Vinny Baxter, the two men sent by Marshall Johnson to the farm rode at a leisurely pace.

It was a long ride from the town to the farm. The day was warm and both men wanted nothing more than to return to the town and report that everything was all right.

They stopped about eight miles outside the town, ate their lunch, and allowed the mounts to rest. They watered and fed their mounts and then started their journey to the farm. They were about a half-mile away when they spotted the first signs of trouble. Moving closer to the farm they saw smoke coming from that direction.

Jack said, "It's a little warm for a fire, something must be wrong."

Vinny said, "The woman might have a cooking fire."

"There is too much smoke for a cooking fire."

The two of them put their horses into a trot and rode toward the farm. They arrived one day too late. There was nothing that they could do.

Vinny and the deputy reported to the Marshal and told him what they had found.

"There was a pregnant woman and a young boy dead in the front yard, both shot twice. I found the black man hanging from a tree. He was shot many times. We buried them in the cornfield. Marshal they even killed the dog, the mule, and some of the chickens."

"Damn that Tommy."

"Marshal it's a shame what Tommy did."

"His men killed a boy and a pregnant woman. He had no reason to bother those people".

"They never bothered anyone".

"That black man must have put up some fight. I counted eight graves on the side of the house. He shot eight of them before they got him."

"He shot 10, I just got back from the Stanton Ranch. I was too late to stop Tommy and his men. All that I could do was talk to his father. His father had tried to stop him but couldn't. My hands were tied it was outside my jurisdiction.

"We only counted eight graves."

"Two of the men were returning just as I got there. Fourteen men went to that black man's farm. Two of the fourteen that rode to the farm returned and two of them were injured. They brought the bodies of Tommy and the foreman back to the ranch. The rest they buried at the farm. That black man outdrew Tommy and shot most of the others as they went for their guns. That black man was one fast man with a six shooter."

The End

About The Author

Ben A. Watford received his Bachelor of Science degree in Chemistry from Howard University in 1957 and his Master's degree from Tuskegee University in 1960. He taught Chemistry at Smithtown High School in St. James, New York. He taught Science Techniques and Elementary Mathematics at Long Island University in the Graduate Education Department as an Associate Professor. Born in Winton, North Carolina, he now lives in Fairfield Harbour near New Bern, North Carolina with his wife Barbara. His last published work was a novel, "The Coming of the Comet." He is an active Potter making pottery on his potter's wheel. He has had several one-man shows at Art Galleries in Eastern Carolina. He is an avid golfer.

Printed in the United States
23671LVS00004B/406-468

9 781418 485436